WOMEN

WOMEN

BY
BOOTH TARKINGTON

GARDEN CITY   NEW YORK
DOUBLEDAY, PAGE & COMPANY
1925

CONTENTS

v

PREAMBLE

B UT why not?" Mrs. Dodge said, leading the
"Discussion" at the Woman's Saturday Club
after the reading of Mrs. Cromwell's essay,
"Women as Revealed in Some Phases of Modern
Literature." "Why shouldn't something of the actual
life of such women as ourselves be the subject of a
book?" Mrs. Dodge inquired. "Mrs. Cromwell's paper has pointed out to us that in a novel a study of
women must have a central theme, must focus upon a
central figure or 'heroine,' and must present her as a
principal participant in a centralized conflict or drama
of some sort, in relation to a limited group of other
'characters.' Now, so far as I can see, my own life
has no such centralizations, and I'm pretty sure
Mrs. Cromwell's hasn't, either, unless she is to be
considered merely as a mother; but she has other
important relations in life besides her relations to her
three daughters, just as I have others besides that I
bear to my one daughter. In fact, I can't find any
central theme in Mrs. Cromwell's life or my own; I
can't find any centralized drama in her life or mine,

and I doubt if many of you can find such things in yours. Our lives seem to be made up of apparently haphazard episodes, some meaningless, others important, and although we do live principally with our families and friends and neighbours, I find that people I hardly know have sometimes walked casually into my life, and influenced it, and then walked out of it as casually as they came in. All in all, I can't see in our actual lives the cohesion that Mrs. Cromwell says is the demand of art. It appears to me that this very demand might tend to the damage of realism, which I take to mean lifelikeness and to be the most important demand of all. So I say: Why shouldn't a book about women, or about a type of women, take for its subject some of the actual thoughts and doings of women like ourselves? Why should such a book be centralized and bound down to a single theme, a single conflict, a single heroine? The lives of most of us here consist principally of our thoughts and doings in relation to our children, our neighbours, and the people who casually walk into our lives and our children's and neighbours' lives and out again. It seems to me a book about us should be concerned with all of these almost as much as with ourselves."

"You haven't mentioned husbands," Mrs. Cromwell suggested. "Wouldn't they——"

"They should be included," Mrs. Dodge admitted. "But I would have husbands and suitors represented in their proper proportion; that is to say, only in the proportion that they affect *our* thoughts and doings. In challenging the rules for centralization that you have propounded, Mrs. Cromwell, I do not propose that all rules of whatever nature should be thrown over. One in particular I should hold most advisable."

"What rule is it?" a member of the club inquired, for at this point Mrs. Dodge paused and the expression of her mouth was somewhat grim.

"It is that a book about women should not be too long," Mrs. Dodge replied. "Especially if it should be by a man, he would be wise to use brevity as a means of concealing what he doesn't know. And besides," she added, more leniently, "by brevity, he might hope to placate us a little. It might be his best form of apology."

WOMEN

I

MRS. DODGE AND MRS. CROMWELL

WE LEARNED in childhood that appearances are deceitful, and our subsequent scrambling about upon this whirling globe has convinced many of us that the most deceptive of all appearances are those of peace. The gentlest looking liquor upon the laboratory shelves was what removed the east wing of the Chemical Corporation's building on Christmas morning; it was the stillest Sunday noon of a drowsy August when, without even the courtesy of a little introductory sputtering, the gas works blew up; and both of these disturbances were thought to be peculiarly outrageous because of the previous sweet aspects that prevented any one from expecting trouble. Yet those aspects, like the flat calm of the summer of 1914, should have warned people of experience that outbreaks were impending.

What could offer to mortal eye a picture of more

secure placidity than three smiling ladies walking homeward together after a club meeting? The particular three in mind, moreover, were in a visibly prosperous condition of life; for, although the afternoon was brightly cold, their furs afforded proof of expenditures with which any moderate woman would be satisfied, and their walk led them into the most luxurious stretch of the long thoroughfare that was called the handsome suburb's finest street. The three addressed one another in the caressively amiable tones that so strikingly characterize the élite of their sex in converse; and their topic, which had been that of the club paper, was impersonal. In fact, it was more than impersonal, it was celestial. "Sweetness and Light: Essay. Mrs. Roderick Brooks Battle"—these were the words printed in the club's year book beneath the date of that meeting, and Mrs. Roderick Brooks Battle was the youngest of the three placid ladies.

"You're all so sweet to say such lovely things about it," she said, as they walked slowly along. "I only wish I deserved them, but of course, as everyone must have guessed, it was all Mr. Battle. I don't suppose I could write a single connected paragraph without his telling me how, and if he hadn't kept helping me I just wouldn't have been ready with any paper at all.   Never in the world!"

"Oh, yes, you would, Amelia," the elder of the two other ladies assured her.   "For instance, dear, that beautiful thought about the 'bravery of silence'— about how much nobler it is never to answer an attack—I thought it was the finest thought in the whole paper, and I'm sure that was your own and not your husband's, Amelia."

"Oh, no, Mrs. Cromwell," Mrs. Battle returned, and although her manner was deferential to the older woman she seemed to be gently shocked;— her voice became a little protesting.   "I could never in the world have experienced a thought like that just by myself.   It was every bit Mr. Battle's.   In fact, he almost as much as dictated that whole paragraph to me, word for word.   It seemed a shame for me to sit up there and appear to take the credit for it; but I knew, of course, that everybody who knows us the least bit intimately would understand I could never write anything and it was all Mr. Battle."

"My dear, you'll never persuade us of it," the third lady said.   "There were thoughts in your paper so characteristically feminine that no one but a woman could possibly——"

"Oh, but *he* could!" Mrs. Battle interrupted with an eagerness that was more than audible, for it showed itself vividly in her brightened eyes and the sudden glow of pink beneath them. "That's one of the most wonderful things about Mr. Battle: his intellect is just as feminine as it is masculine, Mrs. Dodge. He's absolutely—well, the only way I can express it is in his own words. Mr. Battle says no one can be great who isn't universal in his thinking. And you see that's where he excels so immensely;— Mr. Battle is absolutely universal in his thinking. It seems to me it's one of the great causes of Mr. Battle's success; he not only has the most powerful reasoning faculties I ever knew in any man but he's absolutely gifted with a woman's intuition." She paused to utter a little murmur of fond laughter, as if she herself had so long and helplessly marvelled over Mr. Battle that she tolerantly found other people's incredulous amazement at his prodigiousness natural but amusing. "You see, an intellect like Mr. Battle's can't be comprehended from knowing other men, Mrs. Dodge," she added. "Other men look at things simply in a masculine way, of course. Mr. Battle says that's only seeing half. Mr. Battle says women live on one hemisphere of a globe and men on the other, and neither can look round the circle, but from the stars the whole globe is seen—so that's why we should keep our eyes among the stars! I wanted to work that thought into my paper, too. Isn't it beautiful, the idea of keeping our eyes among the stars? But he said there wasn't a logical opening for it, so I didn't. Mr. Battle says we should never use a thought that doesn't find its own logical place. That is, not in writing, he says. But don't you think it's wonderful—that idea of the globe and the two hemispheres and all?"

"Lovely," Mrs. Dodge agreed. "Yet I don't see how it proves Mr. Battle has a feminine mind."

"Oh, but I don't mean just that alone," Mrs. Battle returned eagerly. "It's the thousand and one things in my daily contact with him that prove it. Of course, I know how hard it must be for other women to understand. I suppose no one could hope to realize what Mr. Battle's mind is like at all without the great privilege of being married to him."

"And that," Mrs. Cromwell remarked, "has been denied to so many of us, my dear!"

Mrs. Dodge laughed a little brusquely, but the consort of the marvellous Battle was herself so marvellous that she merely looked preoccupied. "I know," she said, gravely, while Mrs. Dodge and Mrs. Cromwell stared with widening eyes, first at her and then at each other. "How often I've thought of it!" she went on, her own eyes fixed earnestly upon the distance where, in perspective, the two curbs of the long, straight street appeared to meet. "It grows stranger and stranger to me how such a miracle could have happened to a commonplace little woman like me! I never shall understand why I should have been the one selected."

Thereupon, having arrived at her own gate, it was with this thought that she left them. From the gate a path of mottled flagstones led through a smooth and snowy lawn to a house upon which the architect had chastely indulged his Latin pleasure in stucco and wrought iron; and as Mrs. Battle took her way over the flagstones she received from her two friends renewed congratulations upon her essay, as well as expressions of parting endearment; and she replied to these cheerfully; but all the while the glowing, serious eyes of the eager little brown-haired woman remained preoccupied with the miracle she had mentioned.

Mrs. Cromwell and Mrs. Dodge went on their way with some solemnity, and were silent until the closing door of the stucco house let them know they were out of earshot. Then Mrs. Cromwell, using a hushed voice, inquired: "Do you suppose she ever had a painting made of the Annunciation?"

"The Annunciation?" Mrs. Dodge did not follow her.

"Yes. When the miracle was announced to her that she should be the wife of Roderick Brooks Battle. Of course, she must have been forewarned by an angel that she was 'the one selected.' If Battle had just walked in and proposed to her it would have been too much for her!"

"I know one thing," Mrs. Dodge said, emphatically. "I've stood just about as much of her everlasting 'Mr. Battle says' as I intend to! You can't go anywhere and get away from it; you can hear it over all the chatter at a dinner; you can hear it over fifty women gabbing at a tea—'Mr. Battle says this,' 'Mr. Battle says that,' 'Mr. Battle says this *and* that'! When Belloni was singing at the Fortnightly After-noon Music last week you could hear her 'Mr. Battle says' to all the women around her, even during that loud Puccini suite, and she treed Belloni on his way out, after the concert, to tell him Mr. Battle's theory of music. She hadn't listened to a note the man sang, and Belloni understands about two words of English, but Amelia kept right on Mr. Battle-saying him for half an hour! For my part, I've had all I can stand of it, and I'm about ready to do something about it!"

"I don't see just what one could do," Mrs. Cromwell said, laughing vaguely.

"*I* do!" her companion returned.   Then both were silent for a few thoughtful moments and wore the air of people who have introduced a subject upon which they are not yet quite warm enough to speak plainly.   Mrs. Cromwell evidently decided to slide away from it, for the time being, at least.   "I don't think Amelia's looking well," she said.   "She's rather lost her looks these last few years, I'm afraid.   She seems pretty worn and thin to me;—she's getting a kind of skimpy look."

"What else could you expect?   She's made herself the man's slave ever since they were married.   She was his valet, his cook, and his washerwoman night and day for years.   I wonder how many times actually and literally she's blacked his boots for him! How could you expect her *not* to get worn out and skimpy looking?"

"Oh, I know," Mrs. Cromwell admitted;—"but

all that was in their struggling days, and she certainly doesn't need to do such things now. I hear he has twenty or thirty houses to build this year, and just lately an immense contract for two new office buildings. Besides, he's generous with her; she dresses well enough nowadays."

"Yes," Mrs. Dodge said, grimly. "They'd both see to that for *his* credit; but if he comes in with wet feet you needn't tell me she doesn't get down on her knees before him and take off his shoes herself. I know her! Yes, and I know him, too! Rich or poor, she'd be his valet and errand girl just the same as she always was."

"Perhaps," said Mrs. Cromwell. "But it seems to me her most important office for him is the one she's just been filling."

"Press agent? I should say so! She may stop blacking his boots, but she'll never stop that. It's just why she makes me so confounded tired, too! She thinks she's the only woman that ever got married!"

"Amelia *is* rather that way," the other said, musingly. "She certainly never seems to realize that any of the rest of us have husbands of our own."

"'Mr. Battle can't be comprehended from knowing

other men!'" Here Mrs. Dodge somewhat bitterly
mimicked the unfortunate Amelia's eager voice.
"'Other men look at things in simply a masculine
way!' 'I know how hard it must be for other women
to understand a god like my husband just from knowing their own poor little imitation husbands!'"

"Oh, no," Mrs. Cromwell protested. "She didn't
quite say that."

"But isn't it what she meant? Isn't it exactly
what she felt?"

"Well—perhaps."

"It does make me tired!" Mrs. Dodge said, vigor-
ously, and with the repetition she began to be more
than vigorous. Under the spell of that rancour which
increases in people when they mull over their injuries,
she began to be indignant. "For one thing, outside
of the shamelessness of it, some of the rest of us
could just possibly find a few enthusiastic things to
say of our husbands if we didn't have some regard
for not boring one another to death! I've got a
fairly good husband of my own I'd like to mention
once in a while, but——"

"But, of course, you'll never get the chance,"
Mrs. Cromwell interrupted. "Not if Amelia's in
your neighbourhood when you attempt it."

"What I *can't* understand, though," Mrs. Dodge went on, "is her never having the slightest suspicion what a nuisance it is. I should think the man himself would stop her."

But Mrs. Cromwell laughed and shook her head. "In the first place, of course, he agrees with her. He thinks Amelia's just stating facts—facts that ought to be known. In the second, don't you suppose he understands how useful her press-agenting is to him?"

"But it isn't. It makes us all sick of him."

"Oh, it may have that effect on you and me, Lydia, but I really wonder——" Mrs. Cromwell paused, frowning seriously, then continued: "Of course, he'd never take such a view of it. He instinctively knows it's useful, but he'd never take the view of it that——"

"The view of it that what?" Mrs. Dodge inquired, as her friend paused again.

"Why, that it may be actually the principal reason for his success. When he left the firm that employed him as a draughtsman and started out for himself, with not a thing coming in for him to do, don't you remember that even then everybody had the impression, somehow, that he was a genius and going to do wonders when the chance came? How do you suppose that got to be the general impression except through Amelia's touting it about? And then, when he *did* put up a few little houses, don't you remember hearing it said that they represented the first real Architecture with a capital 'A' ever seen in the whole city? Now, almost nobody really *knows* anything about architecture, though we all *talk* about it as glibly as if we did, and pretty soon—don't you remember?—we were all raving over those little houses of Roderick Brooks Battle's. What do you suppose made us rave? We must have been wrong, because Amelia says now that Battle thinks those first houses of his were 'rather bad'—he's 'grown so tremendously in his art.' Well, since they were bad, what except Amelia made us think then that they were superb? And look at what's happened to Battle these last few years. In spite of Amelia's boring us to death about him, isn't it true that there's somehow a wide impression that he's a great man? Of course there is!"

"And yet," Mrs. Dodge interposed, "he's not done anything that proves it. Battle's a good architect, certainly, but there are others as good, and he's not a bit better as an architect than Mr. Cromwell is as a lawyer or than my husband is as a consulting engineer."

"Not a bit," Mrs. Cromwell echoed, carrying on the thought she had been following. "But Mr. Dodge and Mr. Cromwell haven't had anybody to go about, day after day for years, proclaiming them and building up a legend about them. Nobody has any idea that they're great men, poor things! Don't you see where that puts you and me, Lydia?"

"No, I don't."

"My dear!" Mrs. Cromwell exclaimed. "Why, even Battle himself didn't know that he was a great man until he married Amelia and *she* believed he was —and *told* him he was—and started her long career of going about making everybody else sort of believe it, too."

"I think it's simply her own form of egoism," said the emphatic Mrs. Dodge. "She'd have done exactly the same whoever she married."

"Precisely! It's Amelia's way of being in love— she's a born idolizer. But you didn't answer me when I asked you where that puts *us*."

"You and me?" Mrs. Dodge inquired, frowning.

"Don't you see, if she'd married my husband, for instance, instead of Battle, everybody'd be having the impression by this time that Mr. Cromwell is a great man? He'd have felt that way himself, too, and I'm afraid it would give him a great deal of pleasure. Haven't we failed as wives when we see what Amelia's done for *her* husband?"

"What an idea!" The two ladies had been walking slowly as they talked;—now they came to a halt at their parting place before Mrs. Cromwell's house, which was an important, even imposing, structure of the type called Georgian, and in handsome conventional solidity not unlike the lady who lived in it. Across the broad street was a newer house, one just finished, a pinkish stucco interpretation of Mediterranean gaiety, and so fresh of colour that it seemed rather a showpiece, not yet actually inhabited though glamoured with brocaded curtains and transplanted arbor vitæ into the theatrical semblance of a dwelling in use. Mrs. Dodge glanced across at it with an expression of disfavour. "I call the whole thing perfectly disgusting!" she said.

II

A LADY ACROSS THE STREET

MRS. CROMWELL also looked at the new house; then she shook her head. "It's painful, rather," she said, and evidently referred to something more than the house itself.

"Outright disgusting!" her friend insisted. "I suppose he's there as much as ever?"

"Oh, yes. Rather more."

"Well, I'll say one thing," Mrs. Dodge declared; "Amelia Battle won't get any sympathy from me!"

"Sympathy? My dear, you don't suppose she dreams she needs *sympathy!* Doesn't she show the rest of us every day how she pities us because we're not married to Roderick Brooks Battle?"

"Yes, and that's what makes me so furious. But she *will* need sympathy," Mrs. Dodge persisted, with a dark glance at the new house across the street. "She will when she knows about that!"

"But maybe she'll never know."

"What!" Mrs. Dodge laughed scornfully. "My

dear, when a woman builds a man into a god he's going to assume the privileges of a god."

"And behave like the devil?"

"Just that," Mrs. Dodge returned, grimly. "Especially when his idolater has burnt up her youth on his altar and her friends begin to notice she's getting a skimpy look. What chance has a skimpy-looking slave against a glittering widow rich enough to build a new house every time she wants to have tête-à-têtes with a godlike architect?"

"But she's only built one," Mrs. Cromwell cried, protesting.

"So far!" her pessimistic companion said; then laughed at her own extravagance, and became serious again. "I think Amelia ought to know."

"Oh, no!"

"Yes, she ought," Mrs. Dodge insisted. "In the first place, she ought to be saved from making herself so horribly ridiculous. Of course, she's always been ridiculous; but the way she raves about him when *he's* raving about another woman—why, it's *too* ridiculous! In the second place, if she knew something about the Mrs. Sylvester affair now it might help her to bear a terrific jolt later."

"What terrific jolt, Lydia?"

"If he leaves her," Mrs. Dodge said, gravely. "If Mrs. Sylvester decides to make him a permanent fixture. Men do these things nowadays, you know."

"Yes, I know they do." Mrs. Cromwell looked as serious as her friend did, though her seriousness was more sympathetically a troubled one than Mrs. Dodge's. "Poor Amelia! To wear her youth out making a man into such a brilliant figure that a woman of the Sylvester type might consider him worth while taking away from her——"

"*Look!*" Mrs. Dodge interrupted in a thrilled voice.

A balustraded stone terrace crossed the façade of the new house, and two people emerged from a green door and appeared upon the terrace. One was a man whose youthful figure made a pleasing accompaniment to a fine and scholarly head;—he produced, moreover, an impression of success and distinction obvious to the first glance of a stranger, though what was most of all obvious about him at the present moment was his devoted, even tender, attention to the woman at his side. She was a tall and graceful laughing creature, so sparklingly pretty as to approach the contours and colours of a Beauty. Her rippling hair glimmered with a Venetian ruddiness,

and the blue of her twinkling eyes was so vivid that a
little flash of it shot clear across the street and was
perceptible to the two observant women as brightest
azure.

Upon her lovely head she had a little sable hat,
and, over a dress of which only a bit of gray silk
could be glimpsed at throat and ankle, she wore a
sable coat of the kind and dimensions staggering to
moderate millionaires She had the happy and
triumphant look of a woman confident through experience that no slightest wish of hers would ever
be denied by anybody, herself distinctly included;
and, all in all, she was dazzling, spoiled, charming,
and fearless.

Certainly she had no fear of the two observant
women, neither of their opinion nor of what she
might give them cause to tell; —that sparkle of azure
she sent across the intervening street was so carelessly amused it was derisive, like the half nod to
them with which she accompanied it. She and her
companion walked closely together, absorbed in
what they were saying, her hand upon his arm; and,
when they came to the terrace steps, where a closed
foreign car waited, with a handsome young chauffeur
at the wheel and a twin of him at attention beside

the door, she did a thing that Mrs. Dodge and Mrs. Cromwell took to be final and decisive.

Her companion had evidently offered some light pleasantry or witticism at which she took humorous offense, for she removed her white-gloved hand from his arm and struck him several times playfully upon the shoulder—but with the last blow allowed her hand to remain where it was; and, although she might have implied that it was to aid her movement into the car, the white fingers could still be seen remaining upon the shoulder of the man's brown overcoat as he, moving instantly after her, took his seat beside her in the gray velvet interior.   Thus, what appeared to be a playful gesture protracted itself into a caress, and a caress of no great novelty to the participants.

At least, it was so interpreted across the street, where Mrs. Dodge gave utterance to a sound vocal but incoherent, and Mrs. Cromwell said "Oh, *my!*" in a husky whisper.   The French car glided by them, passing them as they openly stared at it, or indeed glared at it, and a moment later it was far down the street, leaving them to turn their glares upon each other.

"That settles it," Mrs. Dodge gasped.   "It ought to have been a gondola."

"A gondola?"

"A Doge's wife carrying on with a fool poet or something;—she always has that air to me. What a comedy!"

Mrs. Cromwell shook her head; her expression was of grief and shock. "It's tragedy, Lydia."

"Just as you choose to look at it. The practical point of view is that it's going to happen to Amelia, and pretty soon, too! Some day before long that man's going to walk in and tell her she's got to step aside and let him marry somebody else. Doesn't what we just saw prove it? That woman did it deliberately in our faces, and she knows we're friends of his wife's. She deliberately showed us she didn't care what we saw. And as for him——"

"He didn't see us, I think," Mrs. Cromwell murmured.

"*See* us? He wouldn't have seen Amelia herself if she'd been with us—and she might have been! That's why I say she ought to know."

"Oh, I don't think I'd like to——"

"*Somebody* ought to," Mrs. Dodge said, firmly. "Somebody ought to tell her, and right away, at that."

"Oh, but——"

"Oughtn't she to be given the chance to prepare herself for what's coming to her?" Mrs. Dodge asked, testily. "She's made that man think he's Napoleon, and so she's going to get what Napoleon's wife got. I think she ought to be warned at once, and a true friend would see to it."

In genuine distress, Mrs. Cromwell shrank from the idea. "Oh, but I could never——"

"Somebody's *got* to," Mrs. Dodge insisted, implacably. "If you won't, then somebody else."

"Oh, but you—you wouldn't take such a responsibility, would you? You—you *wouldn't*, would you, Lydia?"

The severe matron, Lydia Dodge, thus flutteringly questioned, looked more severe than ever. "I shouldn't care to take such a burden on my shoulders," she said. "Looking after my own burdens is quite enough for me, and it's time I was on my way to them." She moved in departure, but when she had gone a little way, spoke over her shoulder, "*Somebody's* got to, though! Good-bye."

Mrs. Cromwell, murmuring a response, entered her own domain and walked slowly up the wide brick path; then halted, turned irresolutely, and glanced to where her friend marched northward upon the pavement. To Mrs. Cromwell the outlines of Mrs. Dodge, thus firmly moving on, expressed something formidable and imminent. "But, Lydia——" the hesitant lady said, impulsively, though she knew that Lydia was already too distant to hear her. Mrs. Cromwell took an uncertain step or two, as if to follow and remonstrate, but paused, turned again, and went slowly into her house.

A kind-hearted soul, and in a state of sympathetic distress for Amelia Battle, she was beset by compassion and perplexity during what remained of the afternoon; and her husband and daughters found her so preoccupied at the dinner table that they accused her of concealing a headache. But by this time what she concealed was an acute anxiety; she feared that Lydia's sense of duty might lead to action, and that the action might be precipitate and destructive. For Mrs. Cromwell knew well enough that Amelia's slavery was Amelia's paradise—the only paradise Amelia knew how to build for herself—and paradises are, of all structures, the most perilously fragile.

Mrs. Cromwell was the more fearful because, being a woman, she understood that more than a sense of duty would impel Lydia to action: Lydia herself might interpret her action as the prompting of duty,

but the vital incentive was likely to be something
much more human; for within the race is a profound
willingness to see a proud head lowered, particularly
if that head be one that has displayed its pride.
Amelia had displayed hers too long and too gallingly
for Lydia's patience;—Lydia had "really *meant* it,"
Mrs. Cromwell thought, recalling the fierceness of
Mrs. Dodge's "I've had all I can stand of it!" that
afternoon. A sense of duty with gall behind it is
indeed to be feared; and the end of Mrs. Cromwell's
anxieties was the conclusion that Amelia's paradise
of slavery was more imminently threatened by the
virtuous Lydia than by that gorgeous pagan, Mrs.
Sylvester.

III

PERVERSITY OF A TELEPHONE

THE troubled lady began to wish devoutly that the sight of Mrs. Sylvester caressing Mr. Battle had not shocked her into a fluttering and indecisive state of mind;—she should have discussed the event more calmly with Lydia; should have argued against anything precipitate;—and so, as soon as she could, after her preoccupied dinner, she went to the telephone and gave Mrs. Dodge's number.

Mr. and Mrs. Dodge were dining in town, she was informed; they were going to the theatre afterward and were not expected to return until midnight. This blank wall at once increased Mrs. Cromwell's inward disturbance, for she was a woman readily tortured by her imagination; and in her mind she began to design terrible pictures of what might now be happening in the house of the Battles. Until she went to the telephone she thought it unlikely that Lydia had acted with such promptness; but after receiving through the instrument the information that no information was to be had for the present, Mrs. Cromwell became certain that Mrs. Dodge had already destroyed Amelia's peace of mind.

She went away from the telephone, then came back to it, and again sat before the little table that bore it; but she did not at once put its miraculous powers into operation. Instead, she sat staring at it, afraid to employ it, while her imaginings became more piteous and more horrifying. Amelia had no talk except "Mr. Battle says"; she had no thought except "Mr. Battle thinks"; she had no life at all except as part of her husband's life; and if that were taken away from her, what was left? She had made no existence whatever of her own and for herself, and if brought to believe that she had lost him, she was annihilated.

If the great Battle merely died, Amelia could live on, as widows of the illustrious sometimes do, to be his monument continually reinscribed with mourning tributes; but if a Venetian beauty carried him off in a gondola, Amelia would be so extinct that the act of self-destruction might well be thought gratuitous;— and yet Mrs. Cromwell's imagination pictured Amelia in the grisly details of its commission by all the usual processes. She saw Amelia drown herself variously; saw her with a razor, with a pistol, with a rope, with poison, with a hat-pin.

Naturally, it became impossible to endure such pictures, and Mrs. Cromwell tremulously picked up the telephone, paused before releasing the curved nickel prong, but did release it, and when a woman's voice addressed her, "What number, please?" she returned the breathless inquiry: "Is that you, Amelia?" Then she apologized, pronounced a number, and was presently greeted by the response: "Mr. Roderick Battle's residence. Who is it, please?"

"Mrs. Cromwell. May I speak to Mrs. Battle?"

"I think so, ma'am."

In the interval of silence Mrs. Cromwell muttered, "I *think* so" to herself. The maid wasn't certain;— that was bad; for it might indicate a state of prostration.

"Yes?" said the little voice in the telephone. "Is it Mrs. Cromwell?"

Mrs. Cromwell with a great effort assumed her most smiling and reassuring expression. "Amelia? Is it you, Amelia?"

"Yes."

"I just wanted to tell you again what a lovely impression your essay made on me, dear. I've been thinking of it ever since, and I felt you might like to know it."

"Thank you, Mrs. Cromwell."

"Lydia Dodge and I kept on talking about it after you left us this afternoon," Mrs. Cromwell continued, beaming fondly upon the air above the telephone. "We both said we thought it was the best paper ever read at the club. I—I just wondered if—if Lydia called you up to tell you so, too. Did she?"

"No. No, she didn't call me up."

"Oh, didn't she? I just thought she might have because she was so enthusiastic."

"No. She didn't."

Mrs. Cromwell listened intently, seeking to detect emotion that might indicate Amelia's state of mind, but Amelia's voice revealed nothing whatever. It was one of those voices obscured and dwindled by the telephone into dry little metallic sounds; language was communicated, but nothing more, and a telegram from her would have conveyed as much personal revelation. "No, Mrs. Dodge didn't call me up," she said again.

Mrs. Cromwell offered some manifestations of

mirth, though she intended them to express a tender cordiality rather than amusement; and the facial sweetness with which she was favouring the air before her became less strained; a strong sense of relief was easing her. "Well, I just thought Lydia *might*, you know," she said, continuing to ripple her gentle laughter into the mouthpiece. "She was so enthusiastic, I just thought——"

"No, she didn't call me up," the small voice in the telephone interrupted.

"Well, I'm gl——" But Mrs. Cromwell checked herself sharply, having begun too impulsively. "I hope I'm not keeping you from anything you were doing," she said hastily, to change the subject.

"No, I'm all alone. Mr. Battle is spending the evening with Mrs. Sylvester."

"What!" Mrs. Cromwell exclaimed, and her almost convivial expression disappeared instantly; her face became a sculpture of features only. "He is?"

"Yes. He's finishing the interior of her new house. With important clients like that he always interprets them into their houses you know. He makes a study of their personalities."

"I—see!" Mrs. Cromwell said. Then, recovering

herself, she was able to nod pleasantly and beam again, though now her beaming was rigidly automatic. "Well, I mustn't keep you. I just wanted to tell you again how immensely we all admired your beautiful essay, and I thought possibly Lydia might have called you up to say so, too, because she fairly raved over it when we were——"

"No." The metallic small voice said; and it informed her for the fourth time: "She didn't call me up." Then it added: "She came here."

"No!" Mrs. Cromwell cried.

"Yes. She came here," the voice in the instrument repeated.

"She *did?*"

"Yes. Just before dinner. She came to see me."

"Oh, my!" Mrs. Cromwell murmured. "What did she say?"

"She was in great trouble about Mr. Dodge."

"What?"

"She was in a tragic state," the impersonal voice replied with perfect distinctness. "She was in a tragic state about her husband."

"About John *Dodge?*" Mrs. Cromwell cried.

"Yes. She was hurried and didn't have time to tell me any details, because they had a dinner engagement in town, and he kept telephoning her they'd be disgraced if she didn't come home and dress; but that's what she came to see me about. It seems he's been misbehaving himself over some fascinating and unscrupulous woman, and Mrs. Dodge thinks he probably intends to ask for a divorce and abandon her. She was in a most upset state over it, of course."

"*Amelia!*" Mrs. Cromwell shouted the name at the mouthpiece.

"Yes. Isn't it distressing?" was the response. "Oh course, I won't mention it to anybody but you. I supposed you knew all about it since you're her most intimate friend."

Mrs. Cromwell made an effort to speak coherently. "Let me try to understand you," she said. "You say that Lydia Dodge came to you this afternoon——"

"It was really evening," the voice interrupted, in correction. "Almost seven. And their engagement was in town at half past. That's why he kept calling her up so excitedly."

"And she told you," Mrs. Cromwell continued, "Lydia Dodge told you that her husband, John Dodge, was philandering with——"

"There was no doubt about it whatever," the voice interrupted. "Some friends of hers had seen an actual caress exchanged between Mr. Dodge and the other woman."

"*What!*"

"Yes.   That's what she told me."

"Wait!" Mrs. Cromwell begged.   "Lydia Dodge told you that John Dodge——"

"Yes," the voice of Amelia Battle replied colourlessly in the telephone.   "It seems too tragic, and it was such a shock to me—I never dreamed that people of forty or fifty had troubles like that—but it was what she came here to tell me.   Of course, she didn't have time to tell me much, because she was so upset and Mr. Dodge was in such a hurry for her to come home.   I never dreamed there was anything but peace and happiness between them, did you?"

"No, I didn't," gasped Mrs. Cromwell.   "But Amelia——"

"That's all I know about it, I'm afraid."

"Amelia——"

"Probably she'll talk about it to you pretty soon," Amelia said, at the other end of the wire.   "I'm surprised she didn't tell you before she did me; you really know her so much better than I do.   I'm afraid I'll have to go now.   One of Mr. Battle's assistants has just come in and I'm doing some work with him. It was lovely of you to call me up about the little essay, but, of course, that was *all* Mr. Battle. Good-night."

Mrs. Cromwell sat staring at the empty mechanism in her hand until it rattled irritably, warning her to replace it upon its prong.

IV

A GREAT MAN'S WIFE

SHE had a restless night, for she repeatedly woke up with a start, her eyes opening widely in the darkness of her bedroom; and each time this happened she made the same muffled and incomplete exclamation: "Well, of all——!" Her condition was still as exclamatory as it was anxiously expectant when, just after her nine-o'clock breakfast the next morning, she went to her Georgian drawing-room window and beheld the sterling figure of Mrs. Dodge in the act of hurrying from the sidewalk to the Georgian doorway. Mrs. Cromwell ran to admit her; brought her quickly into the drawing room. "Lydia!" she cried. "What on earth *happened?*" For, even if telephones had never been invented, the early caller's expression would have made it plain that there had been a happening.

"I'd have called you up last night," the perturbed Lydia began;—"but we didn't get back till one o'clock, and it was too late. In all my life I never had such an experience!"

"You don't mean at the theatre or——"

"No!" Mrs. Dodge returned, indignantly. "I mean with that woman!"

"With Amelia?"

"With Amelia Battle."

"But *tell* me," Mrs. Cromwell implored. "My dear, I've been in such a state of perplexity——"

"Perplexity!" her friend echoed scornfully, and demanded: "What sort of state do you think *I've* been in? My dear, I went to her."

"To Amelia?"

"To Amelia Battle," Mrs. Dodge said. "I went straight home after I left you yesterday; but I kept thinking about what we'd seen——"

"You mean——" Mrs. Cromwell paused, and glanced nervously through the glass of the broadpaned window beside which she and her guest had seated themselves. Her troubled eyes came to rest upon the pinkish Italian villa across the street. "You mean what we saw—over there?"

"I mean what was virtually an embrace between Roderick Brooks Battle and Mrs. Sylvester under our eyes," Mrs. Dodge said angrily. "And she looked us square in the face just before she did it! I also mean that both of them showed by their manner that such caresses were absolutely familiar and habitual—and that was all *I* needed to prove that the talk about them was only too well founded. So, when I'd thought it over and over—Oh, I didn't act in haste!— I decided it was somebody's absolute *duty* to prepare Amelia for what I plainly saw was coming to her. Did you ever see anything show more proprietorship than Mrs. Sylvester's fondling of that man's shoulder? So, as you had declared *you* wouldn't go, and although it was late, and Mr. Dodge and I had an important dinner engagement, I made up my mind it had to be done immediately and I went."

"But what did you *tell* her?" Mrs. Cromwell implored.

"Never," said Mrs. Dodge, "never in my life have I had such an experience! I tried to begin tactfully; I didn't want to give her a shock, and so I tried to begin and lead up to it; but it was difficult to begin at all, because I'd scarcely sat down before she told me my husband had got home and had telephoned to see if I'd reached her house, and he'd left word for me to come straight back home because he was afraid we'd be late for the dinner—and all the time I was trying to talk to her, her maid kept coming in to say he was calling up again, and then I'd have to go and *beseech* him to let me alone for a minute—but he wouldn't——"

Mrs. Cromwell was unable to wait in patience through these preliminaries. "Lydia! What did you *tell* her?"

"I'm trying to explain it as well as I can, please," her guest returned, irritably. "If I didn't explain how crazily my husband kept behaving you couldn't possibly understand. He'd got it into his head that we *had* to be at this dinner on time, because it was with some people who have large mining interests and——"

"Lydia, *what* did you——"

"I told you I tried to be tactful," said Mrs. Dodge. "I tried to lead up to it, and I'll tell you exactly what I said, though with that awful telephone interrupting every minute it was hard to say *anything* connectedly! First, I told her what a deep regard both of us had for her."

"Both of you? You mean you and your husband, Lydia?"

"No, you and me. It was necessary to mention you, of course, because of what we saw yesterday."

"Oh," said Mrs. Cromwell. "Well, go on."

"I told her," Mrs. Dodge continued, complying. "I said nobody could have her interests more at heart than you and I did, and that was why I had come. She thanked me, but I noticed a change in her manner right there. I thought she looked at me in a kind of bright-eyed way, as if she were on her guard and suspicious. I *thought* she looked like that, and now I'm *sure* she did. I said, 'Amelia, I want to put a little problem to you, just to see if you think I've done right in coming.' She said, 'Yes, Mrs. Dodge,' and asked me what the problem was."

"And what was it, Lydia?"

"My dear, will you let me tell you? I said in the kindest way, I said, 'Amelia, just for a moment let us suppose that my husband were not true to me; suppose he might even be planning to set me aside so that he could marry another woman; and suppose that two women friends of mine, who had my interests dearly at heart, had seen him with this other woman; and suppose her to be a fascinating woman, and that my friends saw with their own eyes that my husband felt her fascination so deeply that anybody could tell in an instant he was actually in love with her;—and, *more* than that,' I said, 'suppose that these friends of mine saw my husband actually exchanging a caress with this woman, and saw him go off driving with her, with her hand on his shoulder and he showing that he liked it there and was used to having it there;—Amelia,' I said, 'Amelia, what would you think about the question of duty for those two friends of mine who had seen such a thing? Amelia,' I said, 'wouldn't you think it was the true duty of one or the other of them to come and tell me and warn me and give me time to prepare myself?' That's what I said to her."

"And what did she——"

"She jumped right up and came and threw her arms around me," said Mrs. Dodge in a strained voice. "I never had such an experience in my life!"

"But what did she *say?*"

"She said, 'You poor *thing!*'" Mrs. Dodge explained irascibly. "She didn't 'say' it, either; she shouted it, and she kept on shouting it over and over. 'You poor *thing!*' And when she wasn't saying that, she was saying she'd never *dreamed* Mr. Dodge was that sort of a man, and she made such a commotion I was afraid the neighbours would hear her!"

"But why didn't you——"

"I *did!*" Mrs. Dodge returned passionately. "I told her a *hundred* times I didn't mean Mr. Dodge;

but she never gave me a chance to finish a word I began; she just kept taking on about what a terrible thing it must be for me, and how dreadful it was to think of Mr. Dodge misbehaving like that—I tell you I never in my *life* had such an experience!"

"But why didn't you *make* her listen, at least long enough to——"

Mrs. Dodge's look was that of a person badgered to desperation. "I *couldn't!* Every time I opened my mouth she shouted louder than I did! She'd say, 'You poor thing!' again, or some more about Mr. Dodge, or she'd want to know if I didn't need ammonia or camphor, or she'd offer to make beef *tea* for me! And every minute my husband was making an idiot of himself ringing the Battles' telephone again. You don't seem to understand what sort of an experience it was at *all!* I tell you when I finally had to leave the house she was standing on their front steps shouting after me that she'd never tell anybody a thing about Mr. Dodge unless I wanted her to!"

"It's so queer!" Mrs. Cromwell said, bewildered more than ever. "If I'd been in your place I know I'd never have come away without making her understand I meant her husband, not mine!"

"'Making her understand!'" Mrs. Dodge re-

peated, mocking her friend's voice—so considerable
was her bitterness. "You goose! You don't suppose she didn't understand *that*, do you?"

"You don't think——"

"Absolutely! She had been expecting it to
happen."

"What to happen?"

"Somebody's coming to warn her about Mrs.
Sylvester. She did the whole thing deliberately.
Absolutely! She understood I was talking about
Battle as well as you do now. Of course," said
Mrs. Dodge, "of *course* she understood!"

Then both ladies seemed to ponder, and for a
time uttered various sounds of marvelling; but suddenly Mrs. Cromwell, whose glance had wandered
to the window, straightened herself to an attentive
rigidity. Her guest's glance followed hers, and instantly became fixed; but neither lady spoke, for a
sharply outlined coincidence was before them, casting
a spell upon them and holding them fascinated.

Across the street a French car entered the driveway of the stucco house, and a Venetian Beauty
descended, wrapped in ermine too glorious for the
time and occasion. Out of the green door of the
house eagerly came upon the balustraded terrace

a dark man, poetic and scholarly in appearance, dressed scrupulously and with a gardenia, like a bridegroom's flower, in his coat. In his hand he held an architect's blue print; but for him and for the azure-eyed lady in ermine this blue print seemed not more important, nor less, than that book in which the two lovers of Rimini read no more one day. They glanced but absently at the blue print; then the man let it dangle from his hand while he looked into the lady's eyes and she into his; and they talked with ineffable gentleness together.

Here was an Italian episode most romantic in its elements: a Renaissance terrace for the trysting place of a Renaissance widow and a great man, two who met and made love under the spying eyes of female *sbirri* lurking in a window opposite; but it was Amelia Battle who made the romantic episode into a realistic coincidence. In a vehicle needful of cleansing and polish she appeared from down the long street, sitting in the attentive attitude necessary for the proper guidance of what bore her, and wearing (as Mrs. Cromwell hoarsely informed Mrs. Dodge) "her market clothes." That she was returning from a market there could be no doubt; Amelia had herself this touch of the Renaissance, but a Renais-

sance late, northern, and robust. Both of the rear
windows of her diligent vehicle framed still-life stud-
ies to lure the brush of sixteenth- and seventeenth-
century lowland painters: the green tops of sheaved
celery nodded there; fat turnips reposed in baskets;
purple ragged plumes of beets pressed softly against
the glass; jugs that suggested buttermilk and cider,
perhaps both, snugly neighboured the hearty vegetables, and made plain to all that the good wife in the
forward seat had a providing heart for her man and
her household.

The ladies in the Georgian window were truly
among those who cared to look. "Oh, *my!*" Mrs.
Cromwell whispered.

Amelia stopped her market machine and jumped
out in her market clothes at the foot of the driveway, where stood Mrs. Sylvester's French car in
the care of its two magnificent young men. There
was an amiable briskness, cheerful and friendly, in the
air with which Amelia trotted up the terrace steps
and joined the romantic couple standing beside the
balustrade. The three entered into converse.

Mrs. Cromwell and Mrs. Dodge became even more
breathless; and then, with amazement, and perhaps a
little natural disappointment, they saw that the

conversation was not acrimonious—at least, not outwardly so. They marked that Amelia, smiling, took the lead in it, and that she at once set her hand upon her husband's arm—and in a manner of ownership so masterful and complete that the proprietorship assumed by Mrs. Sylvester in the same gesture, the preceding day, seemed in comparison the temporary claim of a mere borrower. And Mrs. Cromwell marked also a kind of feebleness in the attitude of the Venetian Beauty: Mrs. Sylvester was smiling politely, but there was a disturbed petulance in her smile. Suddenly Mrs. Cromwell perceived that beside Amelia, for all Amelia's skimpiness, Mrs. Sylvester looked ineffective. With that, glancing at the sturdy figure of Lydia Dodge, Mrs. Cromwell came to the conclusion that since Amelia had been too much for Lydia, Amelia would certainly be too much for Mrs. Sylvester.

"Look!" said Lydia.

Amelia and her husband were leaving the terrace together. Battle walked to the "sedan" with her and held the door open for her; she climbed to the driver's seat and seemed to wait, with assurance, for him to do more than hold the door. And at this moment the seriousness of his expression was so emphasized that it was easily visible to the Georgian window, though only his profile was given to its view as he looked back, over his shoulder, at the glazing smile of the lady upon the terrace. He seemed to waver, hesitating; and then, somewhat bleakly, he climbed into the "sedan" beside his wife.

"*Open it!*" Mrs. Dodge was struggling with a catch of the Georgian window.

"What for?"

"She's shouting again! I've *got* to hear her!" Mrs. Dodge panted; and the window yielded to her exertions.

Amelia's attitude showed that she was encouraging her machine to begin operations, while at the same time she was calling parting words to Mrs. Sylvester. "Good-bye!" Amelia shouted. "Mr. Battle says he's been *so* inspired by your sympathy in his work! Mr. Battle says that's *so* necessary to an architect! Mr. Battle says *no* artist can ever even *hope* to do anything great without it! Mr. Battle says——"

But here, under the urging of her foot, the engine burst into a shattering uproar: ague seized the car with a bitter grip; convulsive impulses of the apparatus to leap at random were succeeded by more decorous ideas, and then the "sedan" moved mildly forward; the vegetables nodded affably in the windows, and the Battles were borne from sight.

"I see," said Lydia Dodge, moving back to her chair. "I understand now."

"You understand what?" her hostess inquired, brusquely, as she closed the Georgian window.

"I understand what I just saw. I can't tell you exactly how or why, but it was plainly *there*—in Roderick Brooks Battle's look, in his slightest gesture. We were absolutely mistaken to think it possible. He'll never ask Amelia to step aside: he'll never leave her. And however much he philanders, *she'll* never leave *him*, either. She'll go straight on the way she's always gone. *He's* shown us that, and *she's* shown us that."

"Well, then," Mrs. Cromwell inquired; "why is it? You say you understand."

"It's because he knows that between his Venetian romance and his press agent he's got to take the press agent. He's had sense enough to see he mightn't be a great man at all without his press agent—and he'd rather keep on being a great man. And Amelia knows she's getting too skimpy-looking to get a chance to make a great man out of anybody *else;* so she wouldn't let me tell her about him, because she's going to stick to him!"

At this Mrs. Cromwell made gestures of negation and horror, though in the back of her mind, at that moment, she was recalling her yesterday's thought that Lydia's sense of duty was really Lydia's pique. "Lydia Dodge!" she cried, "I won't listen to you! Don't you know you're taking the lowest, unchristianest, vilest possible view of human nature?"

Mrs. Dodge looked guilty, but she decided to offer a plea in excuse. "Well, I suppose that may be true," she said. "But sometimes it does seem about the only way to understand people!"

V

ONE OF MRS. CROMWELL'S DAUGHTERS

IN THE spacious suburb's most opulent quarter, where the houses stood in a great tract of shrubberies, gardens, and civilized old woodland groves, there were many happily marriageable girls; and one, in particular, was supremely equipped in this condition, for she had what the others described as "the best of everything." In the first place, they said, Anne Cromwell had "looks"; in the second place, she had "money," and in the third she had "family," by which they meant the background prestiges of an important mother and several generations of progenitors affluently established upon this soil.

Sometimes they added a word or two about her manners, though a middle-aged listener might not have divined that the allusion was to manners.

"She manages wonderf'ly," they said. Amiably reserved, and never an eager contestant in the agonizing little competitions that necessarily engage maidens of her age, she was not merely fair but generous to her rivals. "She can afford to be!" they cried, thus paying tribute. Her fairness prevailed, too, among her suitors: not one could say she favoured him more than another; but like a young princess, as politic as she was well bred and genuinely kind, she showed an impartial friendliness to everybody.

Even without her background she was the most noticeable young figure in the suburb, but never because she did anything to make herself conspicuous. At the Green Hills Country Club the eye of a stranger, watching the dancing on a summer night, would not immediately distinguish an individual from the mass. As the dancers went lightly interweaving over the floor of a roofless pavilion, where the foliage of great beech trees hung trembling above white balustrades and Venetian lamps, the spectator's first glance from the adjoining veranda caught only the general aspect of carnival: the dancers were like a confusion of gaily coloured feathers blowing and whirlpooling across a dim tapestry. But presently, as he looked, rhythms and shifting designs would appear in the sparkling fluctuation; points of light would separate themselves, taking individual contour, and the brightest would be a lovely girl's head of "gold cooled in moonlight."

Then it would be observed that toward this bright head darker ones darted and zigzagged through the crowd more frequently than toward any other, as the ardent youths plunged to "cut in"; and when the music stopped the lovely girl was not for an instant left to the single devotion of her partner. Other girls, as well as the young men, flocked about her, and wherever she moved there seemed to be something like a retinue. Thus the first question of the stranger, looking on, came to be expected as customary—almost inevitable, "Who is that?" The reply was as invariable, delivered with the amused condescension of a native receiving tribute to his climate or public monuments. "That's what visitors always ask first. It's Anne Cromwell."

Mrs. Cromwell, sitting among contemporaries on the veranda that overlooked the dancing floor, had often heard both the question and the answer, and although she was one of those mothers known as "sensible," she never heard either without a natural thrill of pride. But she was tactful enough to conceal her feeling from the mothers of other girls, and usually laughed deprecatingly, implying that she knew as well as any one how little such ephemeral things signified. Anne had her own deprecating laughter for tributes, and the most eager flatterer could not persuade her to the air of accepting them seriously; so that both mother and daughter, appearing to set no store by Anne's triumphs, really made them all the more secure. It was a true instinct guiding them, the same that prevailed with Cæsar when thrice he refused the crown; for what hurts our little human hearts, when we watch a competitor's triumph, is his pride and his pleasure in it. If he can persuade us that it brings him neither we will not grudge it to him, but may help him to greater.

Moreover, both Anne and her mother believed themselves to be entirely genuine in their deprecation of Anne's preëminence, and, when they were alone together, talked tributes over with the same modest laughter they had for them in company. Yet Mrs. Cromwell never omitted to tell Anne of any stranger's "Who is that?" nor of all the other pleasing things said to her, or in her hearing, of her daughter. And, on her own part, Anne laughed and told of the like things that had been said to her, or that she had overheard.

"Of course, it doesn't mean anything," she would add. "I just thought I'd tell you."

For the truth was that Anne's triumphs were the breath of life to both mother and daughter, and they were doomed to make the ancient discovery that our dearest treasures are those that are threatened.

The threat was perceived by Mrs. Cromwell upon one of those summer nights so exquisite that we call them "unreal," because they belong to perished romance, and we have learned to imagine that what is real must be unlovely. Only the relics of a discredited sentimental epoch could go forth under the gold-pointed canopy of such a night, and sigh because the stars are ineffable. Mrs. Cromwell was such a relic, and, being in remote attendance upon her daughter at the country club, she had gone after dinner to walk alone upon the links in the starlight. In an old-fashioned mood, she naturally wanted to get away from the dance music of the open-air pavilion; but, when she returned, her shadow from the rising moon preceded her, and she decided that even the tomtoms and war horns of the young people's favourite "orchestra" could never entirely ruin the moon. Then, instead of joining any of the groups upon the veranda, she went to an easy chair, aloof in a shadowy corner, where she could see the dancers and be alone to watch Anne.

She looked down a little wistfully. Only a year or so ago she had thus watched her oldest daughter, Mildred, now a matron, and in time she would probably see her youngest, the schoolgirl, Cornelia, dancing here. But Anne, though the mother strove not to know it, was her dearest, and the period of eligible maidenhood, like any other period, is not long. Mrs. Cromwell was wistful because she thought it would not be really long before Anne might sit here to watch the maiden dancing of a daughter of her own.

The pavilion was a little below the level of the veranda, and almost at once her eye found the dominant fair head it sought. Anne was talking as she danced, smiling serenely, a graceful young figure, shapely and tall, with a hint of the contented ampleness that would come later, as it had come to her mother. Mrs. Cromwell, seeing Anne's smile, smiled too, in her seclusion, and with the same serenity; though an enemy might have said that these two smiles partook of the same complacency. However, at that moment Mrs. Cromwell could not have imagined the existence of an enemy: she had no conception that there could be in the world such a thing as an enemy to herself or to her daughter.

She was a little sorry that Anne wasn't dancing with young Harrison Crisp. She liked to see Anne dancing with any "nice boy," but best of all with young Crisp, and this was not only because the two were harmoniously matched as dancers, as well as in other ways, but because the mother had comprehended that this young man might prove to be her daughter's preference for more than dancing. Mrs. Cromwell was not anxious to see Anne married; she wished her to prolong the pretty time of girlhood; but any mother must have been pleased to see so splendid a young man place himself at her daughter's disposal. Mrs. Cromwell wondered where he was this evening, and she had just begun to look for him among the dancers when strangers intruded upon her retreat.

She heard unfamiliar voices behind her, and then a small group of middle-aged people drew up wicker chairs to the veranda railing that overlooked the dancing-floor. Mrs. Cromwell gave them a side glance and perceived that they were visitors, "put up" at the club, for this was an organization closely guarded, and she knew all of the members. The newcomers sat near her, and though she would have preferred her seclusion to remain secluded, she could not help waiting, with a little motherly satisfaction, to hear them speak of her Anne, as strangers inevitably must.

And presently she smiled in the darkness, thinking herself rewarded; for a man's voice, deeply impressed, inquired: "Who *is* that wonderful girl?"

In the light of the moment's impending revelation, the mother's smile upon Mrs. Cromwell's half-parted lips, as she waited for the reply, becomes a little pathetic.

"Why, it's *Sallie*, of course!"

This strange answer arrested Mrs. Cromwell's smile, of which reluctant and mirthless vestiges remained for a moment or two before vanishing into the contours that mark an astounded disapproval. Then she slowly turned her head and looked at these queer visitors, and her strong impression was that the two middle-aged women and their escort, a stout elderly man in white flannels, were "very ordinary looking people."

Their chairs were within a dozen feet of hers, but

they sat in profile to her, and possibly were unaware of her, or were aware of her but vaguely. For strangers in a strange place are often subject to such an illusion of detachment as these displayed, and seem to feel that they may speak together as freely as if they alone understood language. But, of course, to Mrs. Cromwell's way of thinking, the greater illusion of the present group was in believing that somebody named Sallie was a wonderful girl. She failed to identify this pretender: none of her friends had a daughter named Sallie, and Anne had never spoken of any Sallie.

"I declare I didn't recognize her!" the elderly man said, chuckling. "Who'd have thought it? Sallie!"

The woman who sat next him laughed triumphantly. "I don't wonder you didn't recognize her," she said. "It's six years since you saw her, and she was only fourteen then. I guess she's changed *some*—what?"

"Well, 'some'!" he agreed. "She makes the rest of 'em look like flivvers."

The second of the two women tapped his head with her fan. "George, I guess you never thought you'd be the uncle of a peach like that!"

"Well, I'm not as surprised to be the uncle of a peach," he said, with renewed chuckling, "as I am to see you the aunt of one! I'm kind of surprised to have Jennie, here, turn out to be the mother of one, too. You certainly never showed any such style as that when you were young, Jennie! Why, there ain't a girl in that whole bunch to hold a candle to her! She's a two-hundred-carat blazer and makes the rest of 'em look like what you see on a ten-cent-store counter! You heard me yourselves: the very first thing I said was, 'Who *is* that wonderful girl?' And I didn't even know it was Sallie. I guess that shows!"

Sallie's mother laughed excitedly. "Oh, we're used to it, George! She's never gone a place these last three years she didn't put it all over the other girls in two shakes of a lamb's tail! The boys go crazy over her as soon as they see her, even the ones that are engaged to other girls, and a few that are married to the other girls, too! We've had some funny times, I tell you, George!"

"I expect so!" he chuckled. "I guess you're fixing for her to pick a good one, all right, Jennie!"

"She don't need me to do any fixing for her," Sallie's mother explained, gaily. "She's got a mighty good head on her, and I guess she knows she can choose anything she decides she wants. Look at her now." She laughed in loud triumph as she spoke, and pointed to the pavilion.

Mrs. Cromwell's eyes followed the direction of the pointing forefinger and saw a stationary nucleus among the swirl of dancers—a knot of young men gathered round a girl and engaged in obvious expostulation. The disagreement was so pronounced, in fact, as to resemble a dispute; for it involved more gesturing than is usually displayed in the mere arguments of members of the northern races;—"cutting in" to dance with this girl was apparently a serious matter.

She was a laughing, slender creature, with hints of the glow of rubies in the corn-silk brown of her hair; and the apple-green thin silk of her sparse dancing dress was the right complement for her dramatic vividness. Brilliant eyed, her face alive with little ecstasies of merriment as the debaters grew more and more emphatic, she might well have made an observer think of "laughing April on the hills"—an April with July in her hair and a ring of solemn young fauns disputing over her.

She did not allow their disagreement to reach a

crisis, however, though the fauns were so earnest as
to seem to threaten one;—she placed a slim hand
upon the shoulder of her interrupted partner, whose
arm had been all the while tentatively about her
waist, and began to dance with him. But over her
shoulder as she went, she flung a look and a word to
the defeated, who dispersed thoughtfully, with the air
of men not by any means abandoning their ambitions.

Then the coronal of ruby-sprinkled hair was seen
shuttling rhythmically among the dancers; and
such a glowing shuttle the eye of a spectator must
follow. This pagan April with her flying grace in
scant apple-green emerged from the other dancers as
the star emerges from the other actors in a play;
and only mothers of other girls could have failed to
perceive that any stranger's first question must
inevitably be, "Who is *that?*"

Mrs. Cromwell had no such perception;—her
glance, a little annoyed, sought her daughter and
easily found her. Anne was dancing with young
Hobart Simms, long her most insignificant and
humblest follower. Mrs. Cromwell thought of
him as "one of the nice boys"; but she also thought
of him as "poor little Hobart," for only two things

distinguished him, both unfortunate. His father had lately failed in business, so that of all the "nice boys," Hobart was the poorest; but, what was more to the point in Mrs. Cromwell's reflections just then, of all the "nice boys" he was the shortest. He was at least four inches shorter than Anne, and it seemed to the mother that the contrast in height made Anne look too large and somehow too placid. Mrs. Cromwell wanted Anne to be kind, but she decided to warn her against dancing with Hobart: there are contrasts that may bring even the most graceful within the danger of looking a little ridiculous.

Anne was at her best when she danced with the tall and romantically dark Harrison Crisp; but unfortunately this delinquent had been discovered: he was the triumphing partner who had carried off the young person called Sallie. Mrs. Cromwell might have put it the other way, however: she might have looked upon the episode as the carrying off of young Crisp by this froward Sallie.

Sallie's mother appeared to take this view, herself. "Look at that!" she cried. "Look at the state she's got that fellow in she's dancing with! Look at the way he's *looking* at her, will you!" And again she gave utterance to the loud and excitedly triumphant laugh that not only offended the ears of Mrs. Cromwell but disquieted her more than she would have thought possible, half an hour earlier. It seemed to her that she had never before heard so offensive a laugh.

"Did you ever see anything to beat it?" Sallie's mother inquired hilariously. "He looks at her that way the whole time—except when she's dancing with somebody else. Then he stands around and looks at her as if he had an awful pain! She's got him so he won't dance with anybody else. It's a scream!" And here, in her mirthful excitement, she slapped the stout uncle's knee; for Sallie's mother made it evident that she was one of those who repeat their own youth in the youth of a daughter, and perhaps in a daughter's career fulfil their own lost ambitions. She became more confidential, though her confidential air was only a gesture; she leaned toward her companions, but did not take the trouble to lower her voice.

"He's been to the house to see her four times since Monday. Last week he had her auto riding every single afternoon. The very day he *met* her he sent her five pounds of——"

"Who is he?" the uncle inquired. "He's a fine *looking* fellow, all right, but is he——"

Sallie's mother took the words out of his mouth. "*Is* he?" she cried. "I guess you'll *say* he is! Crisp Iron Works, and his father's made him first vice-president and secretary already—only two years out of college!"

"Sallie like him?"

"She's got 'em *all* going," the mother laughed;—"but he's the king. I guess she don't mind keeping him standing on his head awhile though!" Again she produced the effect of lowering her voice without actually lowering it. "They say he was sort of half signed up for somebody else. When we first came here you couldn't see anything but this Anne Cromwell. She's one of these highbrow girls—college and old family and everything—and you'd thought she was the whole place. Sallie only needed about three weeks!" And with that Sallie's mother was so highly exhilarated that she must needs slap George's knee once more. "Sallie's got her in the back row to-night, where she belongs!"

The aunt and uncle joined laughter with her, and were but vaguely aware that the lady near them had risen from her easy chair. She passed by them, bestowing upon them a grave look, not prolonged.

"Who's all that?" the stout uncle inquired, when she had disappeared round a corner of the veranda. "Awful big dignified looking party, *I'd* call her," he added. "Who is she?"

"There's a lot of that highbrow stuff around here," said Sallie's mother;—"but, of course, I don't get acquainted as fast as Sallie. I don't know who she is, but probably I'll meet her some day."

If Mrs. Cromwell had overheard this she might have responded, mentally, "Yes—at Philippi!" For it could be only on the field of battle that she would consent to meet "such rabble." She said to herself that she dismissed them and their babblings permanently from her mind; and, having thus dismissed them, she continued to think of nothing else.

Her old-fashioned mood was ruined; so was the moon, and so was her evening. She went home early, and sent her car back to wait for Anne.

VI

SALLIE EALING

IT DID not wait so long as it usually did: Anne
came home early, too, at eleven; though the
dancing would go on until one, and it was her
habit to stay as long as the musicians did. Distant
throbbings of dance music from across the links came
in at the girl's open window as she undressed in her
pretty room; but she listened without pleasure, for
perhaps she felt something unkind in these faraway
sounds to-night—something elfish and faintly jeering.

Her mother, coming in, and smiling as she always
did when she came for their after-the-party talks,
saw that Anne looked serious: her eyes were grave
and evasive.

"Did you get tired—or anything, Anne?"

"It wasn't very exciting—just the same old crowd
that you always see there, week after week. I
thought I might as well get to bed a little early."

"That'll please your father," Mrs. Cromwell assured her. "I noticed you danced several times

with young Hobart Simms. You were dancing with him when I left, I think."

"Yes?" Anne said, inquiringly, but she did not look toward her mother. She stood facing her dressing-table, apparently preoccupied with it. "I shouldn't?"

"'Shouldn't?'" Mrs. Cromwell echoed, laughing indulgently. "He's commonplace, perhaps, but he's a nice boy, and everybody admires the plucky way he's behaved about his father's failure. I only thought——" she hesitated.

"Yes?"

"I only thought—well, he *is* a little shorter than you——"

"I see," Anne said; and with that she turned eyes starry with emotion full upon her mother. The look was almost tragic, but her voice was gentle. "Did we seem—ridiculous?"

"No, indeed! Not at all."

"I think we did," Anne murmured and looked down at the dressing-table again. "Well—it doesn't matter."

"Don't be so fanciful," Mrs. Cromwell said. "You couldn't look ridiculous under any circumstances, Anne."

"I understand," said Anne. "You don't think I danced with Hobart Simms because I *wanted* to, do you, Mother?"

"No, it was because you're kind," Mrs. Cromwell returned, comfortingly; then continued, in a casual way, "It just happened you were with poor little Hobart during the short time I was looking on. I suppose you weren't *too* partial to him, dear. You danced with all the rest of the customary besiegers, didn't you?"

"Oh, I suppose so," Anne said, wearily. In profile to her mother, she stood looking down upon the dressing-table, her hands moving among little silver boxes and trumperies of ivory and jade and crystal; but those white and shapely hands, adored by the mother, were doing nothing purposeful and were only pretending to be employed—a signal to mothers that daughters wish to be alone but do not know how to put the wish into tactful words. Mrs. Cromwell understood; but she did not go.

"I'm glad you danced with all of 'em," she said. "You did dance with them all, did you, Anne?"

"I guess so."

"I'm glad," the mother said again, and then, as in a musing afterthought, she added, "I only looked on for a little while. I suppose Harrison was there?"

The daughter's hands instantly stopped moving among the pretty trifles on the dressing-table; she was still from head to foot; but she spoke in a careless enough tone. "Harrison Crisp? Yes. He was there." And then, as if she must be scrupulously honest about this impression, she added, "At least, I *think* he was."

"Oh!" Mrs. Cromwell exclaimed, enlightened. "Anne, didn't you dance with him at *all?*"

"With Harrison?" the girl asked, indifferently. "No; I don't believe I did, now I come to think of it."

"Didn't he ask you at all?"

Anne turned upon her with one of those little gasps that express the exasperated weariness of a person who makes the same explanation for the hundreth time. "Mother! If he didn't ask me, isn't that the same as not asking me 'at all'? What's the difference between not dancing with a person and not dancing with him 'at all'? What's the use of making such a commotion about it? Dear me!"

The unreasonableness of this attack might have

hurt a sensitive mother; but Mrs. Cromwell was hurt only for her daughter:—petulance was not "like" Anne, and it meant that she was suffering. Mrs. Cromwell was suffering, too, but she did not show it.

"What in the world was Harrison doing all evening?" she asked. "It seems strange he didn't come near you."

"There's no city ordinance compelling every man in this suburb to ask me to dance. I don't know what he was doing. Dancing with that girl from nowhere, probably."

"With whom?"

"Nobody you know," Anne returned, impatiently. "A girl that's come here lately. He seemed to be unable to tear himself away from her long enough to even say 'How-dy-do' to anybody else. He's making rather an exhibition of himself over her, they say."

"I heard something of the kind," her mother said, frowning. She seated herself in a cushioned chair near the dressing-table. "Is she a commonish girl named Sallie something?"

"Yes, she is," Anne replied, and added bitterly: "Very!" Having reached this basis, they found that they could speak more frankly; and both of them felt a little relief. Anne sat down, facing her mother. "She's a perfectly horrible girl, Mother —and that's what he seems to like!"

"I happened to hear a little about her," Mrs. Cromwell said. "I noticed some relatives of hers who were there—her mother was one—and they were distinctly what we call 'common.' I was so surprised to find such people put up as guests at the club that before I came home I asked some questions about them. The mother and daughter have come here to live, and they're apparently quite well-to-do. Their name is Ealing, it seems."

"Yes," said Anne. "Sallie Ealing."

"What surprised me most," Mrs. Cromwell continued, "I learned that they'd not only been given guests' cards for the club, but had actually been put up for membership."

"Yes," Anne said huskily. "It's Harrison. He did it himself and he's got about a dozen people to second them. Several of the girls thought it their duty to tell me about that to-night."

"You poor, dear child!" the mother cried; but her compassion had an unfortunate effect, for the suave youthful contours of the lovely face before her were at once threatened by the malformations of anguish: Anne seemed about to cry vociferously, like a child. She got the better of this impulse, however; but she stared at her mother with a luminous reproach; and the light upon the dressing-table beside her shone all too brightly upon her lowered eyelids, where liquid glistenings began to be visible.

"Oh, Mamma!" she gasped. "What's the matter with me?"

"The matter with you?" her mother cried. "You're perfect, Anne! What do you mean?"

Anne choked, bit her lip, and again controlled herself, except for the tears that kept forming steadily and sliding down from her eyes as she spoke. "I mean, why do I mind it so much? Why do I care so about what's happening to me now? I never minded anything in my life before, that I remember. I was sorry when Grandpa died, but I didn't feel like *this*. Have I been too happy? Is it a punishment?"

Her mother seized her hands. "'Punishment'? No! You poor lamb, you're making much out of nothing. Nothing's happened, Anne."

"Oh, but it has!" Anne cried, and drew her hands away. "You don't *know*, Mamma! It's been coming on ever since that girl first came to one of the summer dances, a month ago! Mamma, to-night, if it hadn't been for little Hobart Simms, there were times when I'd have been stranded! Absolutely! It's such a horribly helpless feeling, Mamma. I never knew what it was before—but I know now!"

"But you *weren't* 'stranded,' dear, you see."

"I might have been if I hadn't come away," Anne said, and her tears were heavier. "Mamma, what can I do? It's so unfair!"

"You mean this girl is unfair?"

"No; she only does what she thinks will give her a good time.' There was sturdiness in Anne's character; she was able to be just even in this crisis of feeling. "You can't blame her, and it wouldn't do any good if you did. I mean it's unfair of human nature, I guess. I honestly never knew that men were so stupid and so—so *soft!* I mean it's unfair that a girl like this Sallie Ealing can turn their heads."

"I just caught a glimpse of her," Mrs. Cromwell said. "What is she like?"

"She's awful. The only thing she hasn't done is bob her wonderful hair, but she's too clever about

making the best of her looks to do that.   She smokes
and drinks and 'talks sex' and swears."

"Good heavens!"   Mrs. Cromwell exclaimed.
"And such a girl is put up for membership at our
quiet old family country club."

Anne shook her head, and laughed tearfully.
"She'll never be blackballed for that, Mamma!
Nobody thinks anything about those things any
more; and besides, she only does them because she
thinks they're 'what goes.'   *They* aren't what's made
the boys so wild over her!"

"Then what has?"

"Oh, it's so crazy!" Anne cried. "I could imagine
little boys of seven or even ten, being caught that
way, at a children's party, but to see grown *men!*"

"Anne!"   Mrs. Cromwell contrived to smile,
though rather dismally. "How are these 'grown
men' caught by Miss Sallie Ealing?"

"Why, just by less than *nothing*, Mamma! Of
course, she's got a kind of style and anybody'd
notice her anywhere, but what makes you notice
her so much is her being so triumphant: the men are
all rushing at her every instant, and that makes you
look at her more than you would.   But what *started*
them to rushing and what keeps them going is the

thing I feel I can never forgive them for. Mamma, I feel as if I could never respect a man again!"

"Remember your father," Mrs. Cromwell said indulgently. "Your father——"

"No; if a man like Harrison Crisp can become just a girl's slave on that account——" Anne interrupted herself. "Why, it's like Circe's cup!" she cried. "I suppose that meant Circe's kiss, really."

"They don't do that, do they, Anne?"

"I don't know," Anne said. "It's not that at first, anyhow."

"Well, how does she enslave them?"

"It's like this, Mamma. The first time I ever saw her, I was dancing with Harrison, and he happened to point her out to me. He'd just met her and didn't take any interest in her at all. He really didn't. Well, a minute or two later she danced near us and spoke to him over her partner's shoulder as they passed us. 'I heard something terrible about you!' was what she said, and she danced on away, looking back at him over her shoulder. Pretty soon some one cut in and took me away, and Harrison went straight and cut in and danced with Sallie Ealing almost all the rest of the evening. The next day he and I were playing over the course and when we finished she was just starting out from the club in a car with one of the boys. She called back to Harrison, 'I dreamed about you last night!' and he was terribly silly: he kept calling after her, 'What was the dream?' And she kept calling back, 'I'll *never* tell you!' Mamma, that's what she does with them *all*."

"Tells them she's dreamed about them?"

"No," Anne said. "That's just a sample of her 'line.' When she dances near another girl and her partner, she'll say to the other girl's partner, 'Got something *queer* to tell you,' or 'I *heard* something about you last night,' or 'Wait till you *hear* what I know about *you*,' or something like that; and, of course, he'll get rid of the girl he's with as soon as he can and go to find out. She almost never passes a man at a dance, or on the links, without either calling to him if he's not near her, or whispering to him if he is. It's always some absolutely silly little mystery she makes up about him—and almost her whole stock in trade is that she's heard something about 'em, or thought something curious about 'em, or dreamed about 'em. It's always something about *them*, of course. Then they follow her around to find out, and she doesn't tell 'em, so they keep *on*

following her around, and she gets them so excited
about themselves that then they get excited about
her—and she makes 'em think she's thinking about
them mysteriously—and they get so they can't *see*
anybody but Sallie Ealing! They don't know what
a cheap bait she's caught 'em with, Mamma;—
they don't even guess she's *used* bait! That's why
I don't feel as if I could ever respect a man again.
And the unfairness of it is so *strange!* The rest of
us could use those tricks if we were willing to be that
cheap and that childish; but we can't even tell the
men that we wouldn't stoop to do it! We can't do
anything because they'd think we're jealous of her.
What *can* we do, Mamma?"

Mrs. Cromwell sighed and shook her head. "I'm
afraid a good many generations of girls have had
their Sallie Ealings, dear."

"You mean there isn't anything we can do?"
Anne asked, and she added, with a desolate laugh,
"I just said that, myself. But *men* do things when
they feel like this, don't they, Mamma? Why is it
a girl can't? Why do I have to sit still and see men
I've respected and looked up to and thought so wise
and fine—why do I have to sit still and see them
hoodwinked and played upon and carried off their

feet by such silly little barefaced tricks, Mamma? And why don't they see what it is, themselves, Mamma? Any girl or woman—the very stupidest— can see it, Mamma, so why doesn't the cleverest man? Are men *all* just *idiots*, Mamma? Are they?"

This little tumult of hurried and emotional questions pressed upon the harassed mother for but a single reply. "Yes, dear," she said. "They are. It's a truth we have to find out, and the younger we are when we find out, the better for us. We have to learn to forgive them for it and to respect them for the intelligence they show in other ways—but about the Sallie Ealings and what we used to call 'women's wiles,' we have to face the fact that men are— well, yes—just idiots!"

"*All* men, Mamma?"

"I'm afraid so!"

"And there's nothing to do about it?"

"I don't quite say that," Mrs. Cromwell returned thoughtfully. "There's one step I shall certainly be inclined to take. I'm certain these Ealing people would *not* make desirable members of the club and I——"

"No, no!" Anne cried, in terrified protest. "You mustn't try to have them blackballed, Mamma.

You couldn't do a single thing about it that Harrison would hear of, because he's proposed them himself, and he'd insist on knowing where the opposition came from. Don't you see what he'd think? It would look that way to everybody else, too. Don't you *see*, Mamma?"

Mrs. Cromwell was forced to admit her helplessness to help her daughter even by this stroke of warfare. "It's true, I'm afraid, Anne. But what an outrageous thing it is! We can't even take measures to protect a good old family institution like the Green Hills club from people who'll spoil it for us— and all because a silly boy was made sillier by a tricky girl's telling him she'd dreamed about him!"

"Yes," Anne said, while new tears sidled down her cheeks;—"he must have been silly all the time. I didn't think he was—not until this happened—but he must have been, since it *could* happen." She put out a hand to her mother's. "Mamma," she said, piteously, "why does any one have to care what a silly person does? If he's silly and I know it, why does it matter to me what he does? Why don't I get over it?"

And with that, the sobbing she had so manfully

withheld could be withheld no longer. Her mother soothed her in a mother's way, but found nothing to say that could answer the daughter's question. They had an unhappy half-hour before Anne was able to declare that she was ashamed of herself and apologize for "making such an absurd scene"; but after that she said she was "all right," and begged her mother to go to bed. Mrs. Cromwell complied, and later, far in the night, came softly to Anne's door and listened.

Anne's voice called gently, "Mother?"

The door was unlocked, and Mrs. Cromwell went in. "Dearest, I've been thinking. You and I might take a trip somewhere abroad perhaps. Would you like to?"

"We can't. We can't even do that. Don't you see if we went now it would look as if I couldn't stand it to stay here? We can't do anything, Mother!"

Mrs. Cromwell bent over the bed. "Anne, this isn't serious, dear. It will pass, and you'll forget it."

"No. I think I must have idealized men, Mother. I believe I thought in my heart that they're wiser than we are. *Are* they *all* such fools, Mother? That's what I can't get over. If you were in my place and Papa not engaged to you yet, and he saw Sallie Ealing and she tried for him—oh, Mamma, do you think that even *Papa*——"

Mrs. Cromwell responded with a too impulsive honesty; she gave it as her opinion that Sallie would have found Mr. Cromwell susceptible. "I'm afraid so, Anne," she said. "Perhaps this Ealing girl's way would be too crude for him now, at his age, but I shouldn't like him to be exposed to her system in the hands of Madame de Staël, for instance. Somewhere in the world there may be a man who wouldn't feel any fascination in it, but if there is he'd be a 'superman,' and we aren't likely to meet him. You must go to sleep now."

"I'll try to, Mother," the unhappy girl said obediently. "I'll *try* not to think."

VII

NAPOLEON WAS A LITTLE MAN

ON AN afternoon of June sunshine, a week later, Mrs. Cromwell sat with a book beside one of the long windows of her drawing-room. The window was open, and just outside it a grass terrace, bordered by a stone balustrade, over-looked the lawn that ran down to the shady street. Anne reclined in a wicker *chaise longue* upon the ter-race, protected by the balustrade and a row of plants from the observation of the highway. She, also, had a book; but it lay upon her lap in the relaxed grasp of a flaccid hand. Her eyes were closed, though she was not asleep; and the mother's frequent side glances took anxious and compassionate note of darkened areas beneath the daughter's eyelids, of pathetic shapings about her mouth.

The street was lively with motorists on the way to open country, for it was Saturday, and the auto-mobiles were signalling constantly; out among all the signals, so alike, there was one that Anne recognized. Suddenly she opened her eyes, drew herself up, and looked across the top of the balustrade at a shining gray car just then approaching. It was a long, fleet-looking thing, recognizably imported, and impressive in its intimations of power, yet it selfishly had seats for but two people. One was not occupied; and in the other reclined a figure appropriate to the fine car, for, like the car, the figure was long, fleet-looking, and powerful. The young man was bareheaded; his dark hair shone in the sunlight, and his hands were gracefully negligent, but competent, upon the wheel. One of them gave Anne a cordial though somewhat preoccupied wave of greeting.

She waved in return, but did not smile; then she sank back in her chair and closed her eyes again. Her mother sent a hard glance down the street after the disappearing car, looked at Anne, and breathed a deep, inaudible sigh.

A moment later a straw hat upon a head of short sandy hair appeared above the balustrade and little Hobart Simms came up the stone steps that led from the lawn to the terrace. "I hope I'm not disturbing a nap," he said, apologetically.

Mrs. Cromwell was sorry to see him. There are

times when the intrusions of the insignificant are
harder to bear than those of the important, and she
felt that Anne's suffering would be the greater for the
strain of talking to this bit of insignificance in particular.   However, both mother and daughter gave
the youth a friendly enough greeting; he sat down in a
chair near Anne, and Mrs. Cromwell returned her
eyes to her book.

"It's such a fine day," Hobart said, fanning himself with his straw hat.   "I thought maybe after I
get my breath you might like to take a walk, maybe."

"I believe not," Anne said, smiling faintly.   "How
did you lose your breath, Hobart?"

"Hurrying," he explained.   "I'm working with
the receiver that's in charge of my father's business,
you know.   As soon as I found he wasn't coming
this afternoon I left.   I hurried because I was afraid
you'd be out somewhere.   We haven't any car, you
know;—they're in the receiver's hands, too."

"I'm so sorry, Hobart."

"Not at all," he returned, cheerfully.   "It's a
good thing.   There are lots of families that ought to
learn how to use a sidewalk again.   It's doing all of
our family good.   We'd got like too many other
people; we'd got to believing the only place where we

could walk was a golf course. Bankruptcy's been a great thing for my father—I believe it'll add ten years to his life."

Anne laughed and Mrs. Cromwell was pleased, for although the laugh was languid, it was genuine. The mother's glance passed from her daughter to the caller and lingered with some favour upon his shrewd and cheerful face. Perhaps it was just as well that he had come, if he could amuse Anne a little.

"I never heard of any one who took that view before," the girl said. "It's pretty plucky of you, I think."

"Not at all," he said. "We're all of us having a great time. Never had to do anything we didn't want to before, and it's such a novelty it's more fun than Christmas. If it hadn't happened I doubt if I'd ever have found out that I like to work."

"But you did work, Hobart."

"Yes," he said, dryly. "For my father. This is a pretty good receiver we've got, and he's showed me the difference between working for my father and working for other people." He paused and chuckled. "Best thing ever happened to me!"

Anne did not hear him. The automobile signal that had caught her attention a little while before

was again audible from the street, and she had
turned to look.   The long, gray, foreign car came
slowly by, moving flexibly through a momentary
clustering of other machines, and it seemed to guide
itself miraculously, for the driver had no apparent
interest in where it went.   His attention was all
upon the occupant of the seat that had been vacant
a few minutes before;—upon her he gazed with such
aching solicitude that he could be known for a lover
at a distance all round about him of fifty paces
and more.   And not only he, but his companion
also seemed enclosed within the spell that comes
upon lovers, shutting out the world from them;
for, as he gazed upon her, so she likewise gazed
receptively upon him.   But, being a girl, she was in
fact aware of certain manifestations in the world outside the spell, which he was not, and she knew that
she was observed from a Georgian terrace.

She detached her eyes from Harrison's long enough
to wave her slim hand, and received in return a
beaming smile from Anne, across the balustrade,
and a wave of the hand most cordial.   Harrison
remained in his trance, incapable of making or receiving any salutation, and Hobart Simms, looking
after the car as it passed northward, did not see how

bleak and blank Anne looked as she sank back in her chair.

He laughed. "Poor old Harry Crisp!" he said. "He didn't even see us, so it's all up with him. It's too bad: he might have got something out of life; but it's all over now."

"I don't follow you, I'm afraid," Anne said, coldly, in a tired voice.

"No? Well, in the first place, he's working for his father. That's bad, but it can be got over. What's really fatal, he's going to marry that Miss Ealing. I've heard it rumoured, and after looking at 'em just now I see it's true. That's something he can't get over."

"Can't he?" Anne's tired voice was a little tremulous. "You mean he'll always be in love with her? I should think that rather desirable if they're to marry."

"Oh, he'll get over *that*," Hobart said, briskly. "I mean he'll never get over his having married Miss Ealing."

Anne looked puzzled; but she did not try to make him be more explicit. Instead, she asked indifferently, "Don't you call her 'Sallie,' Hobart? I thought all the men called her 'Sallie' by this time. She's been here several weeks."

"No, I don't," he answered. "I haven't called her anything, in fact."

"What? Didn't she take the trouble to fascinate you, Hobart?"

He laughed. "You'd hardly think she would, but she did—a little. I don't suppose you could say she went out of her way to do it, or took any trouble, exactly; but she did invite me to join, as it were."

Anne was more interested. Since the passing of Harrison Crisp's car she had been leaning back in her long chair, but now she sat upright and looked frowningly at her caller.

"'Invited you to join?'" she said. "What do you mean?"

"I mean she invited me to get on the band-wagon," he explained. "Not right up on a front seat, of course; but anyhow I was given a ticket to hang on behind somewhere."

"I don't understand you."

"Probably you don't," Hobart said, and he looked thoughtful. "You're always so above the crowd, Anne, probably you wouldn't understand Miss Ealing's invitations. You see I'm in a pretty good position to see things that you wouldn't, so to speak. Of course, strangers never pay any atten-

tion to the little shrimps in a crowd, and when Miss
Ealing did pay me a slight attention I wasn't so grateful as I should have been;—I thought it was pretty
funny."

"'Funny'!" Anne exclaimed. "Why?"

"Because it only showed her up, you see. Of
course, it didn't mean she had any interest in me; it
only meant she had a use for me. She already had
most of the rest of 'em excited about her; but she's a
real collector and she wanted the *whole* collection—
even me! You see, the girl that makes 'em *all* think
she's thinking about them isn't thinking about *any*
of 'em, of course. She's only thinking about herself,
like any other selfish little brute."

"Hobart!"

"Of course, I don't mean to say she gave me a
pressing invitation to join," he explained, laughing
cheerfully at himself. "Naturally, that couldn't be
expected. The big, hand-painted, gilt-edged card
was for Harrison Crisp, of course; and then there were
a number of handsomely engraved ones for tall
eligibles. She just slipped me a little one printed on
soft paper—a sort of handbill, you know, when she
was delivering 'em around to the residue."

Anne's languor had vanished now. She stared at

him incredulously. "Hobart Simms," she cried, "what do you mean by 'handbills'?"

"It's simple enough," he began. "That is, it is to me. Taller men with fathers that aren't in the hands of a receiver wouldn't have much of a chance to understand it, I imagine. She's made a real stir in our little Green Hills midst with her handbills and——"

Anne interrupted sharply: "I asked you what you meant by her 'handbills.'"

"Yes; I'm trying to tell you, but it's so ridiculous I'm afraid you won't be able to see what I mean. It's like this: she'll be passing you, for instance, dancing with some other man, or hanging to his arm, and she'll whisper to you quickly over his shoulder, 'I *heard* something about you,' or, 'I've found *out* something about you,' or, maybe, 'Can't you even *look* at me?' Something like that, you know,—and you're supposed to get excited and follow up the mystery. You're supposed to wonder just how much she *is* thinking about you, you see. That's what I mean by her handbills, because if you *don't* get excited, but look around a little, you'll notice she's passing 'em pretty freely. That's why I thought it was funny when she even gave me one!"

"Hobart!" Anne cried, and her voice was free and loud, "Hobart Simms!"

"Yes?" he said, inquiringly, not comprehending the vehemence of her exclamation.

Anne did not respond at once. Instead, she sat staring at him, and her mother marked how a small glow of red came into the daughter's cheek. Then Mrs. Cromwell also stared at little Hobart Simms; and for the first time noticed what a good profile he had and what a well-shaped head. Slowly and wonderingly the daughter's eyes turned to meet the mother's, and each caught the marvel of the other's thought: that it was this unconsidered little Hobart Simms who fitted Mrs. Cromwell's definition of a "superman."

"Why, yes," Anne said, slowly. "If you really care to go for a walk, I'd like to go with you, Hobart."

Mrs. Cromwell watched them as they went forth, outwardly the most ill-assorted couple in her sight that day; for Hobart was a full "head" the shorter. They talked amiably together as they went, however, and Mrs. Cromwell's heart was lightened by the sound of Anne's laughter, which came back to her even when the two had gone but a little distance.

The mother's heart might have known less relief, that afternoon, had she suspected this walk to be the beginning of "anything serious." And yet, had she been a good soothsayer and seeress she might well have been pleased; for not many years were to pass before Hobart Simms's electrified fellow citizens were to remind one another frequently that Napoleon was a little man, too.

VIII

MRS. DODGE'S ONLY DAUGHTER

THAT capable and unsentimental matron, Mrs. Dodge, was engaged in the composition of an essay for the Woman's Saturday Club (founded 1882) and the subject that had been assigned to her was "Spiritual Life and the New Generation." Her work upon it moved slowly because the flow of her philosophical thinking met constant interference, due to an anxiety of her own connected with the New Generation, though emphatically not (in her opinion) with its Spiritual Life. Anxiety always makes philosophy difficult; but she sat resolutely at her desk whenever her apprehensions and her general household duties permitted; and she was thus engaged upon a springtime morning a week before her "paper" was to be presented for the club's consideration.

She wrote quotations from Ruskin, Whitman, Carlyle, and Schopenhauer, muttering pleasantly to herself that the essay was "beginning to sound right well"; but, unfortunately for literature, the window beside her desk looked down upon the street. Nothing in the mild activities of "the finest suburb's finest residential boulevard" should have stopped an essay, and yet a most commonplace appearance there stopped Mrs. Dodge's. Her glance, having wandered to the window, became fixed in a widely staring incredulity; then rapidly narrowed into most poignant distaste. She dropped her pen, and from her parted lips there came an outcry eloquent of horror.

Yet what she saw was only a snub-nosed boy shambling up the brick path to her front door, walking awkwardly, and obviously in a state of embarrassment.

At the same moment Mrs. Dodge's only daughter, Lily, aged eighteen, standing at a window of the drawing-room downstairs, looked forth upon precisely the same scene; but discovered no boy at all upon the brick path. Where her mother saw a snub-nosed boy shambling, Lily beheld a knight of Arthur's court, bright as the sun and of such grace that he came toward the house like a bird gliding in a suave curve before it lights. Merlin wafted him;

she had no consciousness that feet carried him; no consciousness that he wore feet at all. She knew only that this divine bird of hers was coming nearer and nearer to her, while her heart melted within her.

Then, investing him with proper human feet for the purpose of her desire, she wanted to throw herself down before the door, so that he would step upon her as he entered. But, instead, she ran to admit him, and, gasping, took him by the hand, led him into the drawing-room, moaned, and cast herself upon his bosom, weeping.

"They want to separate us!" she sobbed. "Forever! But you have come to me!"

Upstairs, her mother set a paper-weight upon the manuscript of "Spiritual Life and the New Generation," realizing at once that emotional conflict was to occupy her for the next hour or so, if not longer. She descended fiercely to the drawing-room, where the caller, rosy as fire, removed his arm from Lily's waist, and would have stepped away from her. But Lily moaned, "No!" and clung to him.

"Stand away from my daughter!" Mrs. Dodge said. "Explain what you mean by daring to come here."

"I—I want to," he stammered. "That's just what I—it's what I came for.   I—I want to——"

But Mrs. Dodge interrupted him. "Did you understand me? I said, 'Stand away from my daughter!'"

"I would," he said, deferentially. "I would, but —but——"

He was unable to explain in words a difficulty that was too evident without them: the clinging Lily resisted his effort to detach himself, and it was clear that in order to obey her mother's command he would need assistance. This, however, was immediately forthcoming.

"Lily!" Mrs. Dodge rushed upon her; but Lily clung only the more tragically.

"No, no!" she moaned. "This is my place and it is my right!"

Mrs. Dodge set really violent hands upon her, and unmistakably there hovered a possibility, in the imminent future, that Lily would not only be removed from her lover but would also get a shaking. Rather than be seen under such undignified circumstances, she succumbed upon a sofa, weeping there. "You *see*," she wailed;—"you *see* how they treat me!"

"Now, before you march out of here," her mother said to the intruder, "you explain how you dared to come."

"Well, that's what I came for," he responded. "I wanted to explain."

"You make it perfectly clear in one stroke," Mrs. Dodge said. "You came here to explain why you came here!"

"Yes, ma'am."

"Brilliant!" she cried. "But I hadn't looked for better. I think you may trouble yourself to take your instant departure, Mr. Oswald Osborne!"

As she pronounced this name, which she did with oppressive distinctness, the young man winced as at the twinge of an old wound reopened. "I don't think that's fair," he said, plaintively.

"It isn't 'fair' for me to choose whom I care to see in my own house?" Mrs. Dodge inquired with perfect hypocrisy, for she knew what he meant.

"I'm talking about 'Oswald'," he explained. "I can't help my name, and I don't think it's fair to taunt me with it. My parents did have me christened 'Oswald,' I admit; but they were sorry when I got older and they saw how I felt about it and what it would do to me. You know as well as I do, Mrs.

Dodge, I've struggled pretty long to get people to quit calling me 'Oswald,' and almost everybody calls me Crabbe now. It isn't a very good middle name, but anyhow it's better than——"

"Good heavens!" Mrs. Dodge interrupted. "Are you going to stand here all morning talking about your *name?* I'm afraid you overlook the circumstance that you've been requested to leave my house."

"I know it," he said, apologetically. "But it really isn't fair to call me 'Oswald' any more, when practically nobody else does, and that's what threw me off. What I came here for, I had to see Lily."

"*I* had to see *you!*" Lily cried from the sofa. "If I hadn't, I should have died!" And at a scornful look from her mother, she passionately insisted upon the accuracy of this view. "Oh, yes, I should, Mamma! You don't *know* what you and Papa have been putting me through! You don't *know* what it does to me! You don't know what it's making me suffer! You don't understand!"

"I understand too much, unfortunately," the mother retorted. "I understand that you've got yourself into such a hysterical state over a young man who couldn't possibly buy a pair of shoes for you—or for himself!—and that your father and I daren't let you step out of the house alone for fear you'll try to run away with him again."

Young Mr. Osborne protested with some heat. "Why, I'm not barefooted, Mrs. Dodge!" he said. "What I came here to say this morning is right on the point you're discussing. You and Mr. Dodge haven't once been fair to me during the whole trouble we've had about this matter, and when you say I couldn't even give Lily a pair of shoes——"

"Could you?" Mrs. Dodge inquired, breathing deeply. "Am I misinformed by my husband? I seem to recall he told me that when you and Lily were eloping last week—in a borrowed car—he overtook you at a refilling station, where she was offering her watch and rings for gasoline."

"I didn't ask her to," Crabbe Osborne said, flushing deeper. "I admit she offered 'em, but I was arguing about it with her when Mr. Dodge got there. Anyhow, the gas man wouldn't take 'em."

"Oh, he should have!" Lily moaned. "Then we wouldn't have all this to go through. We'd have been out of it all. We'd have been together for always!"

"Would you?" her mother asked, with a hard

laugh. "Just how would you have obtained a marriage license, since there weren't enough funds for gasoline?"

"I had that all thought out," the young man replied. "We were going to stop and get married at Saline. I've got a cousin living in Saline, and I could have borrowed as much as we needed from him. He'd have trusted me, because he knows I'd pay him back."

"And would you?" Mrs. Dodge inquired.

This brought a protest from both of the afflicted lovers. Young Mr. Osborne said, "Oh, look here, Mrs. Dodge," and swallowed, but Lily made a real outcry. She sprang up, facing her mother angrily.

"Shame!" she cried. "You taunt him with his poverty! Has he ever pretended for one moment to be a rich man? If he had, there might be some point to your taunts, but you know he hasn't. From the very first I defy you to say he hasn't been absolutely frank about it! I do, Mamma! I defy you to say so!"

"Sit down," said her mother.

"'Sit down?' I won't, Mamma; I won't sit down! Indeed, I won't, and you haven't any right to make me! You and Papa order me to do this;

you order me to do that; you order me to do every-
thing; but the time's past when I obeyed you like a
Myrmidon. I don't trust your wisdom any more,
Mamma; nor Papa's, either—not since you've
tried to keep me an absolute prisoner and won't let
Crabbe even step inside the yard!"

"'Inside the yard?'" Mrs. Dodge said. "It strikes
me he's rather farther than that." She turned upon the perplexed young man. "How many times do
you usually have to be requested to leave a house?"

"Why, I expect to go," he responded, feebly. "I
do expect to go, Mrs. Dodge. I think I have a right
to explain, though, and if you'd just listen a
minute——"

"Very well. I'll give you a minute."

"It's like this," he said. "I know you and Mr.
Dodge object to me as—as a son-in-law——"

"We do, indeed!"

"Well, you see," he went on, "that's just the in-
justice of it. I'm twenty-two-and-a-half years old,
and while I admit I've had considerable trouble in
some of the positions I've filled in a business way,
why, you can't expect hard luck to keep on being
against me forever. It's bound to turn, Mrs.
Dodge. Luck doesn't always run just one way, not

by any means. My own father said last night he
wouldn't be surprised if I'd get hold of something
pretty soon that would interest me so much I'd
do mighty well at it. Well, he's been prejudiced
against me a good long while now, and I thought if he
had faith in me to say as much as that, it was certainly time for other people to begin to show a little
faith in me, too. What I came here for this morning,
Mrs. Dodge, was to tell Lily about my father saying that to me. I thought she ought to know about
it. You see, Father speaking that way started me
to thinking, and I've realized with the positions I've
held so far I couldn't get myself interested in the
work. That's just exactly what's been the main
difficulty. So I wanted to tell Lily I've made up
my mind I'm going to look for a position where
the work *will* interest me. I thought if she knew I'd
taken this stand on the question——"

"Excuse me," Mrs. Dodge interrupted, "I believe
the minute I agreed to listen is up. I must remind
you of my request to leave this house."

"Well——" he said, uncertainly, "if you put it like
that——"

"I do, if you please."

"Well——" he said, again, and took a step toward

the door, but was detained by Lily, who made an impassioned effort to reach him in spite of the fact that her large and solid mother instantly placed herself between them.

"You sha'n't go!" Lily cried. "If you do, I'll go with you. I'll die if you leave me! I will, Mamma!"

"Stop that!" Mrs. Dodge commanded, and again found herself in the predicament of a lady who is compelled to use force. Lily struggled, and, unable to pass, looked agony upon her lover, wept at him over her mother's shoulder, and also extended an imploring arm and hand toward him above this same impediment.

"You mustn't leave me!" she begged, hoarsely. "I can't *stand* it! Take me *away* with you!" And to this she added a word that her mother found incredible, even though Mrs. Dodge had been through some amazing scenes lately, and thought the utmost of Lily's extravagance already within her experience. Yet the mother might have been wiser here, might have understood that for a girl of Lily's emotional disposition, and in Lily's condition of tragic love, no limits whatever may be set.

To Lily herself the word she used was not extravagant at all; it was merely her definition of Crabbe Osborne. As he went toward the door Lily saw a brightness moving with him, an effulgence that would depart with him and leave but darkness when he had passed the threshold. No doubt the true being of young Crabbe was neither as Mrs. Dodge conceived it nor as Lily saw it;—no earthly intellect could have defined just what he was: nor, for that matter, can any earthly intellect say what anything is, since all of our descriptive words express nothing more than how the things appear to ourselves; and our descriptions, therefore, are all but bits of auto-biography. Thus, Lily's word really expressed not Crabbe but her own condition, and that was what shocked her mother. Yet Lily sincerely believed that the word described Crabbe; and, in her opinion, since her lover's effulgence was divine, this word was natural, moderate, and peculiarly accurate.

"Take me away with you," she wailed; and then, in a voice beset with tears, she hoarsely called him, "Angel"!

"Oh, murder!" cried Mrs. Dodge. And she was inspired to turn upon Crabbe Osborne a look that expressed in full her critical thought of Lily's term for him.

Unquestionably he found himself in difficulties. Called "angel" in the presence of a third party, he may have been hampered by some sense of personal inadequacy. He produced a few sounds in his throat, but nothing in the way of appropriate response; and under the circumstances the expression of Mrs. Dodge was not long to be endured by any merely human being.

"I guess maybe—maybe I better be stepping along," he murmured, and acted upon the supposition that his guess was a correct one.

Lily cried, "No! Don't *leave* me!" And piteously she used her strange word for him again; but her mother held her fast until after the closing of the front door was heard. "Oh, Heaven!" Lily wailed, "won't you even let me go and watch him till he's out of sight? Won't you even let me *look* at him?"

"No, I won't!"

Upon this the daughter slid downward from the mother's grasp and cast herself upon the floor. "He's gone!" she sobbed. "Oh, he's gone! He's gone, and you drove him out! You drove him! You did! You drove him!"

"Get up from there," Mrs. Dodge said, fiercely. "Be quiet!   Do you want the servants to hear you?"

"What do *I* care who hears me?   You drove him!   You drove him, Mamma!   You did!   You *drove* him!"

IX

MRS. DODGE'S HUSBAND

S PIRITUAL LIFE and the New Generation"
lay meekly upon Mrs. Dodge's desk for all
the rest of that day, and nothing was added
to it. Late in the afternoon Lily consented to take
a little beef tea and toast in her room; but she was
still uttering intermittent gurgles, like sobs too
exhausted for a fuller expression, when her mother
brought her tray to her—or perhaps Lily merely
renewed the utterance of these sounds at sight of
her mother—and all in all the latter had what she
called "a day indeed of it!"

So she told Mr. Dodge upon his arrival from his
office that evening. "*Haven't* I, though!" she added,
and gave him so vivid an account that, although he
was tired, he got up from his easy chair and paced
the floor.

"It comes back to the same old, everlasting question," he said, when she had concluded. "What
does she *see* in him? What on earth makes her act

104

like that over this moron? There's the question I
don't believe anybody can answer. She's always
been a fanciful, imaginative girl, but until this thing
came over her she appeared to be fairly close to
normal. Of course, I supposed she'd fall in love
some day, but I thought she'd have a few remnants of
reason left when she did. I've heard of girls that
acted like this, but not many; and I never dreamed
ours would be one of that sort. I'd like to know what
other parents have done who've had daughters get
into this state over some absolutely worthless cub
like Crabbe Osborne."

"I don't know," Mrs. Dodge said, helplessly.
"I'd ask 'em if I did. I'm sure I'm at my wits'
end about it."

"We both are. I admit I haven't the faintest idea
how to do anything more intelligent than we've been
doing—and yet I see where it's going to end."

"Where, Roger? Where do you think it's going
to end?"

"They've tried twice now," he said, gloomily.
"Last time, if the idiot had taken the precaution
to see that there was plenty of gas in his borrowed
car before they started, they'd have been married.
Some day before long he'll borrow *enough* gas, and

then she's going to slip out and meet him again, and they will."

"No, no!" his wife protested. "I can't bear to hear you say so."

"It'll happen, just the same," he assured her, grimly. "Nothing on earth that we've done has been able to make her see this cub except as an angel —a persecuted angel. She really meant it when she called him that;—on my soul, I believe she did! We've told her the truth about him over and over till the repetition makes us sick. What effect does it have on her? We've told her what his own father said about him, that he's 'absolutely no good on earth and never will be!' What help was that? Then we tried having other people tell her their opinions of Crabbe. It only made her hate the other people. We've tried indulgence; we made the greatest effort to interest her in other things; we've tried to get her interested in other young men; we've tried giving her anything she wanted; we've tried to get her to travel; offered her Europe, Asia, and the whole globe; and then when she wouldn't go and everything else we tried was no good, we tried taking the whole thing as a joke—making good-natured fun of this cub; trying to make her see him as ridiculous—and the end of that was her first attempt to run away with him! Well, she did it again, and if we keep on as we're going she'll do it *again!* What's our alternative? I ask you!"

His wife could only moan that she didn't know;— her mind as well as her emotion was exhausted, she said; and the only thing she could suggest now was that he should try to get Lily to come down to dinner. He assented gloomily, "Well, I'll see, though it makes me sick to listen to her when she's like this," and went upstairs to his daughter's room.

After he had knocked repeatedly upon the door, obtaining only the significant response of silence, he turned the knob, found himself admitted into darkness, and pressed a button upon the wall just inside the door. The light, magically instantaneous, glowed from the apricot-coloured silk shades of two little lamps on slender tables, one at each side of the daintily painted bed;—and upon the soft green coverlet, with her fair and delicate head upon the lace pillow, lay his daughter. With hands pressed palm to palm upon her breast, her attitude was that of a crusader's lady in stone upon a tomb; and the closed eyes, the exquisite white profile, thin with suffering, the slender, long outline of her figure, could not fail to touch a father's heart. For the wasting of long-drawn anguish was truly sculptured there, even though the attitude might have been a little calculated.

"Lily," he said, gently, as he approached the bed, "your mother wants to know if you wouldn't like to come down to dinner."

The dark eyelids remained as they were; but the pale lips just moved. "No, thank you."

"You won't?"

"No."

"Then shall we send your dinner up to you, Lily?"

"No, thank you," she whispered.

He had come into the room testily, in a gloomy impatience; but she seemed so genuinely in pain and so pathetically fragile a contestant against her solid mother and against his own robust solidity that suddenly he lost every wish to chide her, even every wish to instruct her. He became weak with compassion, and the only wish left in him was the wish to make her happier. He sat down upon a painted little chair beside the bed.

"Lily, child," he said, huskily, "for pity's sake, what is it you want?"

And again the pathetic lips just moved.

"You know, Papa."

There was something in the whispered word "Papa" that cried to him of sweetness under torture, and cried of it with so keen a sound that he groaned aloud. "O, baby girl!" he said, succumbing then and there, when he had least expected such a thing to happen to him. "We *can't* let you suffer like this! Don't you know we'll do anything on earth to make you happy?"

"No. You wouldn't do the one thing—Papa?"

"I said anything," he groaned.

X

LILY'S ALMOST FIRST ENGAGEMENT

WHEN he came downstairs to his wife, five minutes later, he told her desperately to what he had consented.

"There isn't any alternative," he said, in his defence against Mrs. Dodge's outcry. "It was going to happen anyhow, in spite of everything we could do, and she's grown so *thin*—I hadn't realized it, but she's lost heaven knows how many pounds! You don't want the child to *die*, do you? Well, when I saw her there, so worn and stricken, it came over me what *that* alternative would mean to us! When it comes to risking her life, I give up. I'd give my own life to keep her from marrying this idiot, but not hers! There's only one thing for us to do, and we've got to go through with it."

"I can't!"

"Yes, you can," he told her, angrily. "And since we've got to do it we'll do it right. Not another word to her from either of us in dispraise of her idiot.

On the contrary! And he's to be asked to dinner to-morrow night, and as often as she wants him afterward. Blast him, I'll put him into my own office and try my darnedest to make it a job that'll interest him. They can be married as soon as he's saved enough to pay his own way. I'll give her enough for hers. We're beaten, Lydia. There's nothing else to do."

She protested despairingly, and in continued despair finally surrendered her "better judgment," as she called it, to his weakness. Thus, after a painful evening of argument, they went unhappily to their uneasy beds, but woke in the morning determined to be thoroughbreds in the manner of their acceptance of Oswald Crabbe Osborne as their daughter's betrothed.

Their encounter with him, when he came to dinner that evening in this recognized capacity, was an almost overwhelming trial of their gameness; but they succeeded in presenting the semblance of a somewhat strained beaming upon him, and were rewarded by the sight of a fading daughter blossoming again.

For Lily was radiant: her eyes and cheeks glowed; her feet danced; she was all light and love and gaiety.

At the table she laughed at every nothing, caressed her father, patted her mother's cheek again and again, and from her eyes poured sunshine upon her lover across the centrepiece of roses.

Crabbe received the sunshine with complacency, for he was accustomed to it; and although his position in regard to her father and mother was a novelty, he appeared to accept their change of front as something he had confidently expected all along. That is to say, he took it as a simple and natural matter, of course, and was not surprised to be shown every consideration by his former opponents.

In truth, they showed him more consideration than he was able to perceive. As was already well known to them, he had not the equipment for what is often spoken of as general conversation; his views upon religious, political, scientific, or literary subjects were tactfully not sought, because of his having omitted to acquire the information sometimes held to be a necessary preliminary to the formation of views;—in fact, as Lily's parents were previously aware, he lacked even those vagrant symptoms of ambition, the views without the information. Therefore, Mr. and Mrs. Dodge kept the talk at first as weatherly, and then as personal, as they could make

it, hoping he might shine a little, or at least that some
faint spark might come from him to brighten their
own impressions of him. They wanted to force
themselves to like him; they had genuine yearnings
to think better of him than had been their habit;
but although they strove within themselves to attain
these ends, they cannot be thought to have succeeded.
The nearest Crabbe came to giving them a spark
was when he spoke of his father; and even that apparent momentary gleam was not a happy one.

"He's well," Crabbe said, replying to Mrs. Dodge's
inquiry. "He's usually well enough. He takes
pretty good care of his health and all. I guess he's
a good deal surprised; but probably not enough to
make him sick."

"Isn't he?" Mr. Dodge said, and he laughed
hopefully, for it seemed to him that here was an
unexpected hint of humour, something he had never
attributed to the young man. "What would surprise him as much as that?"

"I don't know, exactly," Crabbe replied. "But
he told me once he always got sick if anything surprised him too much. He says it injures his diges-
tion. What he's surprised about now, it was when I
told him about Lily's telephoning me this morning

you were going to find me a position that would interest me. He certainly said he was surprised."

Mr. Dodge's expectations collapsed, though his expression remained indomitably genial. "I see," he said. "Well, we'll surprise him more by showing him how well you get on at the work."

"I know I will," Crabbe returned, simply. "I mean I'm certain to if it *is* interesting. It's just like I've been telling Lily: the only reason I ever had any trouble at all in business, it's because the luck's been all one way so far;—it kept against my getting anything to do that had any possibilities in it. But it'll be different from now on, I guess. All anybody needs to do for me, Mr. Dodge, is to find me a position where I'll feel some use in getting my brain to work."

Mr. Dodge said he was sure of it, gave his attention to his plate for a few moments, and then, with the gallant assistance of his wife, returned to the weather. Later, when they were alone together in the library, where they could hear from the drawing-room the pretty sound of Lily's prattling, and, at brief intervals, her happy laughter, the parents faced their misery.

"It's unbelievable," Mr. Dodge said, huskily. "You don't run across these extreme cases of self-satisfied asininity more than a few times in your whole life, even counting all the hundreds and thousands of people you come in contact with. And to think you've got to take such a case into your *family!*"

"It's your idea!" his wife reminded him.

"It isn't! It's not my idea; it's a monstrous delusion that's got hold of our girl and that we failed to show her *is* a delusion. Well, since we couldn't show her it is, and since opposing her in it was injuring her health, what's left for us to do but to act as if it were a reality? It isn't my idea to treat this moron as an angel and take him into our family: it's the dreadful necessity that her delusion has forced upon us."

"Thank you for not ending with, 'Isn't that logical?'" she said. "I've been under such a strain, keeping my face cordial at the table, I don't believe I could have stood it!"

"Under a strain?" he echoed. "I should say so!" He gave her a commiserating and comradelike pat upon her shoulder as he passed behind her to get a book from the shelves. "We've both been under a strain, Lydia, and I'm afraid we've got to go on being under it."

"Yes," she agreed. "That's the prospect—for the rest of our lives!"

"I'm afraid so." Then, with grave faces, they settled down to their books, or, at least, tried to settle down to them, but looked into vague and troubled distance more than they read;—ever and anon, as Lily's merriment was made ripplingly vocal in the drawing-room, the silence of the library would become intensified and then be broken by a mother's sigh. But at ten o'clock the front door was heard to close with soft reluctance; and Lily left upon the air a trail of dance music in slender soprano as she skipped down the hall and into the library. She threw her arms about her mother, then about her father, kissing them in turn.

"Now you've let yourselves begin to know him," she cried, "isn't he wonderful? Isn't he wonderful, Mamma? Isn't he wonderful, Papa?"

The two thoroughbreds proved of what stuff heroism is made. They said Crabbe was wonderful. . . . Upon an evening two weeks later, Mr. Dodge, again alone with his wife in the library, reverted to this opinion. "I think Crabbe Osborne is more than wonderful," he said. "I think he's unique. I hate to be premature, but he's been in my office for several days now, and, though they don't say it, I can see that everyone there agrees with me. He couldn't possibly have a duplicate."

"Isn't he 'interested' in anything you've offered him? Hasn't he been able to get his 'brain' to work?"

"Not yet," Mr. Dodge replied. "He's a little discouraged about it, I'm afraid."

"But you aren't, are you?" She made this inquiry with a pointedness not wasted upon him, for he had already perceived the indications that thenceforth in their private hours, until death did them part, he was to be the defender of their acceptance of Crabbe Osborne. Mrs. Dodge adopted her husband's policy, but could not relinquish her attitude of having been forced to it.

"I'm not discouraged about my daughter's health and spirits," he retorted, a little sharply. "I'm not discouraged about having done the right thing. The 'right thing'? How often do I have to tell you it was the *only* thing? Look what it's done for Lily. She was literally pining away. How many weeks was it that we never once saw her smile? How many dozens and dozens of miserable, agonizing scenes did we have with her? How long was it that every day was only another of weeping and outcries— and untouched food on trays outside her door— and tears on untouched food on the table when she did come to the dining-room? I tell you, this house was nothing but a nightmare!"

"And how would you define most of our dinners during the last fortnight?"

He winced, but continued to defend himself. "At least we've reduced the nightmare. If our dinners with the moron are nightmares for us, they aren't for Lily. Only two of us suffer, where it was nightmare for all three of us before. And it's been easier for us this second week than it was the first one."

"Not for me," his wife said, dismally. "The more I see of him the more terrible it is to think of him as permanent."

"But can't you think only of Lily?"

"Indeed, I can! I'm doing just that!"

"Well, then," he urged, "think of the difference in her these two weeks have made. Now she's interested in everything, happy in everything. How many times did we try to get her to go to the country club dances and be with the other young people of the kind she liked and enjoyed before this spell came upon her? She said she 'hated the horrible old place!' because Crabbe Osborne couldn't go there."

"He didn't mind that," Mrs. Dodge remarked. "He went anyhow until they sent him a note reminding him he wasn't a member. That was why Lily said she hated it and we couldn't get her to go any more. I was surprised she decided to go to-night, since she knows he can't be there."

"There's the very point I'm making," her husband said. "Two weeks ago we'd both have thought it was the last thing in the world she'd consent to do, and this evening we didn't even suggest it to her; she went of her own volition, and cheerfully, too! I ask you if that doesn't show she's a different creature. And isn't it better for two to suffer than three?"

"I ask *you*," she returned, sharply: "How short sighted are you? We're giving her a recess from pain, yes; but what are we thrusting her into? When she does see him as he is, and finds herself bound to him for life, isn't she going to turn to us then, when it's too late, and say: 'Why didn't you save me?'"

"Oh, Lord!" the father groaned, and his gesture

was that of a man who has tried to make the best
of his misery, but abandons the effort. "I don't
know! I can't see! When you put it like that, I
don't know whether we're doing right or wrong." He
paced the library floor, walking heavily, his head
down. "It's a miserable thing any way you look at
it," he said. "I did have just one slight alleviation: it
seemed to me I bore it a little better, having him at
the dinner-table this week, than I did the week before.
It seemed to me maybe it might be because I was
getting to like him a little, perhaps."

"No," Mrs. Dodge said, grimly. "It was because
he was here five times the first week and only three
the second."

"Is that so?" He stopped his pacing and stood
still. "So she asked him five times the first week and
only three the second. Doesn't that look as if
maybe——"

"No, I'm afraid not," his wife interrupted, unhesi-
tatingly destroying this obscure germ of hope.
"When you give a child a toy it'll play with it more at
first than it will later. That doesn't mean the child
won't cry if you try to take the toy away, does it?"

"No, I suppose not." He had relapsed into gloom

again.   "And I suppose my poor little alleviation was——"

"Your 'alleviation,'" Mrs. Dodge informed him, "was in the diminished number of the acute attacks —three instead of five—and not because you began to feel any affection for the disease itself."

"I'm afraid you're right," he said. "And I'm afraid you've found the correct definition for what afflicts us." He sank into a chair, unhappily limp and relaxed, his arms hanging flaccidly over the arms of the chair. "Crabbe Osborne is our disease," he said. "It's a disease the more awful because when a child gets it the parents get it, too, and when they give the child an opiate they only stop her pain for a little while; and then the child and the parents, all three of 'em, have got to have the disease for the rest of their lives! And the greatest mystery of it all is that an absolutely chance boy, with no malice, no harm in him—a mere drifting bit of flesh and nothing, that we'd never heard of a year ago—that a meaningless thing like Crabbe Osborne should do all this to us!"

"It isn't," she said.   "He has nothing whatever to do with it.   It's Lily's imagination. Her imagination was in the state to get the disease, and it just hap-

pened this boy was the nearest thing at a crucial
moment. It might as well have happened to be
someone else."

"If it *had* only been any one else!" Mr. Dodge
exclaimed. "I'm willing to agree with you, though:
Crabbe just happened to be the fatal microbe. Well,
he's done for us, that's sure!"

Mrs. Dodge glanced sidelong at him—she was making intermittent efforts to read, and a table and a
lamp were between them. "'Done for us?' Well,
you said there was no alternative, didn't you? It's
your policy, isn't it?"

"I suppose so," he groaned. "I suppose so,
Lydia." Then, shaking his head ruefully, and with a
grunt of desolate laughter in his throat, he said: "I
know, of course, that you're going to lash me with it
—my 'policy'—for the rest of our lives!"

But this was a prediction unfulfilled, for they had
missed a clew that was in their hands; or, more accurately, it had been in their mouths, and they had
actually spoken it. A toy withheld becomes the uni-
verse to a child, and a lover withheld is life and death;
but toys and lovers freely given are another matter.
What Mr. and Mrs. Dodge failed to see was the significant relation of five to three.

. . . The gloomy parents, despondently communing, were still in the library at midnight when Lily came home. They heard her laughter outside before the latchkey turned in the lock of the front door; and then, with the opening of the door, her voice sounded in a gay chattering like a run of staccato notes in an aria of spring. Accompanying it, interrupting it, there was heard a 'cello obbligato, a masculine voice, young and lively, and this short duet closed with Lily's "See you day-after-tomorrow!"

She came dancing into the library, all white fur and flying silk.

"Oh, you mustn't!" she cried. "You dear things, you mustn't sit up for me!"

"We didn't," her mother said. "We were just reading. Who was it that brought you home? I asked your Aunt Sarah——"

"Oh, no! Aunt Sarah was there, but I didn't want to trouble her to come out of her way." Lily seated herself lightly on the arm of her mother's chair, letting one cheerful foot swing and resting an affectionate hand upon Mrs. Dodge's shoulder. "Freddie Haines brought me home. He's a nice boy."

"Is he?"

"I like him awf'ly," said Lily. "I danced with lots of others, though, too. I didn't want 'em to think I was only going to dance with nobody but Fred."

"Didn't you?"

"Freddie Haines is considerate," said Lily. "He doesn't mind my being an old engaged girl at all." Upon this she looked across to meet her father's frowning glance, and laughed. "Oh, Fred won't tell; he's never going to mention it. I didn't forget I promised you to keep it under cover until we're ready to have it announced. I haven't told any one but Fred, and I'm not going to." Here she jumped down from her mother's chair, took an apple daintily from a bowl on the table, and skipped to the door, laughing reminiscently. "He didn't take it seriously, anyhow!" she said as she went out. Then, humming a dance tune, she ran upstairs to her bed.

In the library the astounded parents gazed long upon each other, and the longer they gazed the wider were their eyes.

"Well, at least there's this much to be said for me," Lily's father said, finally;—"when we decided to adopt my policy——"

"Your what?" cried Mrs. Dodge. "Your policy!"

He perceived that his policy was about to be

claimed by another—not instantly, nor brazenly, but nevertheless with a slowly growing assurance that in time would browbeat him.

To-night his |wife said, "Your *policy!*" The day would come when she would say "*Your* policy?"

XI

CORNELIA CROMWELL, having passed her sixteenth birthday anniversary, had begun to think seriously about life and books, and was causing her parents some anxiety. She declined a birthday party, although in former years such festivals had obviously meant to her the topmost of her heart's desire; and she expressed her reasons for this refusal in a baffling manner. "I simply don't care to have one," she said, coldly. "Isn't that enough?" Then, being further pressed, and informed that this repeated explanation of hers was one of those not uncommon explanations that do not explain, she said with visibly increasing annoyance: "Frankly, it would be a useless expense, because I don't care to have a party."

"She's so queer lately," her mother complained to Cornelia's married sister Mildred. "She won't go to other girls' parties either. Of course, it isn't desirable often, while she's still in school, but there are a few she really ought to go to, especially now, during the holidays. She simply refuses—says she 'doesn't care to.' It isn't natural, and I don't know what to make of it, she's grown so moody."

"Don't you think young girls nearly all get like that sometimes?" Mildred suggested. "Perhaps somebody hurt her feelings at the last party she did go to." She laughed reminiscently. "I remember when I was about her age I was terribly anxious to please that funny little Paul Thompson, who used to live next door. He danced with me twice at somebody's birthday party, and I felt perfectly uplifted about it. Then I overheard him talking to another boy, not thinking I was near him. He said his mother had told him he must be polite to me or he wouldn't have done it, and he certainly never would again, no matter what his mother said, because I'd walked all over his new pumps. It just crushed me, and I know I moped around the house for days afterward; but I wouldn't tell you what was the matter. It's the most terribly sensitive age we go through, Mamma, and I just *couldn't* have told you. Perhaps there's been a Paul Thompson for Cornelia."

"No," Mrs. Cromwell returned. "I'm sure there isn't, and that nobody's hurt her feelings. She came home from the last party she went to, a couple of months ago, in a perfect gale of high spirits; she'd had a glorious time. Then, a week or two later, when I spoke of arranging for her birthday, she got very moody—wouldn't hear of any such thing; and she's been so ever since. Your father's getting cross about it and thinks we ought to do something."

"You don't suppose—you don't suppose she's fallen in love? It does happen, you know, Mamma —even at fifteen and sixteen."

"No," Mrs. Cromwell returned decidedly. "I'm certain it isn't that. She's sensible about the boys she knows, and she's never shown the slightest sentimentality. I've thought over all those things, and it isn't any of them. Nothing's the matter with her health either; so there just isn't any reason at all for a change in her. Yet she *has* changed—completely. In the space of a few weeks—you might almost say a few days—instead of being the bright, romping, responsive girl she's always been, she's become so silent and remote you'd think the rest of her family were mere distant and rather inferior acquaintances. It's mysterious and extremely uncomfortable. Your father thinks we ought to send her away to school where she'd have a complete change, and I've had some correspondence about it with Miss Remy of your old school.   I think perhaps——"

Mrs. Cromwell stopped speaking, her attention arrested by the sound of a door opening and closing. She listened for a moment, then whispered: "There! She's just come in.   See for yourself."

The two ladies were sitting in a room that opened upon the broad central hallway of the house, and their view of that part of the black-and-white marble-floored hall just beyond the open double doors was unimpeded.   Here appeared in profile the subject of their discussion, a plump brunette demoiselle, rosy-cheeked and far from uncomely, but weightily preoccupied with her own thoughts.

She did not even glance into the room where sat her mother and sister, though the doorway was so wide that she must have been conscious of them;— she was going toward the stairway at the other end of the hall, and would have passed without offering any greeting, if her mother's voice, a little strained, had not checked her.

"Cornelia!"

The girl paused unwillingly.   "Yes?"

"Don't you see who's here?"

"Yes."   Cornelia nodded vaguely in the direction

of her sister. "How do you do," she said, not smiling. "I'm glad to see you."

"Is that all you have to say?" Mrs. Cromwell inquired.

"Yes, Mamma, if you please. May I go now? There's something important I want to attend to."

"What is it?"

"Something important."

"You told us that," her mother returned. "What is it?"

Cornelia's voice expressed the strained tolerance of a person who has already reported, over and over, all the known facts in a case. "Mamma, I explained that it's something important. Would you mind letting me go?"

"No! Do!" her mother replied crisply, and, when Cornelia had disappeared, turned again to her oldest daughter, and with widespread hands made the gesture of one displaying strange stuff for inspection.

"You see? That's what she's like all the time."

"What do you suppose it is she says is so important?"

Mrs. Cromwell laughed ruefully. "That's all you'd ever find out about it from her. If I ask her again at lunch what it was, she'll do just what she

did then. Her expression will show that she finds
me a very trying person, and she'll either say, 'Nothing,' or else, 'It was something I wanted to attend
to.' And if we should follow her up to her room
now, we shouldn't learn any more about it. She'd
probably be just pottering at her dressing-table or
looking out of the window. That's all we'd find her
doing."

In this surmise Mrs. Cromwell was correct;—if
she and Mildred had ascended to Cornelia's room,
they would have found her either rearranging the
silver and porcelain trifles on her dressing-table, or
else standing at the window near her desk and looking
down pensively upon the suburban boulevard below.
That is to say, by the time they opened the door
she would have been doing one of those two things:
Cornelia was quick of hearing.

What they would have found her doing, if they
could have entered her room without any forewarning
sound of footsteps, however, was another matter.
While her mother and sister continued to wonder
about her downstairs, Cornelia went to her small
desk of dull mahogany and seated herself before it,
but, having done that, did nothing else for a minute
or two;—instead, she sat listening, a precaution due

to the possibility that her mother might indeed prove so curious as to follow up recent inquiries in person.

Then she opened the desk, and after a final glance at her closed door, took from about her neck, beneath the collar of her brown silk blouse, a tiny key upon a fragile gold chain of links as slim as thin wire. With the key she unlocked a drawer inside the desk, and as she did this her expression altered;—the guarded look vanished, and there came in its place a tenderness, wistful and yet so keen that the colour in her cheeks heightened and her softened eyes grew lustrous.

She took first from the drawer a little notebook bound in black leather, and opened it. All the pages were blank except the first one, upon which she had lately written the opening sentence of a novel that she intended to offer the world when the work had been secretly completed. She read the sentence over fondly and yet with some perplexity. It was this:

Gregory Harlford had just fallen out of his airoplane at a height of 7000 feet and as he possessed no parachute he realized that only a miracle could save him from being dashed to pieces at the end of his descent.

That was the original form of the sentence, but Cornelia had made an alteration. She had scratched

out "7000" and replaced it with "5000." To-day
she looked at the latter figure thoughtfully for some
time, and, having drawn a line through it, wrote
"1000" above it.   Then, for a few moments, she had
an encouraged look and seemed about to begin a
second sentence, but did not do so. Instead, she
rested her elbow upon the desk and her chin upon
her hand; and as she continued her study of the opening of her novel, her air of being encouraged gave
way to a renewed bafflement. It was not that the
opening sentence displeased her;—on the contrary.
Yet whenever she wished to add another and get
on with the story, she came to one of those inexplicable blank gaps in the creative mind, one of those flat
stops that so often set even the most willing novelists
to walking the floor or the links.

She was sure that if she could once surmount the
difficulty of the second sentence, the rest would flow
easily from her. Gregory Harlford was to be the
hero of her story, and she had in her mind's eye a
remarkably definite portrait of him, which she
wished to include in the novel; but she felt that
under the circumstances a description of his person
and attributes would be out of place in the second
sentence. There was a vague but persistent im-

pediment somewhere;—inspiration failed to make an appearance, and, after waiting almost fifteen minutes for it, she sighed, pushed the little book away and turned to the other contents of the drawer.

There were several queer items: the stub of an almost entirely consumed lead pencil; an odd bit of broken amber, not quite cylindrical, and half of an old shoe-lace. There were also a dozen dried violets, a flattened rosebud, and a packet of small sheets of note paper whereon appeared cryptic designs—line drawings most curious. These enigmas were what now occupied Cornelia.

They were her own handiwork; nobody had even seen any of them, and they were of different ages. The oldest of the designs had been drawn long, long ago;—that is to say, long, long ago, according to Cornelia's sense of the passage of time. For she was sixteen now, and she had made the first of the queer drawings four eternal years earlier, when she was only a child.

It appeared to be the representation in profile of a steep stairway, or perhaps a series of superimposed cliffs, each with a small shelf at its base. Beginning at the bottom of the sheet of paper, this stairway, or series of cliffs, rose to a small plateau or summit near the top; and upon each step, or shelf of cliff, there was drawn one of those little figures children call "men";—the body is emaciated to the extent that it becomes a single straight line, the arms and legs being similar lines, and the head a round black dot.

In Cornelia's drawing, each of these little figures was labelled, a name having been written beside it; and in some cases a descriptive word or two had been added beneath the

name.   Thus, under the name "Georgie P.", which evidently belonged to the figure occupying the lowest step or shelf, there appeared in faded purple ink a phrase of qualified admiration, "Half Hand-some."   Another expression of an enthusiasm lim-ited by a defect in its subject seemed to refer to "Harold," midway in the ascent—"Terribly Good Looking But Stingy."   However, the figure upon the summit, named in full, "William Peterson McAvoy," was obviously the symbol of a being without flaw, for here Cornelia had carefully printed, all in capital letters: "ABSOLUTELY PERFECT."

Yet, in the next drawing, which, like all the others, was of the same stairway, or series of cliffs, with little "men" upon the steps or ledges, a sharp disaster had befallen this figure adorning with its perfection the summit of the first design. Cornelia had drawn a straight line from the summit down to the bottom of the page; and evidently this straight line indicated a precipice of catastrophical dimension. At the foot of it lay the dot and five lines representing the head, body, and members of William Peterson McAvoy, again thus denominated, and near by was written the simple explanation, "Too Snooty." The summit was bare.

In a subsequent design, done when Cornelia was thirteen, the half handsome Georgie P., who had sometimes occupied one step and sometimes another, finally made his appearance upon the summit, though without any other explanatory tribute than a date: "Sept. 16th." But Georgie P. did not long remain in his high position. A drawing made only a week later depicted him miserably upon his back at the foot of the precipice, and beside him Cornelia had written: "Perfectly Odious. Well only another dream shatered."

All of the drawings were dated and thus proved that they were made at irregular intervals;—sometimes two or three months had elapsed between them; sometimes three or four would be produced within a week; and the figures upon the steps or ledges varied in name and relative position as greatly, though one or two of the names appeared upon all of the designs except the last and most recent one. This had been drawn only a month ago, and was interestingly different from its predecessors.

One thing that made it different was the fact that it contained a Mister. In the others there were Georgies and Harolds and Williams and Toms and Johnnies; but now, for the first time, with unique dignity, appeared "Mr. Bromley," neither a Mister nor a Bromley having been seen upon any previous step or ledge. Moreover, this début of his was unprecedented. Instead of occupying one ledge and then another, sometimes ascending, sometimes descending, before reaching the final elevation, Mr.

Bromley made his first appearance strikingly upon
the summit. More than this, the ledges below him
were unoccupied;—the lofty plateau alone was
inhabited. The Harolds and
Johnnies and Georgies were
gone utterly from the picture,
as if unworthy to be seen at all upon a
mountain crowned with this supreme
Mister.

For the cliffs, or stairway, meant a
mountain to Cornelia;—she thought of
the drawings as a mountain; and she
called the little packet, kept in the
locked drawer, "My Mountain." Her mountain
was her own picture of her heart and of the impressions made upon it;—no wonder she kept it locked
away! And now it was a deeper secret than ever,
for in its present state it glorified the one name alone,
and would have told her world everything. Mr.
Bromley was the "English Professor," aged forty-
three, at the boarding-school where she was a day
scholar; and not long ago he had told her she ought
to think "less about candy and more about books
and life." That was what was the matter with
Cornelia;—she had begun her novel immediately,

and spent a great deal of time in her room, thinking about life and Mr. Bromley.

Mr. Bromley was the hero of the novel and Cornelia thought of him as Gregory Harlford. The general public would never have supposed Mr. Bromley to be an aviator, and he had no claim, in fact, to be thought anything so dashing, though he was fond of chess and still played tennis sometimes. Nevertheless, he seemed to be a quietly resourceful man, one who would find a way out of almost any difficulty, and it was strange that he remained so long suspended in mid-air, in Cornelia's story, even after the vacancy beneath him had been reduced to a thousand feet. For, after looking over her mountain, Cornelia again took up the little leather-bound notebook and renewed the struggle for a second sentence.

Nothing resulted, and, sighing, she gave over the effort and performed a little daily ceremonial of hers, placing side by side in a row her mementoes of Mr. Bromley—the stub of the pencil he had used, the worn shoe-lace he had broken and carelessly tossed aside, the rosebud she had once asked him to smell, the violets that had dropped from his coat lapel, and the fragment of the amber mouthpiece of his pipe, broken when it fell from his pocket upon the stone steps of the school building. Dreamily, she put them all in a row, touching them gently, one after the other; then she leaned her elbows upon the desk and, with her chin in her hands, thought about life and books in a general way for several minutes.

After that, as the air was warm in the room, she went to the window and opened it. Looking down moodily, she saw her sister Mildred departing. "Going home to mess around with the baby," Cornelia thought. "That's her life. How strange she can be contented with it!"

A large red open car went by, sending forth upon the wintry air some cheerful cadences of song as it passed;—young gentlemen collegians merrymaking not indecorously in this holiday time. Cornelia looked down upon the manly young faces, rosy with the wind. "How terrible!" she murmured, dreamily. For they were no part of her mountain; her sister's baby had nothing to do with Mr. Bromley; neither had the song from the big red car; both were dross.

A negro rattled by upon an ash cart drawn by a lively mule. The negro whistled piercingly to a friend in the distance, and the mule's splendid ears stood high and eager; he was noble in action, worthy of all attention. Cornelia could not bear him. "Oh, dear!" she said, probably thinking of his master, who was proud of him. "What lives these people lead!"

She was in the act of turning away from this barren window when something far down the street caught her attention. It was the figure of a thin, somewhat middle-aged gentleman in gray clothes, approaching slowly upon the sidewalk. For a moment Cornelia was uncertain; then there appeared for an instant, beneath the rim of his soft hat, twin sparklings of reflected light. They vanished, but Cornelia needed no further proof that the gentleman in gray wore the eye-glasses that completed her identification of him.

She said, "*Oh!*" in a loud voice, and clapped her joined hands over her mouth to stifle this too-eloquent revelation. Then the bright eyes above the joined hands semicircled impulsively to the bed, where lay her hat and coat as she had tossed them when she came into the room. The impulse that made her look at them increased overwhelmingly; she seized them, put them on hurriedly; opened her door with elaborate caution, tiptoed to a back stairway, descended it noiselessly, and a moment later left the house by a rear door. No one had seen her except the cook's cat.

XII

HER HAPPIEST HOUR

THUS Cornelia saved herself from replying to intrusive questions about where she was going, and why; but in her impulsive haste she had forgotten something. Upon her desk, upstairs, lay her heart's secret, her mountain, all in loose sheets of paper. Beside the desk was an open window;—she had left the door open, too, and this was a breezy day. Such was instantly her condition at sight of Mr. Bromley; and with no thought but to have more sight of him, she flitted across the back yard and through an alley gate, leaving calamity brooding behind her.

Mr. Bromley, returning homeward with a book under his arm, after his morning's browsing in the suburban public library, was not surprised to see one of his pupils emerge from a cross-street before him, since this was the neighbourhood in which most of the school's day scholars lived; but he wondered why Cornelia Cromwell was so deeply preoccupied. She seemed to look toward him, though vaguely, and he lifted his hand to his hat; but before he could complete his salutation she looked away, apparently unconscious of him. She was walking in a rather elderly manner, with her head inclined forward and her hands meditatively clasped behind her—the right posture for an engrossed statesman philosopher, but not frequently expected of sixteen. At the corner she turned northward upon the boulevard sidewalk, Mr. Bromley's own direction, and went pensively on before him, some thirty yards or so in advance.

His gait was slow, for that was his thoughtful habit; and the distance between them, like Cornelia's attitude, remained unvaried until the next cross-street was reached. Here, without altering that scholarly attitude of hers by a hair's-breadth, she walked straight into what was the proper path and right-of-way demanded by an oncoming uproarious taxicab.

With his hoarse warning signal and with his own hoarse voice, the driver raved; she heeded him not. So, taking his life in his hands, he saved her by charging into the curbstone. The wheels providentially mounted and bore him fairly upon the sidewalk;—

he crashed down again to the pavement of the boulevard and roared onward, Biblically oratorical about
women, let hear him who would.

Mr. Bromley rushed forward and seized Cornelia's
arm. "Miss Cromwell!"

She looked up, smiling absently. "Do you think
there was any danger?" she asked. "I didn't
notice."

"Good gracious!" he cried. "Don't you know
you can't cross streets *any*where, these days, without
looking to see what's coming? What was the matter
with you?"

"The matter?" she repeated, vaguely, as she began
to walk onward with him. "Why, nothing."

"I mean: What on earth were you thinking of to
step right in front of a——"

"Oh, that? Yes," she said, gently. "I see what
you mean now, Mr. Bromley. I was thinking about
life."

"You were, indeed?"

"And books," she added.

"Well, I wouldn't!" he said, for he had long since
forgotten his advice to her in the matter. "If I
were you, I'd put my mind more upon street crossings,
especially during pedestrian excursions."

She accepted the reproof meekly, not replying, and for some moments walked beside him in silence. Then she said gravely: "I believe I haven't thanked you for saving my life."

"What?"

She repeated it: "I haven't thanked you for saving my life."

"Good gracious!" he exclaimed. "I didn't do anything of the kind."

"You did, Mr. Bromley."

"I certainly did not," he said, astonished that she seemed genuinely to believe such a thing. "The taxicab was banging around all over the sidewalk by the time I reached you."

"No," she insisted. "I heard you call my name, and then you took hold of me. If you hadn't, I'd have gone straight on."

"Well, you'd have been all right to go straight on, because by that time the taxicab was twenty or thirty feet away."

"No, I'd have been killed," she said. "If you hadn't caught me, I'd have been killed absolutely."

He stared at her, perplexed, though he knew that people often retain but a confused recollection of exciting moments, even immediately after those

moments have passed. Then, with this thought in
his mind, he was a little surprised to find that she
simultaneously had it in her mind, too.

"Maybe you were a little excited to see a person
in danger," she said. "It might have got you mixed
up or something. When things happen so quickly,
it's hard to remember exactly what *did* happen.
You may not know it, but you saved my life, Mr
Bromley."

He laughed. "I didn't; but if you insist on thinking so, I suppose there's no harm."

This seemed to content her; she nodded her head,
smiled sunnily, then became grave again. "And to
think you'd risk your own life to save—even mine!"
she murmured.

"That's merely absurd, Miss Cromwell. By not
the remotest possibility could it be conceived that I
placed myself in any jeopardy whatever."

"Well"——she returned, indefinitely, but seemed
to reserve the right to maintain her own conviction
in the matter. "I think 'jeopardy' is a beautiful
word, Mr. Bromley," she added, after a moment's
silence. "I mean, whether you admit you were in
jeopardy or not, it's a word I think ought to be used
oftener because it's got such a distinguished kind of

sound." She repeated it softly, to herself. "Jeopardy." Then, in a somewhat louder voice, but as if merely offering a sample sentence in which this excellent word appeared to literary advantage, she murmured: "He placed his life in jeopardy—for me."

"I didn't!" her companion said, sharply. "The word is extremely inappropriate in any such connection."

"I just used it to see how it would sound," Cornelia explained. "I mean, whether you did get in jeopardy or anything, or not, on my account, Mr. Bromley, I was just seeing how it would sound if I said it. I mean, like this." And she began to repeat, "He placed his life in jeopardy——"

"Please oblige me," Mr. Bromley interrupted. "Don't say it again."

His tone was brusque, and she looked up inquiringly to find him frowning with annoyance. She decided to change the subject.

"Do you care much for Christmas, Mr. Bromley?" she asked, in the key of polite small talk. "It strikes me as terribly tiresome, myself. I'm positively looking forward to the next school term."

"Are you?"

"Yes—and oh! there was something I thought of

the other day I wanted to ask you. Are you a
Republican or a Democrat, Mr. Bromley?"

"Neither."

"That's so much more distinguished," Cornelia
said. "I mean it seems so much more distinguished
not to be in politics. Do you believe in woman
suffrage?"

"No."

"Neither do I," she said, and made a serious
decision instantly. "I'm never going to vote,
myself. The more I think about books and life,
Mr. Bromley, the less I care about—about"—she
hesitated, having begun the sentence without fore-
seeing its conclusion—"well, about things in general
and everything," she finally added.

The gentleman beside her looked puzzled; but
Cornelia was unaware of the sweeping vagueness of
her remark. She was not in a condition to take note
of such details, her consciousness being too preoccupied with the fact that she was walking with him
who dwelt upon the summit of her mountain—
walking with him and maintaining a conversation
with him upon an intellectual footing, so to speak.
And as she felt that a special elegance was demanded
by the occasion, she made her voice a little artificial

and obliterated our alphabet's least fashionable consonant from her enunciation entirely.

She waved a pretty little ungloved hand in a gesture of airy languor. "Most things seem such a baw, don't you think?" she said.

"Bore?" he inquired, correctly interpreting her effort. "They certainly shouldn't seem so to you, at your age."

"My *age?*" she echoed, and gave forth an affected little scream. "Don't talk to me about my *age!* Why, half the time I feel I'm at least a hundred."

Her companion's reception of the information was somewhat dry. "Not much *more*, I trust," he said, and looked hopefully forward into the distance as if to some goal or terminus of this excursion.

But Cornelia's exaltation was too high for her to be aware of any slight appearances that might lower it. "Indeed I do," she insisted. "Why, when I look at the classes of younger girls that have come into the school in the years and years I've been there, I feel a thousand. I do, positively, I do assure you."

From beneath a plaintive brow, Mr. Bromley's eyes continued to search the distance hopefully, and he made no response.

Then, as he still remained silent, Cornelia did

what most people do when their ebulliences are received without encouraging comment—she eased herself by a series of repetitions, enthusiastic at first, but tapering in emphasis until she had settled down again into the casual. "It's the positive fact; these younger girls *do* make me feel a thousand—positively, I do assure you! You mayn't believe it, but it's the mere simple truth, I do assure you. It is, I do——" She checked herself, being about to say "I do assure you" again; and although her own ability to use the phrase charmed her, she feared that too much of it might appear to indicate a lack of versatility. She coughed delicately, as a proper bit of punctuation for the unfinished sentence;—then, as further punctuation, uttered sounds resembling a courteous kind of laughter, to signify amusement caused by her own remarks, and thus gradually reached a point where she could regard the episode as closed.

Having successfully passed this rather difficult point, she looked up at him with the air of a person suddenly overtaken by a belated thought that should have arrived earlier. "Oh, by the by," she said, "I suppose I ought to've asked this sooner, but I expect

I forgot it because I was a little excited about your risking your li——"

"I did nothing of the kind," he interrupted, promptly and sharply. "What is it you wanted to ask me?"

"Well, it was this, Mr. Bromley. We got to walking along together after you saved—after I nearly got run over—and I didn't even ask you where you're going."

"I'm on my way to lunch at the Blue Tea Room."

"You—you *are?*" Cornelia said in a strange tone. An impulse, rash and sudden, had affected her throat.

She had never before been quite alone with the solitary inhabitant of her mountain's summit; she had never before walked with him. Her walking was upon air, moreover. She was self-conscious, yet had no consciousness of walking—the rather, she floated in the crystal air of great altitudes; and, rapt in the transcendent presence beside her, she became intoxicated by the experience.

Cornelia had fallen in love with Mr. Bromley sublimely, instantly, upon that day when he told her to think about books and life;—there seemed to be no other reason, though her own explanation defined him as the only man who had ever spoken to her inner self—and now that she found herself alone with him for the first time, she could not bear for that time to be brief. She was already expected at home for lunch, and she knew that her unexplained absence might cause more than mere comment in her domestic circle. Her impulse was, therefore, something more than indiscreet, taking all circumstances and the strictness of her mother into account. But the exciting moment had prevailed with Cornelia before she took anything into account.

"To lunch at the Blue Tea Room?" she cried. "Why, Mr. Bromley, so am I! That's just where I was going. Isn't that *queer?* Why, we can have lunch together."

The hopeful gleam passed out of Mr. Bromley's expression, though perhaps the bright eyes looking up at him so eagerly were able to interpret his gloom as merely the thoughtfulness habitual to a scholar. His was not a practical mind; he had no thought that Cornelia's lunching with him might have any result save to spoil the cozy hour he had planned for himself with his book as a table companion. To him she was one of the hundred pupils at the school— a little girl who had lately developed odd manner-

isms and airy affectations, for no reason except that
many little girls seemed to pass through such phases—
and so far as his interest in her as an individual
human being was concerned, Cornelia might as well
have been eight years old as sixteen.   He saw nothing, except that he would have to listen to her instead of reading his book, for, since she meant to
lunch at the Blue Tea Room, she would probably
talk to him anyhow, whether they sat at the same
table or not.

"Ah—if such be the case, very well," he said,
without enthusiasm.   "Very well, Miss Cromwell."
Then he added hastily, "I mean to say"—and paused
hoping to think of something that might avoid the
proposed tête-à-tête; but he failed.   "I mean to say
—ah—if you wish, Miss Cromwell."

"*Do* I!" she exclaimed, breathlessly; but the radiant face she showed him only gave him the idea that
she was probably excited by the prospect of waffles.

Yet, when waffles—the Blue Tea Room's specialty
—were placed, as a second course, upon the small
blue-and-white painted table between her and Mr.
Bromley, Cornelia showed no avidity for them.
She had resumed her elegant manner, and but toyed
with the food.   Her elegance, indeed, was almost

oppressive to her companion;—she told the blue-
aproned waitress, whose cultivation was betokened
by horn-rimmed spectacles, that forgetting to bring
butter was a "dreadful baw." She said "baw"
as frequently as she could, in fact; and she appeared
to view the people at the other tables through a
frigid though invisible lorgnette.

Her disdain of them as plebeians, beings unknown
and not to be known, was visible in her expression;—
so much so that it made Mr. Bromley uncomfortable;
and here was a small miracle in its way; for in reality
she did not see the other people in the room at all distinctly. They were only blurred planes of far-away
colour to her; she was but dimly aware of their outlines, and failed to recognize two of them whom she
knew very well.

For Cornelia all life and light centred upon
the little painted table at which she sat with
Mr. Bromley. The world to her was like a shadowy
room at sunset, when through a window a last shaft
from the rosy sun illumines one spot alone, making
it glorious, and all else dim and formless. Mr.
Bromley and she sat together in this golden glow,
an aura that shimmered out to nothing all round
about them, so that there was no definite background;

and for anything more than two or three feet away she was astigmatic.

Elation sweet as music possessed her. She was not only lunching at a restaurant with a Distinguished Man, quite as if she were a prima donna in Paris, but that Distinguished Man was Mr. Bromley —Mr. Bromley himself, pale with studious wisdom, yet manly, and incomparably more exciting than the symbol of him drawn with five lines and a dot upon her mountain. She had sometimes trembled when she looked at that emaciated symbol: What wonder could there be that she became a little too elegant, that her laughter rang a little too loudly, or that she showed herself disdainful of lowly presences in a dim background, now, when she sat facing her Ideal made actual in all his beauty?

Beauty it was, in good faith, to Cornelia, and, so far as she was concerned, Praxiteles, experimenting to improve Mr. Bromley, could only have marred him. There was gray in his hair, but it was not emphasized, since he was an ashen blond; and for Cornelia— unaware of his actual years and content to remain so—he had no age, he had only perfection. So beautiful he was in the rosy light with which she encircled him.

"Aren't you going to eat your waffles, now you've got 'em?" he asked, a little querulously.

"Waffles?" she said, as if she knew of none and the word were strange to her. "Waffles?"

"Aren't you going to eat them? I supposed that was why you came here."

She looked down at her plate, appeared surprised to find it occupied, and uttered a courtesy laughter with such grace it seemed almost that she sang the diatonic scale. This effect was so pronounced, indeed, that several people at other tables turned— again—to look at her, and Mr. Bromley reddened. "Oh, yes," she said. "You mean these waffles. Yes, indeed!" And here she repeated her too musical laughter, accompanying it with several excited gestures of amazement as she exclaimed, "*Imagine* my not noticing them when they're absolutely my favourite food! Absolutely they are, my dear man, I do assure you!"

Then, having touched a waffle with her fork, she set the fork down, placed her elbows on the table, rested her chin in her hands and gazed upon her companion lustrously. "Mr. Bromley," she said, "how did your father and mother happen to choose 'Gregory' for your first name? Were you named for somebody else, or did they just have kind of an inspiration to call you Gregory."

"I was named for an uncle," he replied briefly.

"How beautiful!" she murmured.

"What?"

"It's a beautiful name," she said, and, not changing her attitude, continued to gaze upon him.

"Why in the world don't you eat your food?" he asked, impatiently. He had become but too well aware that Cornelia was attracting a covertly derisive attention; and he began to think her a bothersomely eccentric child. Following her noticeable elegance and her diatonic laughter, her dreamy attitude in the presence of untouched waffles was conspicuous, and he was annoyed in particular by the interest with which two occupants of a table against the opposite wall were regarding him and Cornelia.

One of these interested persons was another of his pupils, a girl of Cornelia's age. He could not fail to note how frequently she glanced at him, and after each glance whispered seriously with her mother across their table; then both would stare surreptitiously at him and his rapt vis-à-vis. There was something like a disapproving surveillance—even something inimical—in their continuing observation, he thought; nor was he remote from the truth in this impression.

Cornelia's schoolmate was enjoying herself, excited by what she had easily prevailed upon a nervous mother to see as a significant contretemps. Moreover, the daughter had just imparted to the mother a secret known to half the school, but not to Mrs. Cromwell.

"Crazy about him!" the schoolmate whispered. "Absolutely! She picked up the stub of his pencil and kept it, and a piece of an old broken pipe. We teased her, and she got red and ran away. She won't speak to us for days if we say anything about him she doesn't like. Everybody knows she's simply frantic. Did you ever see such airs as she's been putting on, and did you hear her calling him her 'dear man' and talking about 'I do assure you'? And then looking at him like *that*—the poor smack!"

"I never in all my life saw anything like it!" the mother returned, her brow dark and her eyes wide. "She looked straight at us and never made the slightest sign when we bowed to her! The idea of as careful a woman as Mrs. Cromwell allowing her daughter to get into such a state, in the first place, is very shocking to me; and in the second, to permit her to come here, at her age, and lunch in public with a man she's in such a state *about*—a man supposed to be her teacher and old enough to be almost her grandfather—I simply can't imagine what she means by it."

The schoolmate giggled. "Cornelia's mother? Don't you believe it. Mrs. Cromwell doesn't know a thing about it."

"Then she *ought* to know, and immediately. If one of my daughters behaved like that, I should certainly be thankful to any one who informed me of it. I certainly——"

"*Look!*" the schoolmate whispered, profoundly stirred. "Look at her *now!*"

Cornelia was worth the look thus advised. Under repeated pressure to dispose of her waffles, she had made some progress with them, but now with the plate removed and a cooling sherbet substituted before her, she had resumed her rapt posture, her elbows upon the table, her chin upon her hands, her wistful bright eyes fixed upon the face of the uncomfortable gentleman opposite her.

"Was your uncle a very distinguished man, Mr. Bromley?" she asked. "I mean the one they named you 'Gregory' after."

"Not in any way," he said. He had finished his own lunch, and moved back slightly but significantly in his chair. "Hadn't you better eat your sherbet?" he suggested. "I believe it's about time for me to go."

She sighed, lowered her eyes, and obediently ate the sherbet; but ate it so slowly that by the time she had finished it they were alone in the room except for a waitress, who made her own lingering conspicuous.

"Now, then," Mr. Bromley said, briskly, "if you've quite concluded your——"

"But I haven't had any coffee," Cornelia interrupted. "I always have a small cup after lunch."

"Does your mother——"

"Mamma?" she said, appearing greatly surprised. "Oh, dear, yes. She takes it herself."

He resigned himself, and the waitress brought the little cup; but as Cornelia conveyed the contents to her lips entirely by means of the accompanying tiny spoon, and her care not to be injured by hot liquid was extreme, he thought that never in his life had he seen any person drink an after-dinner cup of coffee so slowly. And, all the while, Cornelia, silent, seemed to be dreamily yet completely engrossed with this long process of consumption; her lowered eyes were always upon the tiny spoon. The impatient Mr. Bromley sat and sat, and finally lost his manners so far as to begin a nervous tapping upon the rugless floor with the sole of his right shoe.

This was the oddest child in the world, he thought. A little while ago she had looked at him with so intent a curious dreaminess that she had annoyed him; now she seemed to have forgotten him in her epicurean absorption in half a gill of coffee. And so he frowned, and shifted in his chair and tapped the floor with his shoe, and did not know that the tapping had grown rhythmical. For, though her eyes were lowered and her lips were silent, Cornelia was keeping time to it with a song. Each tap of Mr. Bromley's foot was a syllable of the song.

> The hours I spent with thee, dear heart,
>   Are as a string of pearls to me;
> I count them over, every one apart——

. . . But at last her pearls were gone; the little cup was empty. "Now," he said, "if you've finished, Miss Cromwell——" And he pushed back his chair decisively, rising as he did so.

Still she sat and did not look up, but with her eyes

upon the empty cup, she asked: "Would you let this be my lunch, Mr. Bromley? Would you mind if I charged it to Papa?"

"Nonsense," he said. He had already paid the waitress. "Ah—if you intend remaining here——"

"No, I'm coming," she said, meekly. "I just——" She rose, and as she did she looked up at him radiantly, facing him. "You—you've been ever so nice to me, Mr. Bromley."

Her cheeks were glowing, her lifted happy eyes were all too worshipfully eloquent; and for a moment, as the two stood there, Mr. Bromley felt a strange little embarrassment, this time not an annoyed embarrassment. Who can know what is in a young girl's heart? Suddenly, to his own surprise, he felt a slight, inexplicable emotion;—something in Cornelia's look pleased him and even touched him. Just for the five or six seconds that he knew this feeling, something mysterious, something charming, seemed about to happen.

"No," he said. "It's you who were nice to me. I—I've enjoyed it—truly."

She drew a deep breath. "Have you *really?*" she cried. And with that, she turned and ran to the door. all sixteen. But, with the door open, she called back to him over her shoulder, "I'm glad it's Friday, Mr. Bromley."

"Why?"

"Because it's only till Monday when school begins!"

XIII

HEARTBREAK

SHE ran out of the door and to the street, where she turned northward, away from home, with her cheeks afire and her heart still singing; but what it sang now was, "Monday! Monday, Tuesday, Wednesday, Thursday, Friday— Monday again!" All through the year she would see him on every one of those days. Cornelia was happy.

She was altogether happy; and she had just spent the happiest hour of her life. Other happy hours she might know, and many different kinds of happiness, but never again an hour of such untouched happiness as this. Happiness unshadowed cannot come often after childhood, and sixteen is one of the years that close childhood.

She was too happy to be with any one except herself; she could not talk to any one except herself; and so her feet bore her lightly to the open country outside the suburban town, and here, pleased with

164

the bracing winter wind upon her face, she walked and walked—and her walking was more like dancing. She did not come home until the twilight of the short day had begun to verge into dusk; and, when she entered the house she went quickly up to her own room without seeing anybody on the way. In her heart she was singing gaily, "Monday! Monday, Tuesday, Wednesday——"

But as she pressed the light on at a lamp upon her dressing-table, something disquieted her. She flew to her open desk, and, breathless, clasped both hands about her throat, for before her was her sacred mountain, but not as she had left it. The little papers had blown about the room. Someone had closed the window, and gathered the drawings together. Someone had left a paperweight upon them. Someone had seen the mountain.

The door opened behind her, as Cornelia stood staring at this violation, and she turned to face her mother.

Mrs. Cromwell closed the door, but she did not sit down or even advance farther into the room. "Cornelia, where have you been all day?"

"What? Nowhere in particular."

"Where did you lunch?"

"What? Nowhere in particular."

"Cornelia!"

"Yes, Mamma." Cornelia had resumed her armour; her look was moody and her tone fatigued.

"Cornelia, I am asking you where you lunched."

"I said, 'Nowhere in particular,' Mamma."

"I know you did." And upon this Mrs. Cromwell's voice trembled a little. "I wish you to tell me the truth, Cornelia."

Cornelia stood before her, apparently imperturbable, with passive eyes evasive; and Mrs. Cromwell, not knowing that her daughter's knees were trembling, began to speak with the severity she felt.

"Cornelia, your father and I have been talking in the library, and we've made up our minds this sort of thing must come to a stop."

"What sort of thing?"

"This rudeness of yours, this moodiness and secretiveness."

"I'm not secretive."

"You are. You're an entirely changed girl. Last year you'd no more have done what you're doing now than you'd have flown!"

"What am I doing now?"

"You're standing there trying to deceive me,"

Mrs. Cromwell answered sharply. "But I'm not deceived any longer, Cornelia; I've learned the truth. We knew that a change had come over you, and you were moody and indifferent toward your family, but we did at least suppose your mind was on your books. But to-day——"

"To-day!" Cornelia cried out suddenly, her look of moodiness all gone. She pointed to her desk. "Were *you* in here to-day after I went out? Did you——"

"You left your door open and your window, and those sheets of paper were blowing clear out into the hall. Naturally, I——"

"Mamma!" Cornelia's voice was loud now, and her finger trembled violently as she pointed to the mountain. "Mamma, did you—did you——"

Mrs. Cromwell laughed impatiently. "Naturally, as I picked them up I couldn't very well help seeing what they were and drawing certain conclusions."

"You *dared!*" Cornelia cried, fiercely. "Mamma, you *dared!*"

"Cornelia, you will please not speak to me in that tone. I'm very glad it happened because, though of course I shouldn't take those little drawings of yours seriously, and they're of no significance

worth mentioning, there was one of them that did
shed a light on something I heard later in the afternoon."

"What? What did you hear?"

Mrs. Cromwell came a step nearer her, gravely.
"Cornelia, you needn't have tried to deceive me
about where you went when you slipped out of the
house before lunch and caused me so much anxiety.
I telephoned and telephoned——"

Cornelia interrupted; her shaking finger still
pointed to the desk: "I don't care to hear this.
What I want to know is how you dared—how you
dared to——"

"Cornelia, you must not ask your mother how
she 'dares' to do anything. We know where you
lunched, and you might have guessed that you
couldn't do such a thing without our hearing of it.
A lady who saw you came straight here to know if it
was by my consent, and I'm very grateful to her for
it. In conjunction with the drawing I'd just seen,
which surprised me greatly, to say the least, what
this lady told me was a shock to me, as it is to your
father, too, Cornelia. To think that you'd deceive
us like this—to say nothing of the indiscretion of a
schoolmaster who is supposed to be in *charge* of——"

"Mr. Bromley?" Cornelia cried. "Do you mean Mr. Bromley?"

"I certainly do. I think his conduct——"

"I asked him," Cornelia interrupted fiercely. "I saw him from the window and I ran down and walked ahead of him, and almost got run over by a taxicab on purpose, and he saved me, and I asked him to let me have lunch with him and told him I was going there anyway. Mamma, don't you dare——" Her voice broke; she gulped and choked; her trembling was but too visible now. "Mamma, if you ever dare say anything against Mr. Bromley——"

"I agree that we may quite as well leave him out of it," her mother said, sharply. "Your own excitement is all the evidence I need that your father and I have been wise in the decision we've just come to."

Something ominous in this arrested Cornelia's anger; and she stared at her mother incredulously. "'Decision'?" she repeated, slowly. "What 'decision'?"

"We're going to put you into Miss Remy's school on the Hudson," Mrs. Cromwell said. "Your father's already engaged a drawing-room for us on the afternoon train to-morrow. I'm going with you, and you'll begin the new term there on Monday."

Cornelia still stared. "No——" she said. "No, Mamma, no——"

Mrs. Cromwell was touched, seeing the terror that gathered in her child's eyes. "You'll love it there after a little while, dear. You may think it's pleasant to stay here, but after you've been there a week or so, it's such a lovely place that you——"

But Cornelia threw herself down passionately at her mother's feet. "No! No! *No!*" she sobbed, over and over again; and in this half-articulate anguish, Mrs. Cromwell read and understood Cornelia's secret indeed. She was compassionate, yet all the more confirmed in her belief that the decision just made with her husband was a wise one.

Cornelia could bring no eloquence to alter her fate. "No! No! *No!*" was only her protest against what she understood was inevitable, though, as she wept brokenly upon her pillow that night, she thought of one resource that would avoid the inevitable, so desperate she was. But she decided to live, and found living hardest when she was on her way to the train next day, and the route chosen by her father's chauffeur cruelly passed the Blue Tea Room.

On the train, thinking of the flying miles that so bitterly lengthened between her and that sacred little blue-painted room, she came to the end of the song her heart had chanted there in time to a tapping foot;—it was the refrain of the car wheels upon the humming rails all that aching way:

> I tell each bead unto the end and there
> A cross is hung.

XIV

MRS. DODGE'S NEXT-DOOR NEIGHBOUR

A T FIVE o'clock upon a February afternoon
the commodious rooms on the lower floor
of Mrs. Cromwell's big house resounded
with all the noise that a hundred women unaided
by firearms could make. A hundred men, gathered
in a similar social manner, if that were possible,
might either be quiet or produce a few uproariously
bellowing groups, a matter depending upon the
presence or absence of noisy individuals; but a hundred habitually soft-voiced women, brought together
for a brief enjoyment of one another's society and
a trifling incidental repast, must almost inevitably
abandon themselves to that vocal rioting ultimately
so helpful to the incomes of the "nerve specialists."

The strain, of course, is not put upon the nerves
by the overpitched voices alone. At times during
Mrs. Cromwell's "tea" the face of almost every
woman in the house was distressed by the expression
of caressive animation maintained upon it. The

172

most conscientious of the guests held this expression
upon their faces from the moment they entered the
house until they left it; they went about from room
to room, from group to group, shouting indomitably;
and, without an instant's relaxation, kept a sweet
archness frozen upon their faces, no matter how those
valiant faces ached.

Men may not flatter themselves in believing it is
for them that women most ardently sculpture their
expressions. A class of women has traduced the
rest: those women who are languid where there are
no men. The women at Mrs. Cromwell's "tea," with
not a man in sight, so consistently moulded their
faces that the invitations might well have read,
"From Four to Six: a Ladies' Masque."

What gave most truly the colour of a masquerade
was the unmasking. This, of course, was never
general, nor at any time simultaneous, except with
two or three; yet, here and there, withdrawn a little
to the side of a room, or near a corner, ladies might be
seen who wore no expression at all, or else looked
jaded or even frostily observant of the show. Sometimes clubs of two seemed to form temporarily, the
members unmasking to each other, exhibiting their
real faces in confidence, and joining in criticism of

the maskers about them. At such times, if a third
lady approached, the two would immediately resume
their masks and bob and beam; then they might seem
to elect her to membership; whereupon all three
would drop their masks, shout gravely, close to one
another's ears, then presently separate, masking
again in facial shapings designed to picture universal
love and jaunty humour.

But among the hundred merrymakers there was
one of whom it could not be said that she was masked;
yet, strange to tell, neither could it be said of her
that she was not masked; for either she wore no mask
at all or wore one always. Her face at Mrs. Cromwell's was precisely as it was when seen anywhere
else; though where it seemed most appropriately
surrounded was in church.

Calm, pale, the chin uplifted a little, with the
slant of the head always more toward heaven than
earth, this angelic face was borne high by the straight
throat and slender figure like the oriflamme upon its
staff; and so it passed through the crowd of shouting
women, seeming to move in a spiritual light that fell
upon them and illuminated them, yet illuminated
most the uplifted face that was its source. Moreover,
upon the lips the exquisite promise of a smile was

continuously hinted; and the hint foreshadowed how
fine the smile would be: how gentle, though a little
martyred by life, and how bravely tolerant.

The beholder waited for this promised heavenly
smile, but waited in vain. "You always think she's
just going to until you see her often enough to find
she never does," a broad-shouldered matron explained to two of her friends at Mrs. Cromwell's.
The three had formed one of the little clubs for a
temporary unmasking and were lookers-on for the
moment. "It's an old worn-out kind of thing to
say," the sturdy matron continued;—"but I never
can resist applying it to her. Nobody can ever
possibly be so good as Mrs. Leslie Braithwaite looks.
I'll even risk saying that nobody can ever possibly
be so good as she seems to behave!"

"Oh, Mrs. Dodge!" one of the others exclaimed.
"But isn't behaviour the final proof? My husband
says conduct is the only test of character."

"He doesn't know what he's talking about," the
brusque Mrs. Dodge returned. "When we do anything noble, it's in spite of our true character; that's
what makes it a noble thing to do. I've lived next
door to that woman for five years, and, though I
seldom exchange more than a word with her, I can't

help having her in my sight pretty often. She always looks noble and she always sounds noble. Even when she says, 'Isn't it a lovely day,' she sounds noble—and, for my part, I'm sick and tired of her nobility!"

"But my husband says——"

"I don't care what Mr. Battle says," Mrs. Dodge interrupted. "The woman's a nuisance!"

"To me," said the third of the group, gravely, "that sounds almost like sacrilege. I've always felt that even though Mrs. Leslie Braithwaite is still quite a young woman, she's the focus of spiritual life for this whole community. I think the people here generally look upon her as the finest inspiration we have among us."

"I know they do," Mrs. Dodge said, irritably. "That's one reason I think she's a pest. People are always trying to live up to her, and it makes cowards and hypocrites of 'em. Look at her now!"

Mrs. Braithwaite had reached the hostess, who was shouting in concert with several new arrivals; but when Mrs. Braithwaite appeared, the voices of all this group were somewhat lowered (though they could not be lowered much and hope to be audible) and, what was more remarkable, Mrs. Cromwell's expression and her manner were instantly altered

perceptibly:—so were the expressions and manners
of the others about her, as Mrs. Dodge vindictively
pointed out.

"Look at that!" she said. "Every one of those
poor geese is trying to look like *her*;—they feel they
have to seem as noble as she is! Instinctively they're
all trying to take on her hushed sweetness. Nobody
dares be natural anywhere near her."

"But that's because of the affection people feel
for her," Mrs. Battle explained. "Don't you
feel——"

"Affection your grandmother!" the brusque lady
interrupted. "What are you talking about?"

"Well, reverence, then. Perhaps that's the better
word for the feeling people have about her. They
know how much of her life she gives to good works.
She's at the head of——"

"Yes, she certainly is!" Mrs. Dodge agreed,
bitterly. "She's the head and front of every up-
lifting movement among us. You can't open your
mail without finding benefit tickets you have to buy
for some good cause she's chairman of. She's always the girl that passes the hat: she's the one that
makes us feel like selfish dogs if we don't give till it
hurts! She's the star collector, all right!"

"Well, oughtn't we to be grateful that she takes such duties upon herself?"

"Do we ever omit any of our gratitude? Why, the papers are full of it: 'It is the sense of this committee that, except for the noble, unflagging, and self-sacrificing devotion of Mrs. Leslie Braithwaite, this fund could never have reached the generous dimensions necessary for the carrying on of this work. Therefore, be it resolved that the thanks of this entire organization'—and so forth. And, as a matter by the way, you never hear whether she gave any of the fund herself."

"She gives time. She gives energy. Mr. Battle says, 'Who gives himself gives all.' Mrs. Braithwaite gives herself."

"Yes, she does," Mrs. Dodge agreed. "It's her form of recreation!"

Her two auditors stared at her incredulously, so that she could plainly see how shocked they were; but, before either of them spoke, a beautiful change in look and manner came upon them. Both of them elevated their chins a little, so that their faces slanted more toward heaven than toward earth; both of them seemed about to smile angelically, but stopped just short of smiling; a purified softness came into their eyes; and, altogether, by means of various other subtle little manifestations, the two ladies began to look noble.

Mrs. Dodge had turned her back toward the group about the hostess, but without looking round she understood what the change in her two companions portended. "Good-bye, ladies of Shalott," she said. "The curse has come upon you!" And she moved away, just as the ennobled two stepped forward to meet Mrs. Leslie Braithwaite in her approach to them.

"Clever of me!" Mrs. Dodge thought, with some bitterness. "Getting myself the reputation of a 'dangerous woman'!" For she understood well enough that she would do no injury to Mrs. Braithwaite in attacking her;—on the contrary, the injury would inevitably be to the assailant; and yet Mrs. Dodge could not forbear from a little boomerang practice at this shining and impervious mark. The reason, unfortunately, was personal, as most reasons are: Mrs. Dodge had come to the "tea" in an acute state of irritation that had been increasing since morning. In fact, she had begun the day with a breakfast-table argument of which Mrs. Braithwaite was the subject.

Mr. Dodge made the unfortunate admission that he had recently sent Mrs. Braithwaite a check for a hundred dollars, his subscription to the Workers' Welfare League; and he was forced into subsequent admissions: he had no interest in the Workers' Welfare League, and could give no reason for sending a check to it except that Mrs. Braithwaite had written him appealing for a subscription. She was sure he wouldn't like to miss the chance to aid in so splendid a movement, she said. Now, as Mrs. Braithwaite had previously written twice to Mrs. Dodge in almost the same words, and as Mrs. Dodge had twice replied declining to make a donation, the argument (so to call it) on Mrs. Dodge's part was a heated one. It availed her husband little to protest that he had never heard of Mrs. Braithwaite's appeals to his wife; Mrs. Dodge was too greatly incensed to be reasonable.

Later in the day she was remorseful, realizing that she had taken poor Mr. Dodge for her anvil because he was within reach, and what she really wanted to hammer wasn't. Her remorse applied itself strictly to her husband, however, and she had none for her feeling toward the lady next door. Mrs. Dodge and her neighbour had never discovered

any point of congeniality: Mrs. Braithwaite's high
serenity, which Mrs. Dodge called suavity, was of so
paradoxical a smoothness that Mrs. Dodge said it
"rubbed the wrong way from the start." The
uncongeniality had increased with time until it became a settled dislike, so far as Mrs. Dodge was concerned; and now, after Mrs. Leslie Braithwaite's
successful appeal to Mr. Dodge for what Mr. Dodge's
wife had refused, the dislike was rankling itself into a
culmination not unlike an actual and lusty hatred.

Mrs. Dodge realized her own condition;—she
knew hatred is bad for the hater; but she could not
master the continuous anger within her. Fascinated,
she watched Mrs. Leslie Braithwaite at the "tea";
could not help watching her, although, as the victim
of this fascination admitted to herself in so many
words, the sight was "poison" to her. Nor was the
poison alleviated by the effect of Mrs. Braithwaite
upon the other guests: everywhere the angelic presence moved about the capacious rooms it was preceded and followed by deference. And when Mrs.
Braithwaite joined a woman or a group of women,
Mrs. Dodge marked with a hot eye how that woman
or group of women straightway hushed a little and
looked noble.

XV

MRS. DODGE DECLINES TO TELL

MRS. DODGE went home early. "I oughtn't to have come," she told her hostess, confidentially, in parting. "I try to be a Christian sometimes, but this is one of the days when I think Nero was right."

"But what——"

"I may tell you—some day," Mrs. Dodge promised, and gloomily went her way.

At dinner that evening she was grim, softening little when her husband plaintively resumed his defence. Lily inquired why her mother was of so dread a countenance.

"Me," Mr. Dodge explained. "It began at breakfast before you were up, and it's the old culprit, Lily."

"I guessed that much," Lily said, cheerfully. "I haven't been falling in love with anybody foolish for three or four months now; and that's the only thing *I* ever do to make her look like this, so I knew it must be you. What you been up to?"

"Aiding in good causes," he answered, sighing. "She hates me for helping the Workers, Lily. Our next-door neighbour appealed to Cæsar, over your mother's head. I've explained two or three hundred times that I didn't know there'd been any previous request to her; but she hates my wicked plotting just the same."

"No. I only hate your weakness," Mrs. Dodge said, not relaxing her severity. "You were so eager to please that woman you couldn't even wait to consult your wife. Her writing to you and ignoring what I'd twice written her was the rudest thing I've ever had done to me, and your donation puts you in the position of approving of it. She did it because she's furious with me, and so——"

But Lily interrupted her. "Mamma!" she exclaimed. "Why, you're talking just ridiculously! Everybody knows Mrs. Braithwaite couldn't be 'furious.' Not with anybody!"

"Couldn't she? Then why did she do such an insulting thing to me? Don't you suppose she knows it's insulting to show she can get a poor silly husband to do something his wife has declined to do? Is there a cattier trick in the whole cattish repertoire? She did it because she's the slyest puss in this community and she knows I know it, and hates me for it!"

Lily stared in the blankest surprise. "Why, it just sounds like anarchy!" she cried. "I never heard you break out like that before except when you were talking about some boy I liked! When did you get this way about Mrs. Leslie Braithwaite?"

"I've never liked her," Mrs. Dodge said. "Never! I've always suspected she was a whited sepulchre, and now I've got proof of it."

"Proof? That's quite a strong word, Lydia," Mr. Dodge reminded her.

"Thank you!" she said. "I mean exactly what I'm saying. Mrs. Braithwaite did this thing to me out of deliberate spitefulness; and she did it because she knows what I think of her."

"But you said you had 'proof' that she's a 'whited sepulchre,'" he said. "The word 'proof'——"

"May we assume that it means reliable evidence reliably confirmed?" Mrs. Dodge asked, with satirical politeness. "Suppose you've done something disgraceful and another person happens to know you did it. Then suppose you play a nasty trick on this other person. Wouldn't it be proof that you hate him because he knows you did the disgraceful thing?"

"I'm afraid I don't follow you," Mr. Dodge said, uncomfortably. "When did I ever do this disgraceful thing you're talking about? If it's actually disgraceful to subscribe a hundred dollars to the Workers——"

"I'm not talking of that," his wife said. "I'll try to put it within reach of your intellect. Suppose I know Mrs. Braithwaite to be a whited sepulchre; then if she does an insulting thing to me, isn't that proof she's furious with me for finding her out?"

"No," he answered. "It might incline one to think that she resented your poor opinion of her, but it doesn't prove anything at all."

"Doesn't it? You wouldn't say so if you knew what I know!"

Lily's eyes widened in hopeful eagerness.

"How exciting!" she cried. "Mamma, *what* do you know about Mrs. Braithwaite?"

"Never mind!"

"But you said——"

"I said, 'Never mind'!"

"But I do mind!" Lily insisted. "You haven't

got any right to get a person's interest all worked
up like that and then just say, 'Never mind'!"

"That's all I *shall* say, however," Mrs. Dodge
informed her stubbornly, and kept to her word,
though Lily continued to press her until the meal was
over.   Mr. Dodge made no effort to aid his daughter
in obtaining the revelation she sought;—he appeared
to be superior to the curiosity that impelled her; but
this appearance of superiority may have been only
an appearance: he may have foreseen that his wife
would presently be a little more explicit about what
she had implied against their neighbour.

In fact, Lily had no sooner gone forth upon some
youthful junketing, immediately after dinner, than
symptoms of forthcoming revelation were mani-
fested.   Mr. Dodge's physician allowed him one
cigar a day, and it had just begun to scent the library.

"I suppose, of course, you're condemning me for a
reckless talker," Mrs. Dodge said.   "You assume
that I'm willing to hint slander against a woman
with only my own injury for a basis, instead of facts."

"On the contrary, Lydia," he returned, mildly, "I
know you wouldn't have said what you did unless
you have something serious to found it on."

Probably she was a little mollified, but she did

not show it. "So you give me that much credit?"
she asked, sourly. "I imagine it's because you're
just as curious as Lily and hope to hear what I
wouldn't tell her. Well, I'm not going to gratify
your curiosity."

"No?" He picked up a magazine from the table
beside his chair, and began to turn over the pages.
"Oh, very well!"

"I *am* going to tell you *something*, though," she
said. "It's because I think you ought to be told
at least *part* of what I know. It may be good for
you."

"For me?" he inquired, calmly, though he well
understood what she was going to say next.

"Yes; you might find it wiser to consult your wife
next time, even when you're dealing with people
you think are saints."

"Why, I don't think Mrs. Braithwaite's a saint,"
he protested. "She *looks* rather like one—a pretty
one, too—and the general report is that she *is* one;
but I don't know anything more than that about
her. She happens to be a neighbour; but we've
never had the slightest intimacy with her and her
husband. We've never been in their house or they
in ours; I bow to her when I see her and sometimes

exchange a few words with her across the hedge between our two yards, usually about the weather. I don't think anything about her at all."

"Then it's time you did," Mrs. Dodge said with prompt inconsistency.

"All right. What do you want me to think about her, Lydia?"

"Nothing!" she said, sharply. "Oh, laugh if you want to! I'll tell you just this much: I found out something about her by pure accident; and I decided I'd never tell anybody in the world—not even you. I'm not the kind of person to wreck anybody's life exactly; and I decided just to bury what I happened to find out. What's more, I'd have kept it *all* buried if she'd had sense enough to let me alone. I wouldn't even have told you that I know something about her."

"It's something really serious?"

"'Serious'?" she said. "No, it's not 'serious.' It's ruinous."

Mr. Dodge released a sound from his mouth. "Whee-ew!" Whistled, not spoken, it was his characteristic token that he found himself impressed. "You've certainly followed the right course, Lydia. Mrs. Leslie Braithwaite's standing isn't just a high one; it's lofty. I shouldn't care to be the person who blasts that statue off its pedestal;—sometimes statues crush the blasters when they fall. I'm glad you kept your information to yourself." He paused, and then, being morally but an ordinary man, he added, "Not—not that I see any particular harm in your confiding in my discretion in such a matter."

"Didn't I explain I'm not confiding in your discretion?" Mrs. Dodge returned. "Lately, I don't believe you have any. I've told you this much so that next time you won't be so hasty in sending checks to women who are merely using you to annoy your wife."

He sighed. "There's where you puzzle me, Lydia. If you found out something ruinous about Mrs. Braithwaite, as you say, and if she knows you did—you intimated she knows it, I think?"

"Absolutely."

"Then I should think you'd be the last person in the world she'd want to annoy. I should think she'd do everything on earth to please you and placate you. She'd want to keep you from telling. That's the weak point in your theory, Lydia."

"It isn't a theory. I'm speaking of facts."

"But if she knows you're aware of what might

ruin her," he insisted, "she would naturally be afraid of you.   Then why would she do a thing that might infuriate you?"

"Because she's a woman," said Mrs. Dodge. "And that's something you'll never understand!"

"But even a woman would behave with some remnants of caution, under the circumstances, wouldn't she?"

"Some women might.   Mrs. Braithwaite doesn't because she's so sure of her lofty position she thinks she can deliberately insult me and I won't dare to do anything about it.   She wanted to show me that she isn't afraid of me."

Mr. Dodge looked thoughtfully at that point upon his long cigar where a slender ring of red glow intervened between the adhering gray ash and the brown tobacco.   "Well, at least she shows a fiery heart," he said.   "In a way, you'd have to consider her action quite the sporting thing.   You mean she's sent you a kind of declaration of war, don't you?"

"If you want to look at it that way.   I don't myself.   I take it just as she meant it, and that's as a deliberate insult."

"But it isn't an 'insult' if she only meant it to show she isn't afraid of you, Lydia."

"It is, though," Mrs. Dodge insisted. "What she means is derision of me. It's the same as if she said: 'Here's a slap in the face for you. I have the satisfaction of humiliating you as your punishment for knowing what you do know about me, and you can't retaliate, because you aren't important enough to be able to injure me!' It's just the same as if she'd said those words to me."

"It seems quite a message," he observed. "Of course, I can't grasp it myself because I haven't any conception of this ruinous proceeding of hers. You were the only witness, I assume?"

"There was a third person present," Mrs. Dodge said, stiffly. "But not as a witness."

"Then what was the third person present doing?"

Mrs. Dodge looked at him with severity, as if she reproved him for tempting her to do something wrong; then she took from a basket in her lap a square piece of partly embroidered linen and gave it her attention, not relaxing this preoccupation where her husband began to repeat his question.

"What was the third person——"

"I heard you," Mrs. Dodge interrupted, frowning at her embroidery. "If I told you that much I'd be virtually telling the whole thing; and I've decided not to do that, even under her deliberate provocation. If I let myself be provoked into telling, I'd be as as small as she is, so you needn't hope to get another word out of me on the subject. The only answer I'll make to your question is that the third person present was not her husband."

"Oh!" Mr. Dodge said, loudly, and, in his sudden enlightenment, whistled "Whee-ew!" again. "So *that's* it!"

"Not at all," she said. "You needn't jump to conclusions, and you'll never know anything more about it from me. The only way you could ever know about it would be through her husband's making a fuss and its getting into the papers or something."

"I see," Mr. Dodge said, apparently not much discouraged. "And, since it's something he hasn't *yet* made any fuss about, it's evidently because he doesn't know."

"*He!*" Mrs. Dodge cried, and, in her scorn of Mrs. Leslie Braithwaite's consort, dropped the embroidery into the basket and stared fiercely at Mr. Dodge; though it was really at an invisible Mr. Braithwaite that she directed this glare of hers. Apparently the unfortunate gentleman was one of those mere husbands whose existence seems either to amuse or to incense the wives of more dominant men: Mrs. Dodge certainly appeared to be incensed. "That miserable little pale shadow of a man!" she cried. "His name's Leslie Braithwaite, but do you ever hear him spoken of except as 'Mrs. Leslie Braithwaite's husband'? He goes down to his little brass-rod works at eight o'clock every morning and gets money for her until six in the evening. Then he comes home and works on the account books of her uplifts until bedtime. If they go out, he stands around with her wrap over his arm and doesn't speak unless you ask him a question. If you do, he begins his answer by saying, 'My wife informs me'—How could that poor little creature know anything about anything?"

"But *you* know," Mr. Dodge persisted. "You *do* know, do you, Lydia?"

"I know what I know," she replied, and resumed her preoccupation with the embroidery.

"But you couldn't substantiate it by another witness, I take it," he said, musingly. "That is, she feels safe against you because if you should ever decide to tell what you know, she would deny it and put you in the position of an accuser without proofs.

It would simply be your word against hers, and she'd
have the sympathy that goes to the party attacked
and also the advantage of her wide reputation for
lofty character and——"

"Go on," his wife interrupted. "Amuse yourself
all you like; you'll not find out another thing from
me. Perhaps, if you should ever spend the morning
at home digging around in our flower border along
the hedge between her yard and ours, you might
happen to hear her talking to her chauffeur, and
in that case you might get to know something more.
Otherwise, I don't see how you ever will."

"Lydia!"

"What?"

"I'm not going to dig in any flower border! I'm
not going to spy around any hedge just to——"

"Neither did I!" she cried, indignantly. "Did you
ever know me to do any spying?"

"Certainly not. But you said——"

"I said 'If you *happen* to.' You don't suppose I
hid and listened deliberately? I was down on my
hands and knees planting tulip bulbs, and the thick
hedge was between us. That's how it happened,
and why, she never *dreamed* anybody was near her.
I didn't even hear her come in that part of the yard

until I heard her speaking right by me, on the other side of the hedge. Please don't be quite so quick to think your wife would be willing to spy on another woman."

"I didn't," Mr. Dodge protested, hastily. "What did she say to the chauffeur?"

"That," his wife replied, severely, "is something you'll never hear from me!"

"From whom shall I hear it, then?"

"I've just told you how you might hear it," she said, plying her needle and seeming to give it all her attention.

"But I can't spend my time in the tulip bed, Lydia."

"That's not what I meant. I said, 'If her husband ever makes such a fuss that it gets into the papers.'"

"If he does, I might find out what she said to the chauffeur?"

"Oh, maybe," Mrs. Dodge said; and she gave him a sidelong glance of some sharpness, then quickly seemed to be busy again with her work.

"I don't make it out at all," the puzzled gentleman complained. "Apparently you overheard Mrs. Braithwaite saying something to her chauffeur that would be ruinous to her if it were known—something that might cause her husband to make a public uproar if he had heard it himself. Is that it?"

Mrs. Dodge began to hum fragmentarily to herself and seemed concerned with nothing in the world except the selection of a proper spool of thread from her basket.

"Is that it, Lydia?"

"You'll never find out from me," she said, searching anxiously through the basket. "Anyhow, I shouldn't think you'd need to ask such simple questions."

"So that *is* it! What you heard her say to her chauffeur would ruin her if people knew about it. Was she talking to the chauffeur about her husband?"

"Good gracious!" Mrs. Dodge cried, derisively. "What would she be talking to anybody about *that* poor little thing for? She never does. I don't believe anybody ever heard her mention him in her life!"

"Then was she talking to the chauffeur about some other man?"

"Of all the ideas! If a woman were in love with a man not her husband, do you think she'd tell her servants about it? Besides, they've only had this chauffeur about two weeks. Have you noticed him?"

"Yes," said Mr. Dodge. "I've seen him sitting in their car in front of the house several times, and I was quite struck with him. He seemed to be not only one of the handsomest young men I ever saw, but to have rather the look of a gentleman."

"So?" Mrs. Dodge said, inquiringly; and her tone was the more significant because of her appearing to be wholly preoccupied with her work-basket. "You noticed *that*, did you?"

"You don't mean to say——"

"I don't mean to say anything at all," she interrupted, crisply. "I've told you that often enough for you to begin to understand it."

"All right, I do. Well, when she'd said whatever she did say to the chauffeur, what happened?"

"Oh, that," she returned, "I'm perfectly willing to tell you. I got up and looked at her over the hedge. I wasn't going to stay there and listen— and I certainly wasn't going to crawl away on my hands and knees! I just looked at her quietly and turned away and came into the house."

"What did she do?"

"She was absolutely disconcerted. Her face just seemed to go all to pieces;—it didn't look like *her* face at all. She was frightened to death, and I never saw anything plainer. That's one reason she hates me so—because I saw her looking so afraid of me and she couldn't help it. Of course, as soon as I got into the house I looked out through the lace curtains at a window—you could hardly expect me not to—and I saw her just going back into her own house by the side door. She'd braced up and looked all stained-glass Joan of Arc again by that time."

Mr. Dodge sat waggling his head and muttering in wonder. "Of all the curious things!" he said. "Human nature is so everlastingly full of oddities it's always turning up new ones that you sit and stare at and can't believe are real. There they are, right before your eyes, and yet they're incredible. What did she say to the chauffeur?"

"No, no," Mrs. Dodge said, reprovingly. "That's what I *can't* tell you." And she added, "I should think you could guess it, anyhow."

"Was there——" He paused a moment, pondering. "Did she use any specially marked terms of endearment in addressing him?"

"No," Mrs. Dodge replied, returning her attention to her work;—"not terms."

"Oh," he said. "Just one term, then. She used

a single term of endearment in addressing him. Is that correct?"

Again Mrs. Dodge became musical: she hummed a cheerful tune, but her face was overcast with a dour solemnity.

"So she did!" her husband exclaimed. "Did she call him 'dear'?"

"No, she didn't."

"'Dearest'?"

"No, she didn't."

"Not," he said, incredulously, "not—*darling*'?"

Mrs. Dodge instantly resumed her humming.

"By George!" her husband cried. "Why, that's just awful! What else did she say to him besides calling him 'darling'?"

"I didn't say she said anything else," Mrs. Dodge returned, primly. "The rest wasn't so important, anyhow, and she was speaking in a low voice. I thought the rest of it was, 'Rosemary, that's for remembrance.' I couldn't be sure because I didn't hear it distinctly."

"But you *did* distinctly hear her call him 'darling'?"

"What I heard distinctly," Mrs. Dodge replied, "I heard distinctly."

"So what Mrs. Leslie Braithwaite said to the chauffeur was this: 'Rosemary, that's for remembrance, darling'?"

"You must draw your own conclusions," she advised him, severely.

"I do—rather!" he returned, and in a marvelling tone slowly pronounced their neighbour's name, "Mrs. Leslie Braithwaite! Of all the women in the world, Mrs. Leslie Braithwaite! And when you rose up, and she saw you, she just went all to pieces and didn't say a word?"

"I told you."

"What did the handsome chauffeur do?"

"Just stood there."

"It's beyond anything!" Mr. Dodge's amazement was not abated;—he shook his head and uttered groaning sounds of pessimistic wonderment. "I suppose the true meaning of the saying, 'It's the unexpected that happens,' is that life is always teaching us to accept the incredible. How long ago was it?"

"A week ago yesterday."

"Have you seen her since?"

"I never talk to her or she to me. We say, 'How do you do? What lovely weather!' and that's all

we ever do say. We haven't even any neighbourly
contact through congenial servants, because of our
having coloured people;—hers are white. I haven't
caught a glimpse of her since it happened until this
afternoon, when she came to Mrs. Cromwell's tea.
Of course, she knew I was looking at her, and she
knew perfectly what I was thinking—particularly
about her insult to me in making such a goose of my
husband."

"But, Lydia——"

"She was having the time of her life over that!"

"Well," he said, reflectively, "leaving out the
question of whether or not I was a goose especially,
and considering her without personal bias, I must
say that under the circumstances she's shown a
mighty picturesque intricacy of character, as well as a
pretty dashing kind of hardihood. If, as you believe,
she sent her note to me as really a derisive taunt
—a gauntlet flung at you with mocking laughter—
and all the while she knows you know of her philandering with a good-looking varlet——"

"She's a bad woman!" Mrs. Dodge exclaimed,
angrily. "That's all there is to it, and you needn't
be so poetical about her!"

"Good gracious, Lydia, I wasn't——"

"Never mind! We can talk of her just as well without any references to gauntlets and mocking laughter and varlets. That is, if you insist upon talking about her at all. For my part, I prefer just to keep her entirely out of my mind."

"Very well," he assented, meekly. "I don't know that I can keep anything so singular out of my mind; but I won't speak of it if it annoys you. What else shall we talk of?"

"Anything in the world except that detestable woman," Mrs. Dodge replied. Then, after some moments of silence over her embroidery, she added abruptly, "Of course, *you* don't think she's detestable!"

"I only said——"

"'Picturesque' was what you said. 'Dashing' was another thing you said. You're quite fascinated with her derisive gauntlets and her mocking laughter! Dear *me*, if that isn't like men!"

"But I only——"

"Oh, murder!" Mrs. Dodge moaned, interrupting him. "I thought you said you weren't going to *talk* about her any more!"

At this he showed spirit enough to laugh. "You know well enough we're both going to keep on talking about her, Lydia.   What do you intend to do?"

"About what?" Mrs. Dodge looked surprised. "About *her*, you mean?   Why, naturally, I intend to keep on doing what I have been doing, and that's nothing whatever except to hold my peace;—I don't descend to the level of feuds with intriguing women. She gave me a clew, though, this afternoon."

"What sort of a clew, Lydia?"

"I don't suppose a man could understand, but I'll try to give you a glimmering.   When she wrote that note to you, there was one thing she hadn't thought of.   She thought of it this afternoon at that tea: it struck her all of a sudden that I could make things a little unpleasant for her if I took the notion to.   She just happened to remember that Mrs. Cromwell is my most intimate friend, and that she is the grandest old rock-bottomed mountain this community can boast.   That woman all at once remembered, and got afraid I might tell my friends."

"How do you know she did?"

"That's what a man couldn't see.   I knew it by a lot of little things I couldn't put into words if I tried, but principally I knew it by watching her manner with Mrs. Cromwell."

"You mean she tried to ingratiate herself?" he
asked. "Her manner was more winsome or flatter-
ing than usual?"

"No, not exactly. Not so open—you couldn't
understand—but it was perfectly clear to me she
was having the time of her life thinking of what she'd
done to me through my husband's weakness, when all
at once she thought of my influence with the Crom-
wells. Well, she's afraid of it, and it made her wish
she hadn't gone quite so far with me. She'd give a
whole lot to-night, I'll wager, if she'd been just a little
less picturesque with her gauntlet throwing and her
mocking laughter! You asked me what I was going
to do and I told you 'Nothing.' But *she'll* do
something. She's afraid, and she'll make a move of
some sort. You'll see."

"But what? What could she do?"

"I don't know, but you'll see. You'll see before
long, too."

"Well, I'm inclined to hope so," he said. "It
would certainly be interesting; but I doubt her making any move at all. I'm afraid you won't turn out
to be a good prophet."

On the contrary, he himself was a poor prophet;
for sometimes destiny seems to juggle miraculously

with coincidences in order to attract our attention to the undiscovered laws that produce them. In fact, Mr. Dodge was so poor a prophet—and so near to intentional burlesque are the manners of destiny in its coincidence juggling—that at this moment Mrs. Leslie Braithwaite's husband had just rung the Dodges' front-door bell. Two minutes later a mulatto housemaid appeared in the doorway of the library and produced a sensational effect merely by saying, "Mrs. Braithwaite and Mr. Braithwaite is calling. I showed 'em into the drawing-room."

She withdrew, and the staggered couple, after an interval of incoherent whispering, went forth to welcome their guests.

XVI

MRS. LESLIE BRAITHWAITE'S HUSBAND

MRS. BRAITHWAITE was superb;—at least, that was Mr. Dodge's impersonal conception of her. Never before had he seen sainthood so suavely combined with a piquant beauty, nor an evening gown of dull red silk and black lace so exquisitely invested with an angelic presence. For to-night this lady looked not only noble, she looked charming; and either his wife had made a grotesque mistake or he stood before an actress unmatched in his experience. She began talking at once, in her serene and sweet contralto voice—a beautiful voice, delicately hushed and almost imperceptibly precise in its pronunciation. "It seemed to us really rather absurd, Mrs. Dodge, that you and your husband should be our next-door neighbours for so long without even having set foot in our house or we in yours. And as Mr. Dodge has lately been so generous to my poor little Workers' Welfare League—the unhappy creatures do need help so, and the ladies of the committee were so touched by your kindness, Mr. Dodge—we thought we'd just make that an excuse to call, even thus informally and for only a few minutes. We wanted to express the thanks of the League, of course, and we thought it was about time to say we aren't really so unneighbourly as we may have seemed—and we hope you aren't, either!"

"No, indeed," Mr. Dodge responded with a hasty glance of sidelong uneasiness at his wife. Her large face was red and rather dismayingly fierce as she sat stiffly in the stiffest chair in the Dodges' white-walled, cold, and rigidly symmetrical drawing-room; but she said, "No, indeed," too, though not so heartily as her husband did. In fact, she said it grimly; yet he was relieved, for her expression made him fear that she would say nothing at all.

"One of the things I find to regret about modern existence," Mrs. Braithwaite continued, in her beautiful voice, "is the disappearance of neighbourliness even in a quiet suburban life like yours and ours. Of course, this is anything but a new thought, yet how concretely our two houses have illustrated it! So it did seem time, at last, to break the ice, especially as I have good reason to think that just these last few days you must have been thinking of me as quite a naughty person, Mrs. Dodge."

Mrs. Dodge stared at her; appeared to stare not only with astounded eyes but with a slowly opening mouth. "What? What did you say?" she asked, huskily.

"I'm afraid you've been thinking of me as rather naughty," the serene caller said, and her ever promised smile seemed a little more emphatically promised than it had been. "I ought to confess to you that as a collector for my poor little Workers' League I'm terribly unscrupulous. It's such a struggling little organization, and the need of help is so frightfully pressing, I may as well admit I haven't any scruples at all how I get money for it. Yet, of course, I know I ought to apologize for asking Mr. Dodge to contribute to a cause that you didn't feel particularly interested in yourself."

"Oh!" Mrs. Dodge said, and to her husband's consternation she added formidably: "Is *that* what you're talking about!"

No disastrous effect was visible, however. Mrs. Braithwaite nodded sunnily. "I'm sure you'll forgive me for the sake of the happiness the money brought to a pitiful little family—the father hasn't had any work for eight months; there are four young children and one just born. If you could see their joy when——"

"I dare say!" Mrs. Dodge interrupted. "I'm glad it did *some* good!"

"I was sure you'd feel so." Mrs. Braithwaite glanced gently at her host, whose face was a remarkable study of geniality in conflict with apprehension; —then her gaze returned to her hostess. "I wanted to make my peace not only for myself," she added, "but for your husband. I'm sure you're going to forgive him, Mrs. Dodge."

Innocently, Mr. Dodge supposed this to be intended as a kindly effort on his behalf and in the general interests of amiability. He was surprised, therefore, and his apprehensions of an outbreak on the part of his wife were little abated, when he perceived that its effect upon her was far from placative. Her ample figure seemed to swell; she was red but grew redder; her action in breathing became not only visible but noticeable; to his appalled vision she seemed about to snort forth sparks. For several perilous moments she did not speak;—then, after compressing her lips tightly, she said: "Mr. Dodge sent you his check upon my direction, of course. Natur-

ally, he consulted me. I told him that since you
had twice solicited me for a subscription it would be
best for us to send you some money and be done
with it."

Mrs. Braithwaite uttered a soothing sound as of
amused relief. "That's so much nicer," she said.
"I was afraid you might have been annoyed with
both of us—with both poor Mr. Dodge and myself—
but that exculpates us. I'm so very glad." She
turned to the perturbed host. "I was *so* afraid I'd
involved you, Mr. Dodge—perhaps quite beyond
forgiveness."

"Not at all—not at all," he said, removing his
gaze with difficulty from his wife's face. "Oh, no.
Everything—everything's been perfectly pleasant,"
he floundered, and Mrs. Dodge's expression did not
reassure him that he was saying the right thing.
"Perfectly—pleasant," he repeated, feebly.

"I *so* hoped it would be," Mrs. Braithwaite said.
"I hoped Mrs. Dodge wouldn't be *very* hard on you
for aiding in such a good cause."

"No," he returned, nervously. "No, she—she
wasn't. She proved to be entirely—ah—amiable,
of course." And again he was dismayed by Mrs.
Dodge's expression.

"Of course," Mrs. Braithwaite agreed, sunnily, with only the quickest and sweetest little fling of a glance at her hostess, "I was *sure* she'd forgive you. Well, at any rate, we've both made our peace with her now and established the *entente cordiale*, I hope." She turned toward her husband and spoke his name gently, in the tone that is none the less a command to the obedient follower: "Leslie." It was apparently her permission for him to prepare himself for departure; but it may also have been a signal or command for him to do something else;—Mr. Dodge noticed that it brought an oddly plaintive look into the eyes of the small and dark Braithwaite.

Throughout the brief but strained interview he had been sitting in one of the Dodges' rigid chairs as quietly as if he had been a well-behaved little son of Mrs. Braithwaite's, brought along to make a call upon grown people. He was slender as well as short; of a delicate, almost fragile, appearance; and in company habitually so silent, so self-obliterative that it might well have been a matter of doubt whether he was profoundly secretive or of an overwhelming timidity. But as he sat in the Dodges' slim black chair, himself rather like that chair, with his trim, thin little black legs primly uncrossed and his small black back straight and stiff, there were suggestions that he was more secretive than timid. Under his eyes were semicircles of darkness, as if part of what he secreted might have been a recent anguish, either physical or mental. Moreover, if he had been in reality the well-trained little boy his manners during this short evening call had suggested, those semi-circles under his eyes would have told of anguish so acute that the little boy had wept.

When his wife said "Leslie," he swallowed; there came into his eyes the odd and plaintive look his host had noticed—it was the look now not of a good little boy but of a good little dog, obedient in a painful task set by the adored master—and he stood up immediately.

"We really must be running," his wife said, rising, too. "This was just our funny little effort to break the ice. I do hope it has, and that you'll both come in to see us some evening. I *do* hope you'll *both* come." She put an almost imperceptible stress on the word "both" as she moved toward the door; then said "Leslie" again. He was still standing beside his chair.

"Ah—" he said; then paused and coughed. "I—
I wonder——"

"Yes?" his host said, encouragingly.

"I—that is, I was going to say, by the way, I
wonder if you happen to know of a good chauffeur,
Mr. Dodge."

At this, Mrs. Dodge's breathing became audible
as well as visible, there fell a moment of such silence.

"A—a chauffeur? No," Mr. Dodge said. "No,
I don't think I do. We haven't one ourselves; we
do our own driving. A chauffeur? No. I'm afraid
I don't know of any."

"I see," Braithwaite returned. "I just happened
to ask. We've—ah—lost the man we've had lately.
He was a very good driver and we haven't anybody
to take his place."

Mrs. Dodge spoke sepulchrally as she rose from
her chair. "That's too bad," she said, and, to her
husband's relief, stopped there, adding nothing.

"Yes," Braithwaite assented. "He was a very
good driver indeed; but he was a college graduate
and only yesterday he found another position, tutor-
ing, and left us. He was a very good man—Dolling."

"What?" Mr. Dodge said. "Who?"

"Dolling," Braithwaite replied; and followed his wife to the door. "I just happened to mention his name: Dolling. I—I didn't address you as 'darling,' Mr. Dodge, though I see how you might easily have thought I did. The man's name was Dolling. I shouldn't like you to think I'd take the liberty of calling *you*——"

But here he was interrupted by such an uproarious shout of laughter from his host that his final words were lost. Mr. Dodge's laughter continued, though it was interspersed with hearty expressions of hospitality and parting cheer, until the callers had passed the outer threshold and the door had closed behind them. Then the hilarious gentleman returned from the hall to face a wife who found nothing in the world, just then, a laughing matter.

"The worst thing you did," she assured him, "was to be so fascinated that you told her I'd been amiable to you about your sending that check—just after I said I knew all about it *before* you sent it and had *told* you to send it! That was a pleasant position to put your wife in, wasn't it?"

"Lydia!" he shouted, still outrageous in his mirth. "Let's forget that part of it and remember only Dolling!"

"All right," she said, and her angry eyes flashed. "Suppose his name *was* Dolling. What was she talking to him about rosemary and remembrance for?"

"I don't know, and it doesn't seem important. The only thing I can get my mind on is your keeping to yourself so solemnly the scandalous romance of Dolling!" And becoming more respectably sober, for a time, he asked her: "Don't you really see a little fun in it, Lydia?"

"What!" she cried. "Do you? After you saw that wretched little man of hers stand up there and recite his lesson like a trained monkey? Did you look at *her* while he was performing? She stood in the doorway and held the whip-lash over him till he finished! And if this idol of yours is so innocent and pure, why did she go all to pieces the way she did when she saw me that morning by the hedge?"

"Why, don't you see?" he cried. "Of course she saw you thought she'd called the man 'darling'! She knew you didn't know his name was Dolling. Isn't it plain to you *yet?*"

"No!" his wife said, vehemently. "It isn't plain to me and it never will be!"

XVII

"DOLLING"

AGAINST all reason she persisted in a sinister interpretation of her lovely neighbour's conduct;—never would Mrs. Dodge admit that Mr. Dodge had the right of the matter, and after a time she complained that she found his continued interest in it "pretty tiresome."

"You keep bringing it up," she said, "because you think you've had a wretched little triumph over me. It's one of those things that never can be settled either way, and I don't care to talk of it any more. If you want to occupy your spare thoughts I have a topic to offer you."

"What topic?"

Mrs. Dodge shook her head in a certain way. "Lily."

"Oh, dear me!" he said. "It isn't happening again?"

She informed him that it was, indeed. Lily's extreme affections were once more engaged. "We're in for it!" was the mother's preface, as she began the revelation; and, when she concluded, her husband sorrowfully agreed with her.

"It's awful now and will be worse," he said; and thus his "spare thoughts" became but too thoroughly occupied. In his growing anxiety over his daughter, he ceased to think of his neighbours;—the handsome chauffeur passed from his mind. Then abruptly, one day, as the wandering searchlight of a harboured ship may startlingly clarify some obscure thing upon the shore, a chance conjuncture illuminated for him most strangely the episode of Dolling.

He was lunching with a younger member of his firm in a canyon restaurant downtown, and his attention happened to become concentrated upon a debonair young man who had finished his lunch and was now engaged in affable discussion with the pretty cashier. He was one of those young men, sometimes encountered, who have not only a strong masculine beauty, but the look of talent, with both the beauty and the talent belittled by an irresponsible twinkle of the eye. Standing below the level of the cashier's desk, which was upon a platform, there was something about him that suggested a laughing Romeo; and, in response, the cashier was evidently not unwilling to play a flippant Juliet. She tossed her head at him, tapped his cheek with a pencil, chattering eagerly; she blushed, laughed, and at last looked yearningly after him as he went away. Mr. Dodge also looked; for the young man was Dolling, once Mrs. Leslie Braithwaite's chauffeur.

"Fine little bit of comedy, that," the junior member of Mr. Dodge's firm remarked, across their small table. "Talked her into giving him credit for his lunch. She'll have to make it up out of her own pocket until he pays her. Of course, he's done it before, and she knows him. Characteristic of that fellow;—he's a great hand to put it over with the girls!"

"Do you know him, Williams?" Mr. Dodge asked, a little interested.

"Know him? Lord, yes! He was in my class at college till he got fired in sophomore year. Every now and then he comes to me and I have to stake him. He's a reporter just now; but it's always the same—whether he's working or not, he never has any money. He can do anything: act, sing, break horses, drive an airplane, any kind of newspaper work—publishes poetry in the papers sometimes, and he's not such a bad poet, either, at that. But he's just one of these natural-born drifters—too good looking and too restless. He never holds a job more than a couple of months."

"I suppose not," Mr. Dodge said, absently. "I suppose he's tried a good many."

"Rather!" Williams exclaimed. "I've got him I don't know how many, myself. The last time I did he was pretty well down and out, and the best I could get for him was a chauffeur's job for a little cuss I happened to know in the brass trade—Braithwaite. Lives out your way somewhere, I think. O'Boyle *took* it all right; it was chauff or starve!"

"I beg your pardon. Who took what?"

"O'Boyle," said Williams. "Charlie O'Boyle, the man we're talking about—the chap that was just conning the cashier yonder. I was telling you he took a job as chauffeur for a family out your way in the suburbs."

"Yes, I understood," Mr. Dodge returned, with more gravity than Williams expected as a tribute to this casual narrative. "You said this O'Boyle became a chauffeur to some people named Braithwaite and that you obtained the position for him. I merely wondered—I suppose when you recommended this O'Boyle to Mr. Braithwaite you—ah—you mentioned his name? I mean to say: you introduced O'Boyle as O'Boyle."

"Well, naturally," Williams replied, surprised and a little nettled. "Why wouldn't I? I wouldn't expect people to take on a man for a family job like that and not tell 'em his *name*, would I? I don't see what you——"

"Nothing," Mr. Dodge said, hurriedly. "Nothing at all. It was a ridiculous question. My mind was wandering to other things, or I shouldn't have asked it. We'd better get down to business, I suppose."

But that was something his wandering mind refused to do; nor would it under any consideration or pressure "get down to business" during the rest of that afternoon. He went home early, and, walking from his suburban station in the first twilight of a gray but rainless November day, arrived at his own gate just as the Braithwaites' closed car drew up at the curb before the next house.

An elderly negro chauffeur climbed down rustily from his seat at the wheel and opened the shining door; Mrs. Braithwaite stepped gracefully down, and, with her lovely saint's face uplifted above dark furs, she crossed the pavement, entered the low iron gateway, and walked up the wide stone path that led through the lawn to the house. On the opposite side of the street a group of impressed women stopped to stare, grateful for the favouring chance that gave them this glimpse of the great lady.

Mr. Braithwaite descended from the car and followed his wife toward the house. He did not overtake her and walk beside her; but his insignificant legs beneath his overcoat kept his small feet moving in neat short steps a little way behind her.

Meanwhile, the pausing neighbour gazed at them and his open mouth showed how he pondered. It was not upon this strange woman, a little of whose strangeness had so lately been revealed to him, that he pondered most, nor about her that he most profoundly wondered. For, strange as the woman seemed to him, far stranger seemed the little creature pattering so faithfully behind her up the walk.

In so helpless a fidelity Mr. Dodge felt something touching; and perhaps, too, he felt that men must keep men's secrets. At all events, he made a high resolve. It would be hard on Mrs. Dodge, even unfair to her; but then and there he made up his mind that for the sake of Mrs. Leslie Braithwaite's husband he would never tell anybody—and of all the world he would never tell Mrs. Dodge—what he had learned that day about Mrs. Leslie Braithwaite's husband's loyalty.

XVIII

LILY'S FRIEND ADA

INDOORS Mr. Dodge too quickly found other matter to occupy his mind. Mrs. Dodge hurried down the stairs to set before him an account of a new phase in Lily's present romance, and they began their daily discussion of their daughter's beglamoured condition. In a way this was a strange thing for them to do, because, like many other fathers and mothers in such parental mazes, they realized that they struggled with a mystery beyond their comprehension. Lily's condition was something about which they really knew nothing, and least of all did they guess what part her dearest girl-friend had in it.

Lily had formed with the sturdy Ada Corey one of those friendships that sometimes suggest to observers an unworthy but persistent thought upon the profundity of girlish vanity. So often is a beautiful girl's best girl-friend the precise companion piece to set off most abundantly the charms of the beauty, or, if both girls of a pair be well-favoured, so frequently is one dark and the other fair, and each the best obtainable background for the other, that the spectator is almost forced to suppose many such intimacies to be deliberately founded upon a pictorial basis.

But this is not to say that these decorative elections to friendship are unaccompanied by genuine fondness; and although Lily Dodge found her background in the more substantial Ada, she found also something to lean upon and cling to and admire. For Lily was one of those girls we call ethereal, because they do not seem intended to remain long in a world their etherealness makes appear gross. They usually do remain as long as other people do, yet their seeming almost poised for a winging departure brings them indulgences and cherishings not shown to that stouter, self-reliant type to which Ada Corey was thought to belong.

Late on that same gray but rainless November afternoon, Ada, herself, spoke of this elaborate difference between them. "I don't see why *you* worry, Lily," she said. "I believe you could get away with anything! You're the kind that can."

"Oh, not *this!*" Lily protested, in a wailing whisper. No one was near them; but in her trouble she seemed to fear the garrulity of even the old forest trees of the park through which the two were taking an autumnal stroll. "Nobody in the world could get out of such a miserable state of things as I've got myself into *now*, Ada."

But this was by no means Miss Corey's first experience of her friend's confidences of despair. "I wouldn't bother about it at all, if I were you, Lily," she said, cheerfully. "I wouldn't give it a thought."

"You wouldn't?" Lily cried, feebly, and her incredulity was further expressed by her feet, which refused to bear her onward in so amazed a condition. She halted, facing her companion in a stricken manner. "You wouldn't give it a thought? When I've just told you that this time it's *three!*"

"No," Ada returned, stoutly. "I wouldn't. If I were *you*, I wouldn't. I wouldn't even if it were four!"

Lily moaned, and in a hopeless appeal for a higher witness to such folly, cast her eyes to heaven—or at least to as much of the dimming sky as roofed over the tattered brown foliage above her. "You wouldn't give it a thought! Not even if there were four of 'em." Then, as the woodland spot where they had stopped was somewhat secluded and apart from the main-travelled roads of the park, Lily felt at liberty to lean against a tree and apply a hand to her forehead in an excellent gesture of anguish. "I'm a goner this time, Ada," she murmured. "I'm a goner!"

"You aren't anything of the kind," Miss Corey assured her. "I tell ʸou it's not worth bothering about."

"Oh!" Lily uttered a sound of indignation, dropped the dramatic little hand, and spoke sharply. "You stand there, Ada Corey, and tell me that if such a thing happened to you, you wouldn't give it a thought?"

"I didn't say that."

"You did! You just said——"

"No; I said if I were *you*," Ada explained. "A thing like this wouldn't happen to me."

"Why wouldn't it? It might happen to any-body," Lily returned, quickly. "Suppose it did happen to you? Do you mean to tell me that if three separate, individual men all pretty nearly con-sidered themselves practically almost engaged to be married to you at the same time, you wouldn't give it a thought? You wouldn't bother about it at *all?*"

"I said I wouldn't if I were *you*," Ada insisted.

"Why wouldn't you?"

"For just the reason I told you. Because you're the kind that can get away with anything."

"But I can't!" Lily cried. "I'm *always* in some sort of miserable mess or other."

"Yes, pretty often," her friend assented. "But it's always a new one, and nobody ever does anything about the old one, so why should you care? You'll write one of these three boys a little weepy note, and you'll have a little weepy scene with another, and that'll leave only the one you like the best, and——"

"But I don't," Lily interrupted, piteously. "I don't absolutely *know* I like him as much as I thought I did, either."

"What!" Ada cried. "Not even *him?*"

"How can anybody ever be absolutely certain? I mean certain enough to get married. You know it's a thing you've got to look at pretty seriously, Ada—getting actually *married*."

But for the moment Ada did not seem to be sympathetic;—she was staring wide-eyed at her friend. "So you're going to wriggle out of it with all three of them."

"But maybe I can't," Lily moaned. "Suppose they insisted? Suppose they just wouldn't *let* me?"

"Has there ever been anything anybody wouldn't let you do?"

Lily moaned again. "You mean I'm spoiled. You mean people let me make 'em miserable. Oh, it's true, Ada! I do wish I could be more like you."

"Like me?" Ada laughed shortly. "You wouldn't for the world."

"Yes, I would." Lily took her friend's hand in her own. "I'd give anything in the world to be like you. You don't *know* what a trouble I am to my mother and father! They're always in some kind of stew or other over me, and I can't help it, because I'm always getting myself into such fearful messes. You never trouble *your* family; you're always a comfort to 'em. You aren't romantic and imaginative and sentimental and fly-off-the-handle, the way I am. You're steady and reliable, and people always know exactly where to find you."

But upon this, Ada looked puzzled. "Is that so?" she asked, gravely. "Is that how I seem to you, Lily?"

"To me? Good heavens! Don't you know that's the way everybody thinks of you? Everybody knows you're dependable;—you're what they call 'so satisfactory,' Ada. Your family and everybody else know you'll never do anything reckless or susceptible or dreamy. Nobody on earth knows what *I'll* do, because I don't myself. Just *look* at the difference between us!"

With that, as if the bodily contrast of the two expressed the contrast in character she had in mind, Lily extended her arms sidewise from her in an emotional gesture inviting an inspection of herself foredoomed to be damning; then pointed dramatically at Ada. "Just look at you and then look at me," she cried. "See what a *terrible* difference it is!"

She dropped her arms to her sides, submitting her case to an invisible jury, who might well have returned a verdict that at least the outward difference was pleasant rather than terrible. In the twilight beneath the trees the fair-haired and ethereal Lily, in her slim gray dress, seemed to be made of a few wisps of mist and a little gold. About her was a plaintive grace, not a quality of her dark-eyed and more substantial companion; yet both girls were comely; both were of the peach-bloom age that follows the awkward years; each had a grace of her own; and neither had cause to be disturbed by anything wherein she was unlike the other. Yet, as it happened, both were so disturbed.

Ada's gravity had increased. "You're all wrong about it, Lily," she said. "I'd give anything in the world to be like you."

"What!" Lily cried. "You wouldn't! Why?"

"Because of what I said. You can get away with anything, and people expect it. But if *I* ever did anything queer it would upset everybody. There'd be no end to it."

"But you never *will!*" Lily almost shouted.

"Won't I?" Ada returned, her gravity not relaxing. "What makes you so sure?"

"Why, you simply couldn't! *My* life is just one long eternal succession of queernesses. I *never* do anything rational; I don't seem to know *how;* but you're never anything but sensible, Ada. You'll fall in love sensibly some day—not like me, but with just one man at a time—and he'll be exactly the person your family'll think you ought to be in love with. And you'll have a nice, comfortable wedding, without any of the ushers misbehaving because you wouldn't marry *him* instead;—and then you'll bring up a large family to go to church every Sunday

and take an interest in missionary work and everything.   Don't you see how much *I* ought to be like
that, and how much you really are that?   Don't
you, Ada?"

Ada shook her head slowly.   "It doesn't quite
seem so," she said.   Then, beginning to stroll onward,
continuing their walk, she looked even more serious
than before, and inquired: "What are you going to
wear to-morrow night?"

Lines almost tragic appeared upon Lily's forehead,
and her previously mentioned troubles seemed of
light account compared to this one.   "Oh, dear!"
she wailed.   "That's *another* thing that's been on
my mind all day.   I haven't the least idea.   What
would you?"

She was still hopelessly preoccupied with the problem when she reached home, after parting with Ada
at the park gates; and in her own pretty room she
went to one of her two clothes'-closets even before
she went to a mirror.   Frowning, she looked over her
party dresses.

The slim, tender-coloured fabrics, charming even
though unoccupied, hung weightlessly upon small,
shoulderlike shapes of nickeled wire; and as she
restlessly slid the hangers to and fro along the groved

central rail that held them, she produced a delicate swish and flutter among the silks and chiffons before her, so that they were like a little pageant of pretty ghosts of the dances to which their young mistress had worn them. Lily approved of none of them, however; and, hearing her mother's firm step approaching the open door of the room, behind her, she said, desperately, without turning, "I haven't got a thing, Mamma; I haven't got a single thing!"

Mrs. Dodge, that solid matron, so inexplicably unlike her daughter, came into the room breathing audibly after an unusually hurried ascent of the stairs. "Lily," she said, in the tone of one who still controls an impending emotion, "Lily, you must never do this to me again. I can't stand it."

"Do what to you again?" Lily inquired, absently, not turning from her inspection. "I haven't got a thing I could wear to-morrow night, Mamma. Absolutely, I don't see how I can go unless——"

"*Lily!*" Mrs. Dodge exclaimed in a tone so eloquently vehement as to command a part of her daughter's attention. "Listen to me!"

Lily half turned, holding forth for exhibition a dress she had removed from its hanger. "What's the matter, Mamma? This pale blue chiffon is

absolutely the only thing I haven't worn so often
I just couldn't face anybody in again; but it never
was a becoming——"

"Lily, put down that dress and listen to me!"

"I'm sure it won't do," the daughter said, regretfully; but she obeyed and hung the dress over the
back of a chair. Then she turned to her dressing-
table mirror and began to remove her small hat.
"Are you upset or anything, Mamma?"

"Upset? No! I'm indignant," Mrs. Dodge explained, fiercely. "If you ever do such a thing to
me again——"

"What? Why, I haven't even seen you since
lunch time, Mamma. How could I have been doing
anything to you when I wasn't anywhere around to
do it?"

"You know well enough what you did to me!
You broke three separate engagements with three
separate——"

But Lily's light laughter interrupted. "Oh, did
the poor things call up?" she asked, and seemed to be
pleasantly surprised. "Well, my not being here
might be doing something to *them*, maybe," she
added, reflectively;—"but I don't see how it was
doing anything to *you*, Mamma."

"You don't? You break three separate engagements without a word, and leave me here to explain it; and then you say that wasn't doing anything to me!"

"But I didn't leave you to do it. I didn't even know you were going to be home this afternoon. I just thought maybe they'd call up and find I was out, and that'd be the end of it. What in the world did you go to the telephone *for*, Mamma?"

"Because two of them asked for me."

"Did they? What for?"

"To ask where you *were*," Mrs. Dodge said, explosively. "Each of 'em kept me about fifteen minutes."

"That was very inconsiderate," Lily observed. "Especially as I hadn't absolutely promised either of 'em I'd go. I only said to call up about three and *probably* I would. I don't think they ought to have kept you so——"

"That isn't what I'm complaining of," her mother interrupted, grimly. "It was disagreeable, especially as I was unable to give either of them any information and they both seemed to think I could if they kept *at* me long enough! It was trying, but it was bearable. What I refuse to have happen again, though, is what has been happening all the rest of the afternoon."

Lily proved herself strangely able to divine her mother's meaning without further explanation. Pink at once became noticeable upon her cheeks. "Oh, goodness!" she said. "Price didn't come *in*, did he?"

"For two and one-half hours," Mrs. Dodge replied, slowly and harshly. "For that length of time this afternoon I have been favoured with the society and conversation—the continuous conversation, I may say—of Mr. Price Gleason. I am strong enough to bear certain things, but not strong enough to bear certain other things, and I want to tell you that this is something you must never do to me again."

Lily sank into a chair, staring widely. "Oh, goodness!" she said. "When did he go?"

"Not until about five minutes before you came in."

"What did he say?"

"What didn't he?" Mrs. Dodge returned. "He had time enough!"

Upon this Lily's expression, grown grave, became tenderly compassionate. "Was he—was he *terribly* hurt with me, Mamma?"

"Well, I shouldn't say so—no. No, I don't think he was just what one might call stricken. At first he seemed rather depressed—but not for long. I don't think that young man will ever be much depressed about anything while he has a listener. All he asks of life is an audience."

"He talks beautifully," Lily said, with the dreamy look her mother knew so well. "Don't you think he does, Mamma? What did he talk about?"

"About nothing," Mrs. Dodge answered cruelly. "I mean, of course, about himself."

"Mamma!" Lily cried, quickly, and her sensitive face showed the pain she felt. "That isn't kind, and it isn't fair!"

"Isn't it? I never in my life listened to such a conceited and unveracious rigmarole as that young man favoured me with this afternoon. I did everything a Christian woman could to show him I wanted him to go, but he never stopped. You *can't* interrupt him when he's wound up like that, and he's always wound up. He makes an oration of it; he stands up, gestures like an actor, and walks around and up and down when he tells you how he's done all the great things he almost believes in himself when he's talking about 'em. I never knew such a story-teller in my life!"

"Mamma!"

"I never did," Mrs. Dodge said. "He told me he'd killed three men in Mexico."

"But, Mamma, it's true! He did! He was prospecting for silver mines and all sorts of things in Mexico."

"I don't believe a word of it, Lily;—it sounded much too much like 'adventure stories.' I don't think he did it; I think he read it. He said he killed those three men because they tried to 'jump his claim,' while he was away on a visit to his friend, the President of Mexico, and that afterward the President made him a general in the Mexican Army, and he fought in seven battles and was wounded twelve times. That was five years ago, so he must have been a general when he was about nineteen. In all my life I never heard——"

"If you please, Mamma!" Lily interrupted. "I'd rather not hear you accuse him of such things. I prefer——"

"Good gracious!" Mrs. Dodge exclaimed. "I can't see why you're so sensitive about him when you deliberately broke an engagement with h m this very afternoon without a word of explanation."

"That's an entirely different matter," Lily said, primly. "I *had* to do that."

"Why did you?"

"Because I couldn't go with one of 'em without hurting both the others terribly."

"But why didn't you make some excuse?"

"Because I couldn't think of anything I was sure would be satisfactory, or that they mightn't find out," Lily explained, seriously; and she added, "I had to put that *off*."

"Until when?"

"Until I get time to think it out, Mamma. So you see it didn't mean I care any less for Price. It **only** meant I was in a perplexing position." She **rose,** facing her mother gravely. "I like him much better than the others, Mamma, and I don't think it's considerate of you to speak so unkindly of him." Here Lily's lip began to tremble a little. "I think he talks wonderfully, and it's every word true about Mexico, and I think you and Papa ought to respect my feeling for him."

"Your father?" Mrs. Dodge cried. "You know perfectly well what your father thinks of him."

But Lily ignored this interpolation, and continued, "It seems to me it was very unkind of you to sit there just coldly criticizing him in your mind all

afternoon when he was doing his best to entertain
you. He meant nothing except kindness to *you*, and
you were sitting there all the time coldly crit——"

"Yes, I was," her mother interrupted. "I was
certainly sitting there! But I wasn't coldly criticizing him in my mind; you're wrong about that. After
two hours of it, my mental criticism was getting
pretty warm, Lily. In fact, I think it would have
scorched me if I hadn't finally got rid of him."

"Got rid of him?" Lily repeated, slowly.
"Mamma—you—you weren't——" She left the
sentence eloquently unfinished.

"Certainly I wasn't rude to him," Mrs. Dodge
returned, sharply. "I showed him the patience of
an angel as long as I could, and then I merely mentioned something I wish I'd thought of long before;
and he picked up his plush hat and yellow gloves and
went home."

"That's as unjust as everything else you say of
him. It isn't plush; it's velours," Lily said. Then
she asked ominously: "Mamma, what was it you
merely mentioned?"

"I told him it was getting to be about your father's
usual time of returning for dinner; that was all."

"*All!*" Lily cried. "When you *knew* that Papa wrote him to stop coming here, and Price never does come any more when Papa's here."

"Yes," Mrs. Dodge said, grimly. "'I'll admit he's that sensitive! Your father's letter was courteous—but clear."

"Courteous!" Lily echoed, and she became tragically rigid. She breathed visibly; her eyes were luminous with suffering and indignation; her sweet and searching little silver carillon of a voice became tremulous and loud. "It was unspeakable! I never knew Papa had such brutality in him. And *you*—I thought you were my friend, Mamma; but now I *see* what you did this afternoon! Price told you the story of his life because he was *defending* himself; he was trying to make you understand him. And all the while he was trying to, you sat there coldly critical, and then insulted him by telling him Papa might come in. You did, Mamma! You did! That's just what it amounted to."

"You consider it's an insult to a young man to tell him that your father may be arriving home presently?"

"Under the circumstances," Lily returned, bitterly, and quite correctly, "it certainly was a deadly insult.

And you say he isn't sensitive! Nobody understands how sensitive he is! And to think he has to
undergo such humiliations for me—all for me!"
With that, becoming every moment more emotion-
ally dramatic, Lily turned to a silver-framed photograph upon her desk, and addressed it, extending
her arms to it in piteous appeal. "Oh!" she cried,
"when I think of all you have to go through for my
sake—for *me*——"

"Lily!" her mother shouted. "Stop it! Stop that
nonsense this instant. Good heavens! your father
and I both thought you were getting over it. We
thought you'd begun to see the truth about Price
Gleason for yourself. What on earth has started
you all *up* again?"

This was a singular question for Mrs. Dodge to
be asking, since she herself was the origin of the re-
newal she thus lamented. Lily had indeed begun
to question her own feeling for the romantic Gleason,
as she had confessed to Ada within that very hour.
Moreover, there had crept upon her lately some faint
and secret little shadows of doubt in regard to the
tale of Mexican slaughter and other tremendous
narratives included by this new Othello as elements
of his wooing. Left to herself, Lily might have found

her doubt increasing; but her mother had changed all that in a few minutes.

Mrs. Dodge believed she had been accurately describing an unpleasantly absurd and erratic young egoist who had trespassed upon her time, her patience, and her credulity until she at last thought of a fortunate device to get rid of him; but this was not the picture she had painted upon her daughter's mind. What Mrs. Dodge really made Lily see was a darkly handsome poet adventurer, eloquently telling the story of his life, not to a stirred Desdemona such as she herself had been, but to a cynical matron who sat in frosty judgment, disbelieving him, and then put humiliation upon him. Lily's pale doubts of him vanished; Mrs. Dodge had made her his champion, with all ardours renewed.

Moreover, no one in the throes of a championing emotion likes to be asked, "What on earth has started you all *up* again?" Perhaps Lily resented this most of all, for the expression taken by her resentment was the one best calculated to dismay the questioner. "I'm not precisely 'started *up*' again, if you please, Mamma," she said, suddenly icy, as she turned from the photograph. "It is time you and Papa both understood clearly. I have never stopped caring for

Price. I have never cared for any one else." And,
having heard herself say it, she straightway believed it.

Mrs. Dodge uttered a dismal cry. "Oh, murder!" she said. "We've got it *all* to go through
again!"

"You cannot change me," Lily informed her.
"Nothing you could possibly say will ever change
me."

"But you know what he is!" Mrs. Dodge wailed,
despairingly. "Your own father says there isn't a
word of truth in his whole body, and besides that,
didn't he inherit four thousand dollars from his great-
aunt and spend almost every cent of it the day after
he got it on an automobile, and then smash the automobile to pieces after a very wild party? You
know he did, Lily! He's irresponsible and he's
dissipated, too; everybody knows he is; and that's
why Mr. Corey didn't want him to come to *their*
house any more than your father wants him to
come to ours. He was interested in Ada Corey before he began to come to see you, Lily."

"I know all about it," Lily said with dignity.
"He told me, of course, that he'd had a friendship
with Ada; and so did she. But Mr. Corey behaved

so outrageously to him, they both thought it would
be better to give it up."

"Ada's father and mother saw what that young
man is, Lily," Mrs. Dodge said, gravely. "They
told Ada it was their wish that she shouldn't receive
him or encourage him in any way; and she listened
to them and saw that they were right, and she obeyed
them, Lily."

"Yes," said Lily;—"she's that sort of a girl. I'm
not, Mamma."

Mrs. Dodge's eyes suddenly filled with tears.
"I know you're not," she said, simply, out of much
experience.

But at this Lily threw her arms about her.
'Mamma!" she cried. "I wish I *could* be like Ada!
I know how I trouble you, and I'd give anything to
be a steady, philosophical, obedient, comfortable
daughter! Oh, I *do* wish I could!"

"Then why can't you do as she did about this
young man, dear? Why can't you see the truth
about him as everybody else sees it? There aren't
any fathers and mothers of girls in the whole place
that don't feel the same way about him. He may
seem fascinating to a few susceptible girls who
haven't any experience, but he's just a bad sort of

joke to everyone else. Why can't you be as sensible as——"

But the moment of melting had passed. When her mother spoke of young Mr. Gleason as just a bad sort of joke, Lily stepped away from her, trembling. "Mamma," she said, "I wish you never to speak of him to me again until you have learned to respect both him and myself."

Mrs. Dodge stared helplessly; then, hearing her husband closing the front door downstairs, she made gestures as of wringing her hands, but said nothing, and went down to relieve herself by agitating Mr. Dodge with the painful narrative.

XIX

PARENTS IN DARKNESS

UPON its conclusion, he went so far as to pace the floor of the library, and make what his wife called an attack upon herself.

"I've done everything anybody could," she protested in defence. "How could *I* help it if he *has* been here a few times when you weren't in the house? It's all very simple for *you!* You merely write him a letter and then sit in your office, miles away, and expect me to do the rest! You don't have to go through the scenes with Lily when it comes to keeping him out. I believe it would be better, instead of making an attack on your wife, if you'd put your mind on what's to be done about it."

He shook his head gloomily. "I'm not so sure it was wise to write him that letter. I'm not sure we haven't been mistaken in our whole policy with Lily."

"Well, you've always overruled me," Mrs. Dodge returned, defensively. "What mistake do you think you've made?"

"I think we've probably been wrong from the start," he said. "Looking back over all our struggles with Lily, it's begun to seem to me that we never once accomplished anything whatever by opposing her."

"What! Don't you realize that she's still a child, and that children have to be opposed for their own good?"

"Not when they're nineteen, and it's opposition about their love affairs or their friendships," he returned, frowning; and he continued to walk up and down the room, his hands clasped behind him. "I mean open opposition, of course. I've begun to believe it never does the slightest good."

"Why doesn't it?" she asked, challengingly. "Are mothers and fathers supposed to sit aside with folded hands and calmly watch their children ruin their lives?"

He shook his head again, and sighed. "Sometimes it seems to me that fathers and mothers might just as well do that very thing. Certainly you and I could have saved ourselves a great waste of voice and gesticulation ever since Lily's babyhood if we'd never opposed her. And so far as I can see, results would have been just the same. Suppose we go on struggling with her about this Gleason nuisance; trying to keep him away from her, arguing with her, and all the rest of it. Will it change her in the slightest? Will it do any good to anybody?"

"You mean to say that we have no effect whatever upon our own child?"

"No," he answered. "We *might* have an effect. That's just what I'm afraid of."

"You mean we shouldn't keep on telling Lily the *truth* about Price Gleason?" his wife cried, incredulously.

"Yes; I've almost come to that conclusion. It doesn't seem to her to be the truth about him when we tell it. She only sees it as an attack on him. We spoil our own cause by making her his defender, and a defender can't help idealizing what he defends. I've come to believe that's where we parents make a lot of our worst mistakes—we're always throwing our children into the camp of our enemies. And in particular, when a girl is showing signs of being in love with a worthless young *poseur*, like this Gleason, I believe that all our denouncing and arguing and bossing only puts a glamour about the fellow in the girl's eyes, and makes her more certain she's in love with him and wants to marry him."

"Why, no," Mrs. Dodge returned, triumphantly demolishing him at a stroke. "Look at Ada Corey. Her father and mother told her the truth about Price Gleason and declined to let her see him. That was enough for Ada. She just quietly gave him up."

"I know—I know," Mr. Dodge admitted; but clung to his point. "Ada isn't like most girls of her age. I understand her, because she's sensible, and I *don't* understand most of 'em—particularly my own daughter; but I've grown pretty sure of one thing and that is this: If we want to throw Lily into this bounder's arms, we'll keep on telling her the truth about him. Our one chance is to let her alone and see if she won't find it out for herself."

"In other words, you intend to revoke our whole policy toward him?"

"In a manner, yes, I believe we should," Mr. Dodge admitted. "I don't go so far as to say I mean to tell Lily I consent to his coming to the house again; but I propose that we stop mentioning him at all in her presence, and that if she speaks of him we say nothing in dispraise of him. That is, from now on we're no longer actively and openly opposing her; and if you're going with her to that country club affair to-morrow night, and he's there, I suggest that you do and say nothing to make her think you object to her being with him. Let her dance with him all she wants."

"It won't work," Lily's mother predicted ominously. "Ada Corey's father took the right course; he simply put his foot down and that ended the matter. Why can't you do as Mr. Corey did?"

Mr. Dodge uttered sounds of rueful laughter. "I've put my foot down with Lily so many times I've worn the sole off my shoe. Remember, too, it's not so long ago since she cured herself of another infatuation because you thought it would be better for us to withdraw our opposition."

"That was utterly different, and the whole Osborne affair was a mere childish absurdity. Lily's older now, and you're proposing a terribly dangerous thing."

"Nevertheless, let's try it. What else *can* we do but try it?"

"I suppose we've got to, since you've made up your mind," his wife said, stubbornly. "But I consent to it under protest. She's absolutely infatuated, and we're throwing her straight in his arms. You'll see!"

This tragic prophecy of hers was in a fair way to be fulfilled almost immediately, she thought, the next evening, as she sat in the little gallery of the Blue Hills Country Club ballroom and looked down upon the dancers. The radiant Lily danced again and again with the picturesque Gleason; and her posture, as they moved gracefully together, was significant—her vivid, delicate face was always uplifted, so that her happy eyes, sweetly confident, seemed continuously engaged with pretty messages to her partner. The poetically handsome Price, on his part, bent his dark head above her ardently; and a stranger would have guessed them at first sight to be a pair newly betrothed. In fact, Mrs. Dodge was disquieted by much such a guess of her own, and her heart sank as she watched them. Moreover, while her heart sank, her indignation rose. This, then, was the result of Mr. Dodge's new policy! And she wished that he had been beside her to see its result—and to hear her opinion of it!

Her guess, however, like that of the supposititious stranger, was not quite accurate. Lily was not engaged to Mr. Gleason—not "absolutely" so, to report her own feeling in the matter. But she would

have admitted being "almost"—almost engaged—
that night. The Mexican hero had never definitely
proposed marriage, any more than she had felt
herself prepared for a definite consent to such a pro-
posal; but his every persuasive word and look and all
her own reciprocal coquetry pointed to that end.
And as the evening continued and they danced and
danced together, murmuring little piquancies to each
other meanwhile, the haziness implied in "almost"
seemed more and more on the point of being dispersed. Lily preferred that it be not quite; but her
partner was "wonderful" to look up to, and to listen
to as she looked. He had warmly appreciative dark
eyes and a stirring mellow voice; and he danced,
if not like a Mordkin, then at least like a Valentino,
which may sometimes be preferable. All in all, she
might have been swept away if he had pressed the
sweeping.

She was the happier because he did not—the in-
definite "almost" was so much pleasanter and more
exciting—and she had what she defined as a simply
magnificent time. Now and then she knew, in an
untroubled, hazy way, that a mute doomfulness
hovered above her in the gallery; but she felt that
her mother was behaving excellently—most surpris-

ingly, too—in not interfering at all. The one thing to bother Lily—and that only a little, and because it puzzled her—came at the very end of the evening. It was something her friend Ada said to her as they were alone together in the corner of a cloakroom, preparing to go home after the last dance.

XX

DAMSEL DARK, DAMSEL FAIR

IDN'T I tell you that you could get away with anything?" Ada said. "Weren't all three of 'em just as wild about you to-night as if you hadn't done it?"

"Done what?"

"Skipped out to walk with me and didn't leave any word behind, when you'd made engagements with all of 'em." And then, as Lily's flushed and happy face showed a complete vagueness upon the matter, Ada exclaimed, "Good gracious! Yesterday!"

Lily remembered, but as one remembers things of long ago. "Oh, that?" she said, dreamily. "It wasn't anything."

Ada looked at her sharply and oddly; and Lily afterward recalled the strangeness of this look. Ada's eyes, usually placid, were wide and lustrous; her colour was high, and she seemed excited. "Have you done anything to get out of being practically almost engaged to any of them?" she whispered, leaning close. "If you haven't, you don't need to worry anyhow, Lily."

She spoke hurriedly, all in a breath, then kissed Lily's cheek quickly and whispered, "I'm sorry!" She ran out into the crowded hallway, drawing her cloak about her as she ran.

"Why, what in the world——" Lily began, but Ada was already out of hearing, and disappeared immediately among the homeward-bound dancers near the outer doors. Lily followed, but could catch not even a glimpse of her, though she found an opportunity to say good-night—again—to Mr. Gleason, who was departing.

"Good-night, but never good-bye, I hope," he said, with a fervour somewhat preoccupied. "You've been *beautiful* to me. I hope you'll always be my friend." And with the air of a person pressed for time, he touched her hand briefly and passed on. Lily attributed his haste to the approach of her mother, who was ponderously bearing down upon them; but this interpretation may have been a mistaken one. Mr. Gleason had much on his mind at the moment, and Mrs. Dodge carefully withheld herself from joining her daughter until he had gone.

. . . Mr. Dodge had not retired to bed; he was smoking in the library when the two ladies of his household returned from their merrymaking. Lily kissed him enthusiastically, while his wife stood by, pure granite.

"You've had a jolly evening, Lily?"

"Beautiful!" she said. "Oh, simply magnificent!" And she ran upstairs to bed.

That is to say, she was on her way to bed, and she ran up the stairs as far as the landing; but there she paused. The acoustic properties of the house were excellent, and from the stairway landing one could hear perfectly what was said in the library when the library door was open. What stopped Lily was the bitter conviction in her mother's voice.

"Do you see?" Mrs. Dodge demanded. "Do you see what you're *doing?* It's just as I told you it would be. Absolutely!"

"Oh, no!" he protested. "This much isn't a fair trial. You haven't given it a chance."

"Haven't I?" Mrs. Dodge laughed satirically. "It's had chance enough to show where it's certain to end. Don't you see that for yourself?"

"No. What makes you think I should?"

"I'll tell you." But before going on to relate her

impressions of the evening, Mrs. Dodge had a deter-
rent thought.   She stood silent a moment, then went
to the door and called softly upward, "Lily?"

"Yes, Mamma.   I'm just going up to bed," Lily
said, diplomatically, and proceeded upon her way as
her mother closed the library door.

Lily wondered if they were talking about her,
though she was unable to see how giving something
a fair trial could have anything to do with her.
She could no longer hear the words her parents were
uttering, though the sound of their voices still came
to her in the upper hall, and it was evident that they
were beginning a spirited discussion.   Her father's
voice sounded protestive, her mother's denunciatory,
and Lily decided that they probably weren't talking
about her at all.   She was in high spirits and laughed
to herself over their earnestness—older people got
excited and argued so over such dull matters, she
thought.   It would be a terrible thing ever to get
middle-aged like that!

She never would be like that, she said to herself as
she undressed.   Never!   Such a thing couldn't
happen.   "To be like Mamma and not care much
what you wear, or anything, and with a good dry old
husband at home—and all so dusty and musty and

settled—and not able to *look* at another man—I could never in the world be like that! Ada Corey could, but I couldn't. I'd a thousand times rather die!"

And with the thought of Ada she remembered Ada's rather enigmatic remarks to her in the cloak-room and the queer look Ada had given her. The recollection of that oddly sharp look disturbed her, and, when she had gone to bed, kept her awhile from sleeping. There had been something appealing in that look, too, something excitedly reticent, as of strange knowledge withheld, and yet something humble and questing. And what in the world had she meant by saying, "I'm sorry!" as she ran out of the room.

Lily had to give it up, at least for that night, but she made up her mind to call Ada on the telephone early in the morning and reproach her for keeping people awake by suddenly becoming mysterious. Of course, though, the explanation would be simple, and the mystery would turn out to be nothing of any importance. Ada never knew any exciting secrets and probably hadn't intended to be mysterious at all. Having come to this conclusion, Lily let her thoughts go where they wanted to go, though they were not so much thoughts as pictures and dreamy echoes of sounds—pictures of dark and tender eyes bent devotedly upon hers, dreamy echoes of a mellow voice murmuring fond things to the lilting accompaniment of far-away dance music. So, finally, she slept, and slept smiling.

A coloured maid tapped at her door in the morning, and, being bidden to enter, came in and brought to Lily's bedside a note addressed in Ada's hand.

"Must been lef' here in the night-time, Miss Lily, or else awful early this morn'. It was stickin' under the front door when I went to bring in the newspaper."

Lily read the note.

It was the only thing we could do, Lily, to keep my people from guessing what was really going on. We didn't mean to let it go on so long, but we had to wait until we could save up enough to start with. Of course, I know everybody will say I'm hopelessly mad and reckless, and my family will be terribly upset. I *told* you I wished I were like you. If it were you, you could get away with a thing like this and after a day or so nobody would think anything about it, but I know how awful and different it will seem to everybody because *I'm* the one that does it!

I'm glad you told me it didn't really mean anything serious to you—I was sure it wouldn't. I hope you won't feel I ought to have given you my confidence, and I *would* have given it if it hadn't been such a serious matter. Besides, the real truth is,

Lily, our whole friendship seemed to be centred on your affairs and you, never on me or mine. You were so interested in the confidences you made to me, you never even seemed to think I had any to make of my own and you never invited any. Please don't take this for criticism—and *please* wish me happiness!

Lily dressed hurriedly; Ada had indeed mystified and disturbed her now; and she was eager to get to the telephone downstairs and find out what in the world this strange communication portended. But as she passed the dining-room door on her way to the little telephone table in the hall, her mother called to her. Mr. and Mrs. Dodge were at breakfast.

"Not now, Mamma. I'll come in a moment. I want to telephone to Ada first."

"Lily," her father said, urgently, "I wouldn't."

His tone arrested her, and she paused near the doorway.

"You wouldn't telephone to Ada?" she asked, nervously. "Why wouldn't you?"

"Ada's not there," he said, gravely. "Come here, Lily."

She came in slowly, looking at him with an appealing apprehension; and his own look, in return, was compassionate. He held a morning paper in his hand, and moved as if to offer it to her, then withheld it. "Wait," he said. "Your mother and I both think her family have behaved foolishly. If they'd shown a little more discretion—but she's the sort of girl nobody'd have dreamed would be up to this sort of thing, and I suppose they must have been terribly upset. Of course, they might have known the papers would get it, though, when they began calling up the police to look for her and stop the——"

"Police!" Lily gasped. "Papa! What are you *talking* about?"

"Ada Corey," he said. "She never came home from the dance last night. She's run away with that crazy young Price Gleason. They eloped from the Country Club, and the paper says they were married at a village squire's office about an hour afterward."

With that, not looking at her, but at his plate, he offered her the newspaper. Lily did not take it. She stared at it, wholly incredulous; then she reddened with sudden high colour, and, remembering Ada's queer look of last night, needed not even the confirmation of the queerer letter just read to understand that the thing was true.

She said nothing, but after a moment went to her chair at the table, and, although he did not look at her, Mr. Dodge had a relieved impression that she was

about to sit down and eat her breakfast in a customary manner. Then his wife rose suddenly and
moved as if to go to her.

"Let me *alone!*" Lily gasped. She ran out of the
door and up to her own room.

She felt that she could not live. No one *could*
live, she thought, and bear such agony. The dimensions of her anger, too great to be contained,
were what agonized her.

"To think of their daring to make me a mere
blind!" she cried out to her mother, when Mrs.
Dodge followed her. "To think they *dared!* It's
the treachery of it—the *insolence* of it! I can't *live*
and be made a mere blind! I *can't,* Mamma!"

XXI

MRS. CROMWELL'S NIECE

IN THE meantime, touching these mothers and daughters, there was a figure not thus far appeared among them, yet destined to be for a while their principal topic and interest. She was, indeed, at this time, a lonely figure, a niece of Mrs. Cromwell's but not well known to her and living a day's rail journey to the westward. On the November day of Lily Dodge's agony this niece of Mrs. Cromwell's was as agonized as Lily.

Each thought herself the unhappiest soul in the world, and yet, with greater wisdom, each might have known that no girl can ever think herself the unhappiest but that, at the same time, other girls—somewhere—will be thinking the same thing and suffering as sadly. The lonely niece's tragedy was as dark as Lily's, but came about in a different way.

The group of girls who had happened to meet at the corner of Maple Street and Central Avenue that morning was like the groups their mothers had sometimes formed, years before, on the same corner. This is to say, it was not unlike any other group of young but marriageable maidens pausing together by chance at a corner in the "best residence section" of a town of forty or fifty thousand inhabitants, anywhere in the land.

Three of these seven girls were on their way homeward from 'downtown"; three were strolling in the opposite direction; and the seventh, seeing the two parties meet and begin their chatter with loud outcries, had come hurrying from a quiet old house near by to join them. The six made a great commotion. Their laughter whooped on the whirling autumn wind that flapped their skirts about them; their gesturing hands fluttered like the last leaves of the agitated shade trees above them; their simultaneous struggles for a hearing, shattering the peace of the comfortable neighbourhood, were not incomparable to the disorderly uproar of a box of fireworks prematurely exploding on the third of July.

The seventh girl, who had come across the lawn of the quiet old house on the corner to join them, also shouted, begging to be told the cause of so much vociferation.

"What's happened? What on earth's the matter?"

she cried, going from one to another of the clamorous damsels and trying to make herself heard. "What is it? What's going on? What's it all *about?*"

One or two took cognizance of her with a nod and a hasty greeting, "Hello, Elsie," but found no more time for her; and the rest paid no attention whatever to her or to her eager inquiries. They were too busy shouting, "But listen, my dear!" or "I never in all my *life!*" or "My dear, you never *saw* anything like it!" though the smallest of them, a pretty brunette with the most piercing voice of all, did at last begin an explanatory response to the repeated entreaties of this Elsie. "Paul Reamer said——" But, as if realizing the waste of so much energy upon a person unconcerned in the matter, she immediately turned to the others, shrieking, "*Listen!* For Heaven's sake, *listen!* He said he'd be along before we got halfway *home!* He said——"

Then even the small brunette's remarkable voice was merged in the conglomerate disturbance, and Elsie was no wiser than before. She continued to go from one girl to another, shouting, "What *about* Paul Reamer? What's he *done?* What *about* him?" But for all the response she got she might have been both invisible and inaudible.

The uproar the six girls were making had no coherence; it accomplished nothing; it was merely a happy noise; and yet it seemed to be about something that concerned the six and was understood by them— something that had nothing to do with the seventh girl and could not be understood by her. The six were not hostile to her; they were merely unaware of her, or, at least, in their excitement, too dimly aware of her to pay any heed to her.

So, presently, she gave over her efforts and stood silent, a little apart from the shouting group and smiling; but her smiling was only an expression of hers, not a true token of feeling within. She wished to go on making her share of the noise; but a persistently disregarded questioner must always become at last a mere onlooker. Thus, Elsie found herself excluded from the merriment she had come to join; and she felt obliged to maintain a lively and knowing look upon her face, so that passers-by might not think her an outsider, for she did not know how to go away with any grace or comfort. Excluded, she could only stand near the congenial, vociferous six and try to look included—a strain upon her facial expression. The strain became painful as she still lingered and the merry group grew merrier; but what pained her more was her regret that she had rushed out so hopefully to meet an exclusion she should have known enough to expect.

She might have known enough to expect it because this was an old familiar experience of hers, an experience so much worse than customary that it was invariable. And another familiar old experience, or phase of this one, was repeated as she stood there, smiling and somewhat glassily beaming, trying to look knowing and included.

From down the street there came swiftly into nearer view an open touring car, driven by a slender young gentleman of a darkly handsome yet sprightly aspect; and upon this the six clamoured far beyond all clamours they had made before. The debonair motorist steered his machine to the curb, close to them, jumped out, was surrounded by the vociferators, and added his own cheerful shoutings to theirs.

What they all meant to convey was for the most part as unknown to Elsie Hemingway as if they gabbled Arabic, though the name "Paul" was prevalent over the tumult, amidst which the owner of it was seized by his coat lapels, his shoulders, even by his chin, and entreated to "listen!" Finally, however, some sort of coherent communication seemed

to be established among them, and the young man
emerged from the group, though the small girl with
the piercing voice still clung to one of his coat pock-
ets. "Call up Fred!" she screamed. "Tell him we
won't wait one instant!"

He detached himself. "Elsie, can I use your
telephone?" he asked, but evidently regarded the
question as unimportant, for he was already upon
his way and did not pause.

"Oh, *do!*" she cried, enthusiastically, glad to seem
a part of the mystery at last, and she turned to go
with him. "Do you want to call up Fred Patterson
to bring his car? Are you getting up a party, Paul?
What's the——"

He had rushed ahead of her and was at the open
front door of the house. "Where do you keep it?"
he called back to her.

"Wait! It's in the back hall. Wait till I show
you," she cried; but he ran into the house, found
the telephone, and was busy with it before she
reached him.

"Did you get Fred's number?" she asked, eagerly.

He was smiling and his eyes were bright with
anticipations that seemed to concern not Elsie but
the instrument before him. He did not look at her

or seem even to hear her, but moved the nickeled prong up and down impatiently.

"Can't you get him?" Elsie inquired, and she laughed loudly. Her air was that of a person secretly engaged with another upon a jocular enterprise bound to afford great entertainment. "Old Fred *is* the slowest old poke, isn't he? Suppose *I* try, Paul."

Young Mr. Reamer's eyes wandered to her and lost their lustre, becoming dead with absent-mindedness immediately. He said nothing.

"Let me try to get that funny old Fred," Elsie urged in the same eager voice; and she stretched forth a hand for the instrument.

Upon this he moved his shoulder in her way, turning from her, and at the same time a small voice crackled in the telephone. Mr. Reamer's brightness of expression returned instantly. "You bet it's me!" he said. "And if you don't hurry up here in that old tin boat of yours, you're going to get killed! The whole gang's out here on the curbstone, simply raving, right in front of Elsie Hemingway's."

"I believe it *is* Fred!" Elsie exclaimed. "I believe you've got him after all. Does he say——"

"You better hurry!" the young man said to the mouthpiece as he dropped the receiver into its hook. Then, as he turned toward the door, he seemed to become conscious, though vaguely, that he was not alone. "Much 'bliged, Elsie," he said. "Goo'bye!"

"Wait. Wait just a minute, Paul."

"What for?"

"Fred isn't on his way yet, I don't suppose," she said, timidly. "Let's—let's wait in Papa's library till he comes. There are some pretty interesting books in there I'd like to show you. Papa's great on bindings and old editions. Wouldn't you like to see some of 'em?"

"Well, another day maybe," he answered, obviously surprised. "You see Mamie Ford and all the girls are out there, and I——"

"Wait," she begged, for he was in motion to depart. "Aren't you ever coming to see me again, Paul?"

"What?" He appeared to have no comprehension of her meaning.

"Aren't you ever coming to see me again?" She laughed lightly, yet there was a tremor in her voice. "I don't believe you've been in our house for over two years, Paul."

"Oh, yes, I have," he returned. "I must have been here a whole lot in that much time. G'bye, Elsie; the girls are——"

But again she contrived to detain him. "Wait. When will you come to see me again, Paul?"

"Oh, almost any time."

"But when? What day?"

This urgency, though gentle, bothered him, and he wished he hadn't thought of using Elsie's telephone. He was a youth much sought, as he had reason to be pleasantly aware, and life offered him many more interesting vistas than the prospect of an afternoon or an evening or a substantial part of either, to be spent tête-à-tête with Elsie Hemingway. Pressed to give a definite reason why such a prospect dismayed him, he might have been puzzled. Elsie wasn't exactly a bore; she wasn't bad-looking, and nobody disliked her. Probably he would have fallen back upon an explanation that would have been satisfactory enough to most of the young people with whom he and Elsie had "grown up." Elsie was "just Elsie Hemingway," he would have said, implying an otherwise unexplainable something inherent in Elsie herself, and nothing derogatory to the Hemingway family.

"*When* will you come, Paul?"

"Why—why, right soon, Elsie. Honestly I will. I'll try to, that is. Honestly I'll——"

"Paul, it's true you haven't been here in over two years." Elsie's voice trembled a little more perceptibly. "The last time you were here was when you came to Mother's funeral. You had to come then, because you had to bring your mother."

"Oh, no," he said, a little shocked at this strange reference. "I was gl—— I mean I wanted to come. I'll come again, too, some day, before long. I must run, Elsie. The girls——"

"You won't say when?" She spoke gravely, looking at him steadily, and there was more in her eyes than he saw, for he was not interested in finding what was there, or in anything except in his escape to the gaiety outdoors.

He laughed reassuringly. "Oh, sometime before very long. I'll honestly try to get 'round. Honestly, I will, Elsie. Listen!"

There were shriekings of his name from the street and lawn. "G'bye! I'm coming!" he shouted, and dashed out of the house to meet the vehement demand for him. He was asked at the top of several voices "what on earth" he'd been doing all that time;

but no one even jocularly suggested Elsie as a cause of his delay.

When he had gone, she went to the front door and closed it, keeping herself out of sight; then she stood looking through the lace curtain that covered the glass set into the upper half of the door. The amiable youth she had called "old Fred," accompanied by a male comrade, was just arriving in a low car wherein they reclined almost at full length rather than sat. The small but piercing Miss Ford leaped to join them, and the other girls, screaming, each trying to make her laughter dominant, piled themselves into Paul Reamer's car. Both machines trembled into motion at once, and swept away, carrying a great noise with them up the echoing street.

Elsie stood for a little while looking heavily out at nothing; then she went slowly up the old, carpeted stairway to her own room, where she did a singular thing. She took a hand mirror from her dressing-table, looked searchingly into the glass for several long and solemn minutes, then dropped down upon her bed and wept. She might have been a beauty discovering the first gray hair.

It was strange that she should look into a mirror

and then weep because, if the glass was honest with her, its revelation should have been in every detail encouraging. The reflection showed lamenting gray eyes, but long-lashed and vividly lustrous; it showed a good white brow and a neat nose and a shapely mouth and chin. No one could have asked a mirror to be coloured a pleasanter tan brown than where it reflected Elsie's rippling hair; and as for the rest of her, she was neither angular nor awkward, neither stout nor misshapen in any way, but the contrary. Yet this was not the first time she had done that strange thing;—she had come too often silently to her room, looked into her mirror, and then fallen to long weeping.

XXII

WALLFLOWER

THE first time she had done it she was only twelve; but even then her reason for it was the same. At the end of a children's party she realized that she had been miserable, and that she was never anything except miserable at parties. She always looked forward to them; always thought for days about what she would wear; always set forth in a tremor of excitement; and then, when she was there, and the party in full swing, she spent the time being wretched and trying to look happy, so that no one would guess what she felt. She had always the same experience: in the games the children played, if two leaders chose "sides," she was the last to be chosen, except when she was ignored and left out altogether, which sometimes happened. When they danced she usually had no partners except upon the urgency of mothers or hostesses;—the boys rushed to all the other girls and came lagging to Elsie only in duty or in desperation. So at last, being

twelve, she realized what had been happening to her
—and came home to look secretly into her mirror
and then to weep.

As she grew older, and her group with her, nothing
changed; she was a wallflower. The other girls were
all busy with important little appointments
—"dates" they called them—Elsie had none. With
the liveliest eagerness the others talked patteringly
about things that were meaningless to her; and when
she tried to talk that way, too, she failed shamefully.
She tried to laugh with them, and as loudly as they
did, when she had no idea what they were laughing
about; and for a long time she failed to understand
that usually they were laughing about nothing. On
summer evenings the boys and girls clustered on
other verandas, not hers; and, sitting alone, she
would hear the distant frolicking and drifts of song.
At dances for her sixteen and seventeen-year-old
contemporaries, everything was as it had been when
she was twelve. Even when her mother, guessing a
little of the truth, tried to help her, and, in spite of
failing health, worked hard at "entertaining" for
Elsie, the entertaining failed of its object;—Elsie
was not made "popular."

"*Why* not?" she had passionately asked herself a thousand times. "*Why* do they despise me so?"

Yet she knew that they did not even despise her. At times they did despise one of their group, usually a girl; for it seems to be almost a necessity, in an intimate circle of young people, that from time to time there shall be a member whom the rest may privately denounce, and in gatherings vent their wit upon more or less openly.

During the greater part of her seventeenth year the dashing Mamie Ford had been in this unfortunate position without any obvious cause. The others were constantly busy "talking" about her, finding new faults or absurdities in her; snubbing her and playing derisive practical jokes upon her—for it is true that youth is cruel; self-interest takes up so much room. Elsie envied her, for at least Mamie was in the thick of things; and the centre of the stew. That was better than being a mere left-outer, Elsie thought; and Mamie fought, too, and had her own small faction, whereas a left-outer has nothing to fight except the vacancy in which she dwells—a dreary battling. Mamie's unpopularity passed, for no better reason than it had arrived;—she was now, at nineteen, the very queen of the roost, and Elsie, wondering why, could only conclude that it was because Mamie made so much noise.

Elsie had long ago perceived that, of the girls she knew, those who made the loudest and most frequent noises signifying excitement and hilarity were the ones about whom the boys and, consequently, the other girls, most busily grouped themselves. Naturally, the simple males went where vivacious sound and gesture promised merriment; and of course, too, a crowd naturally gathers where something seems to be happening. So far as Elsie could see, the whole art of general social intercourse seemed to rest on an ability to make something appear to be happening where nothing really was happening.

What had always most perplexed her was that the proper method of doing this seemed to be the simplest thing in the world, and was, nevertheless, in her own hands an invariable failure. She had watched Mamie Ford at dances and at dinners where Mamie was the life of the party, and she observed that in addition to shouting over every nothing and laughing ecstatically without the necessity of being inspired by any detectable humour, Mamie always offered every possible evidence—flushed face, sparkling eyes, and unending gesticulations—that she was having a genuinely uproarious "good time" herself. Elsie had tried it; she had tried it until her face ached; but she remained only an echo outside the walls. Nobody paid any attention to her.

Therefore she had no resource but to infer what she had inferred to-day, when the merry impromptu party whirled away without a thought of including her, and when Paul Reamer had so carelessly evaded her urgency—her shameless urgency, as she thought, weeping upon her coverlet. This inference of hers could be only that she had some mysterious ugliness, some strange stupidity, and it was this she sought in her mirror, as she had sought it before. It evaded her as it always did; but she knew it must be there.

"What is *wrong* about me?" she murmured, tasting upon her lips the bitter salt of that inquiry. "They couldn't always treat me like this unless there's *something* wrong about me."

She was sure that the wrong thing must be with herself. The Hemingways were one of the "old families";—they had always taken a creditable part in the life of the town, and the last man of them, her father, owned and edited the principal newspaper of the place. Elsie had no prospect of riches, but she was not poor; and other girls with less than she were "popular." Therefore the wrong thing about her could be identified in nothing exterior. Moreover, when she pursued her search for the vital defect she could not attribute it to tactlessness; for that has some weight, and she was weightless. She danced well, she dressed as well as any of the girls did, and her father told her that she "talked well," too;—he said this to her often, during the long evenings she spent with him in his library. Yet he was the only one who would listen to her, and, though she adored him, he was not the audience she most wanted. She "talked well"; but even by pleading she could not get Paul Reamer to spend five minutes with her.

No wonder! Paul was the great beau of the town, and she the girl least of all like a belle. And, remembering his plain consciousness of this contrast, almost ludicrously expressed in his surprise that she should try to detain him with her for even a few minutes, she shivered as she wept. She hated herself for begging of him; she hated herself for having run out of the house to try for the thousandth time to be one of a "crowd" that didn't want her; she hated herself for "hanging around them," laughing

and pretending that she was one of them, when anybody could see she wasn't. She hated herself for
having something wrong about her, and for not being
able to find out what it was; she hated herself, and she
hated everything and everybody—except her father.

. . . At dinner that evening he reproached her
for being pale. "I don't believe you take enough
exercise," he suggested.

"Yes, I do. I took a long walk this afternoon.
I walked four or five miles."

"Did you?" He smiled under his heavy old-
fashioned, gray lambrequin of a moustache, and his
eyeglasses showed a glint of humorous light. "That
doesn't sound as if you went with a *girl* companion,
Elsie! Four or five miles, was it?"

"I went alone," she said, occupied with her plate.

His humorous manifestations vanished and he
looked somewhat concerned. "Is that so? It
might have been jollier the other way, perhaps. I
sometimes think I monopolize you too much, young
woman. For instance, you oughtn't to spend all
your evenings with me. You ought to keep up your
contemporary friendships more than you do, I'm
afraid. Why don't you ask the girls and boys here
to play with you sometimes?"

"I don't want them."

"Would you like to give a dance—or anything?"

"No, Papa."

He sighed. "I'm afraid your young friends bore you, Elsie."

"No," she said. "It isn't that exactly. I just ——" She left the sentence unfinished.

"You just don't take much interest in 'em," he laughed.

"Well—maybe." Still occupied with the food before her, though her being occupied with it meant no hearty consumption of it, she seemed to admit the charge. "Something like that."

"It shouldn't be so," he said. "From the little I see of 'em I shouldn't spot any of 'em for a lofty intellect precisely, but young people of that sort in a moderate-sized city like this usually do seem to older people just a pack of incomprehensible gigglers and gabblers. I suppose you never hear much from 'em except personalities and pretty slim jokes, and it may get tiresome for a girl as solid on the Napoleonic Period as you are." He paused to chuckle. "I don't suppose you hear much discussion of Madame de Rémusat among 'em, do you?"

"No."

"What I'm getting at," he went on;—"you oughtn't to think too much about intellectual fodder or be bored with people your own age because they can't offer it."

At that she glanced wanly at him across the table. "I'm not, Papa. They don't bore me."

"Then I can't understand your not seeing more of 'em. It isn't normal, and you're missing a lot of the rightful pleasures of youth. It's natural for youth to seek youth, and not to devote all its time to an old codger like me. I believe you need a change." He looked at her severely and nodded. "I'm serious."

"What change?"

"Your aunt Mildred's written me again about your visiting there," he said. "Your cousin Cornelia finished her school last year. Now she's home from eight months abroad and they really want you."

"Oh, no," Elsie said, quietly, and looked again at her plate.

"Why not?"

"I don't care to go, Papa."

"Why don't you?"

Her lip quivered a little, but she controlled it, and he saw no sign of emotion. "Because I wouldn't have a good time."

"I'd like to know why you wouldn't," he returned a little testily. "Your aunt Mildred is the best sister I had. She's a pretty fine person, Elsie, and she's always wanted to know you better. She says Cornelia's turned out to be a lovely young woman, and they both want you to come. She's sure you'll like Cornelia."

"Maybe I would," Elsie said, moodily. "That isn't saying Cornelia'd like me."

"Of all the nonsense!" he cried, and he laughed impatiently. "How could she help liking you? Everybody likes you, of course. Mildred says Cornelia has a mighty nice circle of young people about her; they have such jolly times, it's fun just watching 'em, Mildred says; and she enjoys entertaining a lot. They have that big house of theirs, and they're near enough the city to go in for the theatre when they want to and——"

"I know," Elsie interrupted. "They're great people, and it's a big, fashionable suburb and everything's grand! I'm not dreaming of going, Papa."

"Aren't you? Well, I'm dreaming of making you," he retorted. "You haven't been there since you were a little girl, and your aunt says it's shameful to treat her as if she lived in China, when

it's really only a night or day's run on a Pullman.
They want you to come, and they expect to give
you a real splurge, Elsie."

"No, no," she said, quickly; and if he could have
seen her downcast eyes he might have perceived
that they were terrified. "Let's don't talk of it,
Papa."

"Let's do," he returned, genially. "I suppose
you think that because you're bored by this little
set of young people of yours, here, you'll be bored by
Cornelia's friends. I don't know, but I'd at least
guess that they might be a little more metropolitan,
though of course young people are pretty much the
same the world over nowadays."

"Yes," Elsie said in a low voice. "I'm sure they
would be."

"More metropolitan, you mean?"

"No," Elsie said. "I mean they'd be the same as
these are here."

"Well, at least you might give 'em a try. They
might prove to be more——"

"No," Elsie said again. "They'd be just the
same."

This was the cause of the obstinacy that puzzled
and even provoked him during a week of intermittent

arguing upon the matter. Elsie was sure that one thing he said was only too true: "Young people are pretty much the same the world over nowadays"; and in her imagination she could conjure up no picture of herself occupying among her cousin Cornelia Cromwell's friends a position different from that she held among her own. They would be polite to her for the first hour or so, she knew, and then they would do to her what had always been done to her. They would treat her as a weightless presence, invisible and inaudible, a left-outer.

Her aunt and Cornelia would expect much of her; and they would be kind in their disappointment; but they would have her on their hands and secretly look forward to the relief of her departure. Elsie could predict it all, and in sorry imaginings foresee the weariness of her aunt and cousin as they would daily renew the task of privately goading reluctant young men and preoccupied girls to appear conscious that she was a human being, not air. The visit would mean only a new failure, a new one on a grander scale than the old failure at home. The old one was enough for her; she was used to it, and the surroundings at least were familiar. The more her father urged her, the more she was terrified by what he urged.

"I've made up my mind to compel you," he told her one evening in the library. "I'm serious, Elsie."

She did not look up from her book, but responded quietly: "I'm twenty. Women are of age in this state at eighteen, Papa."

"Are they? I wrote your aunt yesterday that you're coming."

"I wrote her yesterday, too. I told her I couldn't."

"No other explanation?"

"Of course I said you needed me to run the house, Papa."

"I didn't bring you up to tell untruths," he said. "You've learned, it seems; but this one won't do you any good. You're going, Elsie, and if you want some new dresses or hats or things you'd better be ordering 'em. You don't seem to understand I really mean it."

She dropped her book in her lap and sighed profoundly. "What for?" she asked. "Why do you make such a point of it?"

"Because I've been watching you and thinking

about you, and I don't believe I'm doing my duty
by you. Not as"—his voice showed feeling—"not
as your mother would have me do it. Sometimes
you cheer up and joke with me, but I don't believe
you're happy."

"But I *am*."

"You're not," he returned with conviction. "And
the reason is, you lead too monotonous a life. A
monotonous life suits elderliness, but it isn't normal
for youth. Really, you're getting to lead the life
of a recluse, and I won't have it. If these provincial
young people here bore you so that you won't run
about and play with them as the other girls do, why
then you've got to try a different kind of young
people."

"But you said young people were all the same,
Papa, the world over; and it's true."

"At least," he insisted, "your cousin Cornelia's
will have different faces, and you're going to go and
look at 'em. Elsie, you're *not* having a good time,
and one way or another I've got to make you. You
need a new view of some kind; you've got to be
shaken out of this hermit habit you've fallen into."

"Papa, please," she said, appealingly. "I don't
want to go. Don't make me. Please!"

At this he rose from his chair and came to her and took one of her hands in his. The room was warm, and she sat near the fire; but the slender hand he held was cold. "Elsie, I want you to," he said. "I don't want to think your mother might reproach me for not making you do what seems best for you. Let me wire your aunt to-morrow you'll come next week."

Her lower lip moved pathetically, and along her eyelids a liquid tremulousness twinkled too brightly. "I couldn't——" she began.

"Don't tell me that any more, Elsie."

"No," she said, meekly. "I meant I couldn't get ready until week after next, Papa—or the week after that. I couldn't go before December. Not before then, please, Papa."

He patted her hand and laughed; pleased that she would be obedient; touched that she was so reluctant to leave him. "That's the girl! You'll have a glorious time, Elsie; see if you don't!" he said, and, looking down tenderly upon her shining eyes, never suspected the true anguish that was there.

XXIII

THE STRANGE MIRROR

IT WAS still there, and all the keener, when Elsie dressed before the French mirror in the big and luxurious bedchamber to which she had been shown on her arrival at her aunt's house.

"Mrs. Cromwell and Miss Cornelia had an engagement they couldn't break. They said for me to say they're sorry they couldn't be here when you came," a maid told her. "Mrs. Cromwell said tell you she's giving a dinner for you and Miss Cornelia this evening. It's set for early because they're going to theatricals and dancing somewheres else afterward, so she thought p'raps you better begin dressing soon as your trunk gets here. They'll have to dress in a hurry, theirselves, so you may not see 'em till dinner."

But Elsie did not have to wait that long. Half an hour later, when she had begun to dress, Cornelia rushed in, all fur and cold rosy cheeks. She embraced the visitor impetuously. "D'you mind bein' hugged by a bear?" she asked. "I couldn't wait even to take off my coat, because I remembered what an awf'ly nice *little* thing you were! Do you know we haven't seen each other for nine years?" She stepped back with her hands upon Elsie's shoulders. "I've got to fly and dress," she said. "*My* but you're lovely!"

With that, she turned and scurried out of the room, leaving behind her a mingled faint scent of fur and violets, and the impression upon Elsie that this cousin of hers was the prettiest girl she had ever seen.

Cornelia's good looks terrified her the more. Probably there were other girls as pretty as that among Cornelia's friends, the people she was to meet to-night. And Cornelia's rush into the room, her flashing greeting, so impulsive, and her quick flight away were all flavoured with that dashingness with which Elsie felt she could never compete. "*My*, but you're lovely!" was sweet of Cornelia, Elsie thought. But girls usually said things like that to their girl visitors—especially when the visitors had just arrived. Besides, anybody could see that Cornelia was as kind as she was pretty.

"*My*, but you're lovely!" was pleasant to hear,

even from an impulsive cousin, yet it was of no great
help to Elsie.   She went on with her dressing, looking
unhappily into the glass and thinking of what irony
there had been in her father's persistence.   "To
make me have a 'good time'!" she thought.   "As
if I wouldn't have had one at home, if I could!   But
of course he didn't know that."

She was so afraid of what was before her, and so
certain she was foredoomed, that during this troubled
hour she learned the meaning of an old phrase describing fear; for she was indeed "sick with apprehension."   She took some spirits of ammonia in a
glass of water as a remedy for that sickness.   "Oh,
Papa!" she moaned.   "What have you done to me?"

The maid who had brought her to her room re-
appeared with a bouquet of rosebuds and lilies of the
valley, to be worn.   "It's from one of the gentlemen
that's coming to dinner, Miss Cornelia said.   He
sent two.   Pr'aps I could pin it on for you."

Elsie let her render this service, and when it was
done the woman smiled admiringly.   "It certainly
becomes you," she said.   "I might say it looks like
you."

Elsie regarded her with a stare so wide and blank
that the maid thought her probably haughty.   "Ex-

cuse me, ma'am. Could I be of any more assistance?"

"No, thank you," Elsie said, still staring, and
turned again to the mirror as the flatterer left the
room.

The bouquet was beautiful, and, before the evening
was over, the unknown gentleman who had sent it
would be of a mind that the joke was on him, Elsie
thought. The misplaced blarney of an Irishwoman
had amazed but not cheered her; and the clock on
the mantel-shelf warned her that the time was ten
minutes before seven. She took some more ammonia.

The next moment into the room came her aunt,
large, decorously glittering, fundamentally important. She was also warm-hearted, and she took her
niece in her arms and kissed her as if she wanted to
kiss her. Then she did as Cornelia had done—held
her at arm's length and looked at her. "You dear
child!" she said. "I've wanted so long to get hold
of you. A man never knows how to bring up a girl;
she has to do it all herself. You've done it excellently, I can see, Elsie. You have lovely taste;
that's just the dress I'd have picked out for you
myself. And to think I haven't seen you since your
dear mother left us! Cornelia hasn't seen you for

much longer than that—you and she haven't had
a glimpse of each other since you were ten or eleven
years old."

"Yes," Elsie said. "I saw her a little while ago."
She gulped feebly, and by a great effort kept her
voice steady. "Aunt Mildred, how proud of her
you must be! I want to tell you something: I think
Cornelia is the very prettiest girl I've ever seen in
my whole life."

Mrs. Cromwell took her hands from her niece's
shoulders, and, smiling, stepped backward a pace
and shook her head. "No," she said. "Cornelia's
very pretty, but she isn't *that* pretty."

"I think she is."

"No." Mrs. Cromwell laughed; then became
serious. She swept a look over her niece from head
to foot—the accurately estimating scrutiny of an
intelligent and experienced woman who is careful to
be an honest mother. "Of course Cornelia isn't in
your class," she said, quietly.

Then she turned to the door. "Come down to
the drawing-room a minute or so before seven," she
said, and was gone.

Elsie stood, cataleptic.

The words seemed to linger upon the stirred air

of the spacious room. "Of course Cornelia isn't in your class." Cornelia's mother had not intended to be satirical; she had been perfectly serious and direct, and she had really meant that Cornelia, not Elsie, was of the lower class of prettiness. Here were three dumfounding things in a row: "*My*, but you're lovely!" "It certainly becomes you—I might say it looks like you." "Of course Cornelia isn't in your class." The third was the astounding climax that now made the first two almost—almost convincing!

Elsie rushed to the long mirror and in a turmoil of bewilderment gazed and gazed at what she saw there. And as she looked, there slowly came a little light that grew to be a sparkling in those startled eyes of hers; her lips parted; breathlessly she smiled a little;—then, all in a flash, radiantly. For what she saw in the mirror was charming. No fear of hers, no long experience of neglect, could deny it; and at last she was sure that whatever the wrong thing about her was, it could be nothing she would ever see in a mirror. She was actually what at home she had sometimes suspected and then believed impossible.

She was beautiful—and knew it!

Marvelling, trembling with timid and formless

premonitions of rapture, she stood aglow in the revelation. She leaned closer to the mirror and spoke to it in a low voice, almost brokenly: "*My*, but you're lovely—I might say it looks like you— of course she isn't in your class!"

Then, with new and strange stars in her eyes, this sudden Cinderella went out of her room and down the wide stairway, dazed but not afraid. The miracle had already touched her.

Her uncle met her at the doorway of the drawing-room. "This is not little Elsie!" he said. "Why, good heavens, your father didn't write us his Elsie had grown up into anything like *you!*"

Immediately he took her upon his arm and turned to cross the room with her, going toward the dozen young people clustered about Cornelia.

But Cornelia came running to her cousin. "You're dazzling!" she whispered, and it was obvious that Cornelia's friends had the same impression. They stopped talking abruptly as Elsie entered the room, and they remained in an eloquent state of silence until Cornelia began to make their names known to the visitor. Even after that, they talked in lowered voices until they went out to the dining-room.

XXIV

TRANSFIGURATION

THEY were livelier at the table, but not nearly so noisy as Mamie Ford and Paul Reamer and their intimates would have been at a dinner party at home, Elsie thought; though this was but a hasty and vague comparison flitting through her mind. She was not able to think definitely about anything for a time: she was too dazzled by being dazzling. Her clearest thought was an inquiry: Was this she, herself, and, if she was indeed Elsie Hemingway, were these queer, kind, new people now about her quite sane?

The tall young man with the long face who sat at her left talked to her as much as he could, being hampered by the circumstance that the fair-haired short young man on her right did his best to talk to her all the time, except when she spoke. Then both of them listened with deference; and so did a third young man directly across the table from her. More than that, she could not look about her without encountering the withdrawing glances of other guests of both sexes, though some of these glances, not from feminine orbs, were in no polite flurry to withdraw, but remained thoughtfully upon her as long as she looked their way. *Could* it be Elsie Hemingway upon whom fond eyes of youth thus so sweetly lingered?

Too centred upon the strange experience to think much about these amazing people except as adjuncts to her transfiguration, she nevertheless decided that she liked best the tall gentleman at her left. He was not so young as the others, appearing to be as far advanced toward middle-age as twenty-seven—or possibly even twenty-nine—and she decided that his long, irregular face was "interesting." She asked him to "straighten out the names" of the others for her, hoping that he would straighten out his own before he finished.

He began with Lily Dodge. "*Our* prettiest girl," he explained, honestly unconscious of what his emphasis implied. "That is, she's been generally considered so since your cousin Anne was married. The young man on Miss Dodge's right and in such a plain state of devotion is named Henry Burnett just now."

"Just now? Does his name change from time to time?"

"Poor Henry's doesn't, no; nor the condition in which Miss Dodge keeps him—probably because she likes to win golf tournament cups with him. I mean, the next time you see her at a dinner the man beside her in that state may have another name. *She* changes 'em."

"I see," Elsie said. She looked absently at Miss Dodge, not aware that there could be anything in common between them, much less that in a manner they had shared a day of agony, no great while past. "She seems very lovely."

"In her own way, yes," her neighbour returned without enthusiasm. "The man on her left——"

Elsie laughed and interrupted. "What I meant to get at—if you don't mind—was the name of the man on *my* left!"

"Of course you wouldn't have caught it," he said. "You naturally wouldn't remember, hearing it spoken with the others."

"No," she said. "Yet I think I do remember that Cornelia spoke it a little more impressively than she did any of theirs."

"That's only because I'm in her father's firm.

The most junior member, of course. They use me as a waste-basket."

"As what?"

"A waste-basket. When Mr. Cromwell and the really important partners discover some bits of worthless business cluttering up the office they fill me up with it. Every good office has a young waste-basket, Miss Hemingway."

"But you haven't yet told me this one's name."

"Harley."

He laughed ruefully, and she asked why. "Harley doesn't seem a funny name to me," she said. "I don't understand your laughing."

"It's to keep from crying," he explained. "My father was dead before I was born and my mother died just after. I was taken over by my grandfather, and he named me for three of Napoleon's marshals—Berthier Ney Junot Harley. It takes a grandfather to do things like that to you!"

"But Junot wasn't a marshal," Elsie said. "He hoped to be, but the Emperor never made him one; Junot was too flighty."

Mr. Harley stared. "I remember that's true;— I spoke of three marshals hastily. I should have said two and a general. My grandfather brought me

up on 'em, and I still collect First Empire books.
But imagine your knowing!"

"You mean you think I don't look——"

He interrupted earnestly. "I'm afraid it's too
soon for you to let me tell you how I think
you look. But you do laugh at my names, don't
you?"

"No; they don't seem funny to me."

"Don't you ever laugh except when things are
funny?" he asked.

"Yes, I do," she said. "I've laughed thousands
of times when everything was horribly unfunny."

"Then why did you laugh?"

For an instant she looked at him gravely. "To
try to be 'popular,'" she said.

Plainly he thought this funny enough for laughter.
"That *is* a joke!" he said. "But if laughing makes
you any more 'popular' than you would be without
it, I hope for this one evening at least you'll be as
solemn as an obelisk."

Of course Elsie said, "Why?"

"Because if you laugh I won't get to see anything
of you at all. I'm afraid I won't anyhow."

He spoke with gravity, meaning what he said;
and the event proved his fear justified. He got

halfway round the country-club ballroom with her, after the theatricals, a surprising number of times, but seldom much farther. However, he conclusively proved his possession of that admirable quality, dogged persistence, and so did the other young gentlemen of the dinner party. So did more than these, including probably a majority of the men and youths, married or single, present that evening at the Blue Hills Club.

Elsie wondered when the spell would break. It seemed impossible that she wouldn't be found out presently as a masquerader and dropped into her old homelike invisibility. But whether the break came or not, she knew she would never again be so miserable as she had been, because she was every moment more and more confidently daring to know that she was beautiful. She laughed at a great many things that weren't funny during this gracious evening; for laughter may spring as freely from excited happiness as from humour; but she made no effort to be noisy—noisiness appeared to be not a necessity at all, but superfluous. And what pleased her most, the girls were "nice" to her, too, as she defined their behaviour;—they formed part of the clusters about her when the music was silent, and they eagerly competed to arrange future entertainment for her. Elsie loved them all, these strange, adorable people who had not seen the wrong thing about her.

The old walls built round her by her own town, enclosing her with such seeming massive permanence and so tightly, now at a stroke proved to be illusion; she was discovering that they were but apparitions all unreal, and that this world is mysterious and can be happily so. Something of its humorous mysteries in dealing with young hearts another person, near her, also learned that night; for Cornelia Cromwell, by coincidence, had a queer experience of her own.

Beyond the outer fringe of dancers she saw her mother standing among a group of the older people;— one of these was Miss Bailey, the principal of the suburban school in which Cornelia had once been a pupil. Cornelia had not seen her for several years and went conscientiously to greet her. Principal and former pupil made the appropriate exchanges; but Cornelia was rather vague with the grayish gentleman who had Miss Bailey upon his arm.

Mrs. Cromwell said something as in correction of an error; but it was too late, and the couple had moved away before Cornelia understood.

"You called her Miss Bailey," Mrs. Cromwell explained. "She's been married to Professor Bromley for two years."

"What! Was that funny little old——" Cornelia checked herself; but the tactful mother had already turned away to speak to someone else. The daughter stood and gazed at the stiff little old-fashioned gentleman standing punctiliously arm-in-arm with his wife. "Oh, dear *me!*" Cornelia whispered.

Then she ran back, wide-eyed, to rejoin an anxious lad who had arrived late. "Look here," he said. "You've missed another chance to let me meet your cousin. What did you run away like that for?"

"To learn something important," Cornelia told him. "Come on;—I'll get you through to Elsie somehow."

For the unmasking of Elsie, that dreaded break in the spell, still postponed itself as the evening wore on. Her miraculous night continued to be a miracle to the end, and she was a girl grateful for wonders when she talked them over with her cousin in the big bedroom, after two o'clock in the morning.

"I never met such darling people in the whole world!" she declared. "I never knew——"

"What nonsense!" Cornelia laughed. "You must

be perfectly used to being a sensation wherever you go, Elsie."

"A 'sensation'?" Elsie cried. "*I?*"

"Don't tell me you don't know it!"

"Cornelia, you don't understand. Nobody was ever really nice to me at a party before to-night in my whole life."

At that her cousin beamed upon her. "I believe that's what I like best of all about you, Elsie."

"You mean nobody ever being nice to me before?"

"No," Cornelia laughed. "I mean your not admitting that you know it. Of course you do know, because it's impossible for a girl like you not to realize the effect you have on people; but I love you for pretending you don't see it."

"But it's true," Elsie insisted. "Until to-night nobody ever——"

"Yes, yes! Go on! It's very becoming, and it's what placates the other girls so that you get both sexes in your train, you clever thing!"

"I'm not clever, though," the visitor protested. "I'm no good at all at pretending things. I'm not——"

"Aren't you?" Cornelia laughed. "Well, it's nice of you to *try* to be modest, then. Your thinking

you ought to be is one of your charms. It isn't
the biggest one, though. Everybody saw that one
the instant you came downstairs to-night and stood
in the drawing-room doorway, just before Father
went to bring you in. It was very striking, Elsie."

"I don't know what you mean."

"That's right; you oughtn't to know," Cornelia
said, seriously. "It has to be spontaneous, I suppose,
and it probably can't be imitated or done deliberately."

"But I didn't do *anything!*" Elsie cried.

"I know you didn't; that's just what I'm pointing
out. Maybe it was something they call 'magnetism';
but anyhow it was more than just being a beauty.
Of course you're *that*——"

"Nobody ever told me so; not before——"

"Nonsense!" Cornelia interrupted; then she went
on: "It seemed to lie in not only being a beauty, but
in being a beauty with a kind of glow. I don't
know just how else to express it, because it's better
than having what they call the 'come hither' look.
It was—well, *charm*, I suppose. People might never
notice that a beauty *is* a beauty if she doesn't have
something of it. But 'charm' is too vague to express
it exactly. It was a look as if—as if——" Cornelia

hesitated, groping. "Well, I can't find any way to tell it except to say it was as if you knew something mysterious and lovely about yourself. And it makes everybody else crazy to know it, too!"

She jumped up, pointing at the clock upon the mantel. "Good heavens! And we've got engagements for every minute of the next two weeks, beginning at half-past eight to-morrow morning! Don't bother to put those flowers in water, Elsie; it'd only be a waste. There'll be more to-morrow!"

"I'd like to keep these," Elsie said. "I think I'd like to keep them forever."

"Dear me! Did he make that great an impresion on you?"

"Who?"

"Elsie, you *are* a hypocrite! Berthier Ney Junot Harley!"

"I didn't even know it was he that sent them. I wanted to keep them because they'd remind me of —of everything."

And when Cornelia, touched by the way this was spoken, had kissed her fondly and gone out, Elsie put the pretty bouquet in a vase of water. Then she took one of the rosebuds from the cluster of them and pinned it upon her breast for the night.

She had liked Berthier Harley best; but it was not on his account that she wore his rosebud through her dreams; it was to remind her of—of everything!

She awoke early, smiling, and the bright wings of all her new fairy memories were fluttering in her heart. Then, reflecting, she became incredulous. Somewhere she had heard that every girl, no matter what her looks, has one night in her life when she is beautiful. Her own night had come at last; she could never doubt that. But what if it were the only one?

She jumped up and ran to the mirror. No;— tousled and flushed from warm and happy sleep, still drowsy, too, she was beautiful in the early sunshine. She knew it, and it was true. Last night had been her night, but it was not to be her only night;— and so, half laughing in her delight, she nodded charmingly to this charming mirror and began to think about what clothes to wear for the first day of her triumphant visit. She had no serious doubt now that it would remain triumphant, and so long as she kept upon her that glamour Cornelia had described as the look of "knowing something mysterious and lovely" about herself, Elsie was right not to doubt. She kept the look, and the longer she kept it, the easier it was to keep. Her visit was all glorious.

XXV

GLAMOR CAN BE KEPT

YOUNG Mr. Paul Reamer had been away, too, that winter. With no profession or business to localize his attention, and a heritage sufficient to afford him comfortable wandering, he had "tried California for a change," as he said; and on his return he went at once to tell Miss Ford about Hollywood. She was not at home; but he waited;—she came in presently, and made a satisfactory noise over him.

"To think of my not being here when you came!" she exclaimed when she had reached a point of more subdued demonstrations. "I'd just run over to Elsie's for half an hour——",

"Where?"

"To Elsie's. I spend about half my time there, I expect, and——"

"You do?" He looked puzzled and a little amused. "What for?"

"Why, everybody does," Mamie returned, surprised. "That is, when she's home. She's away a good deal of the time, you know."

"You mean Elsie Hemingway?"

"Why, naturally. What other Elsie is there?"

"I don't know." He looked more puzzled and more amused. "You say, 'everybody' spends about half the time there?" He laughed. "That sounds funny! What on earth's made her house such a busy place all of a sudden?"

"Oh, it isn't sudden," Mamie said, and she added, reflectively, "You know Elsie always was about the best-*looking* girl in town."

"Oh, possibly. It never seemed to get anywhere though," he returned. "She's good-looking all right, I suppose, but not the way anybody would ever notice."

"What?" Mamie cried. "Why, you don't know what you're talking about!"

"I don't?" He laughed incredulously. "Look here. What *is* all this about little Elsie Hemingway? When I left town——"

Miss Ford interrupted: "Have you seen old Fred yet?"

"No. I haven't seen anybody."

"Well, you'd better see old Fred and ask him 'What *is* all this about little Elsie Hemingway?' He'll probably fall in your arms and burst right out crying!"

"What for?"

"Why, for the same reason some of the others would do the same thing!"

Paul shook his head. "I don't think it's friendly to try to fill me up with fairy stories, Mamie—not just the first minute after I've come home anyhow. When I went away——"

"Oh, there've been lots of changes," Miss Ford assured him. "You'll have to get used to 'em. We've been used to the change about Elsie so long now I suppose we hardly realize there *was* a change. I guess what happened was that we never used to appreciate her, and she had a way of not seeming to feel she counted much, herself; but now we've got a little older and have more sense, or something, and we all see what a wonderful girl she is. You ought to hear old Fred! When he gets started—well, of course, I think she's great myself, but after I've listened to poor old Fred's babble for a couple of hours I almost hate her!"

Again Mr. Reamer shook his head. "It doesn't seem to me my hearing's exactly right. Are you really telling me——"

"You better go see," Mamie advised him. "Oh, you'll get it, too! You think you won't, but you will. You'll get it as bad as any of 'em, Paul Reamer."

The experienced young man laughed in sheerest incredulity; but that evening, his curiosity being somewhat piquantly aroused, he acted upon Miss Ford's advice and went to find out if it could possibly be true that he had overlooked anything important in so long overlooking Elsie Hemingway. It didn't seem probable, but if it proved to be the fact, he was somewhat amusedly prepared to make good to himself what he had lost by the overlooking.

The moment he saw her, when she came into the old-fashioned living-room of the quiet house that had once been too quiet, he understood that he had much more to repay himself for than he had dreamed could be possible. Elsie's look of knowing something mysterious and lovely about herself was still upon her; and Mr. Reamer set himself ardently and instantly to the task of self-repayment.

"Elsie," he said, "I've been away for a long,

dreary time, and I've just got back.   I've come to spend my very first evening with you."

He was too late.

Following Elsie from the library, where the three had been having coffee and discussing the Battle of Waterloo, came two gentlemen. One was Elsie's father, and he walked with his hand upon the other gentleman's shoulder.

The other gentleman was a tall young man from out of town who had been named for two marshals and a general of the First Empire.

XXVI

DESERT SAND

WE SPEAK now of that parent-troubling daughter of Mrs. Dodge's as she came to be through weltering experience, most of it hurried and all of it crowded. For do we not know that there are maidens of twenty-three who have already lived a lifetime? Such is their own testimony. They have had a view of all the world can offer, and foresee the rest of their existence as mere repetition, not stirring to the emotions. Life henceforth is to be but "drab," they say, several decades of them having strongly favoured the word; and this mood, often lasting for days at a time, usually follows one form or another of amatory anticlimax. Not infrequently the anticlimax is within the maiden herself; she finds herself lacking in certain supremities of feeling that appear not only proper but necessary, if the sentimental passions are to be taken at all seriously.

"It is all over—I shall never care for any man—I

shall never marry—I shall never feel anything about anything again," such a one wrote to a girl confidant abroad, and fully believed what she wrote. "I am tired of everything," she continued. "I am all dead within me. I look at things, but I do not see them. I see nothing—nothing absolutely!"

And yet at that very moment, as she glanced absently out of the window beside her pretty green-painted desk, her attention became concentrated upon a young man passing along the suburban boulevard below. He was a stranger, but a modish and comely one; she could not accurately call him "nothing," nor maintain that he was invisible;—her eyes followed him, in fact, until he had passed out of the range of her window. Then, with perfect confidence that she set forth the truth, she turned back to her letter and continued:

"I cannot by the farthest stretch of my imagination picture myself as feeling the least, the slightest— oh, the most infinitesimal!—featherweight of interest in any man again so long as my life shall last. I broke my engagement last night simply on that account. It was not in the most formal sense an engagement, since it hadn't been announced; but

Henry made as much fuss as if I had turned back at
the altar. He was frantic, especially as I could give
him no reason except that I did not feel for him what
I had expected to. He begged and begged to know
what he had done to change me. I could only tell
him he had done nothing. I had simply become
incapable of caring. I think now that I fell in love
too often and too intensely in my younger days.
My "grand passion" came too soon and since then
I have cared less and less each time that I have
fancied my interest intrigued. The absurd boy was
my Sun-god—and yet I see now that he is and always was a ridiculous person, and I laugh when I
remember how I glorified him to myself. He meant
nothing. Price Gleason meant nothing. Laurence
Grover, Paul Arthur, Capt. Williams, and all the
others meant nothing. Henry, so long and tediously
a pursuer, means nothing now. None of them mean
anything. The spring has gone dry and my heart,
that bloomed once so eagerly, is desert sand—desert
sand, my dear!"

She was rather pleased with this bit of metaphor
and read it over aloud, speaking the words linger-
ingly. Upon the wall beyond the pretty desk there

was a mirror facing her; she could see herself when she chose, and she chose to see herself now in her mood of poetic melancholy. She saw a winsome picture in that mirror, too, when she made this choice—an exquisitely fair, delicate creature, slim, though not so fragile as she had been, and, in spite of her heart of desert sand, all alive indeed. Probably induced by pleasure in the metaphor just written, the young lady in the glass was at the moment more sparkling, in fact, than seemed suitable. Therefore, her face became poignantly wistful—an effect so excellent that a surprised approbation was added, a little incongruously, to the wistfulness. The approbation was removed in favour of an inscrutable pathos, which continued throughout a long exchange of looks between the image and its original; then both of these little blonde heads bent once more above their green-painted desks, in a charmingly concerted action, like two glints of sunshine glancing down through foliage;—and the letter was resumed.

"My dear, our suburb is trembling with excitement. The chief scion of all the McArdles is on the point of being Installed in Residence among us. I think it should be spoken of as at least an Installation, shouldn't it? In our great Plutocracy, surely the McArdle dynasty is Royalty, isn't it? Anyhow, you'd think so if you could see the excitement over the announcement that James Herbert McArdle, III, is coming here to represent the dynasty's interests. That is, he's supposed to be the new manager of the huge McArdle Works, which are the smallest, I believe, of the dozens of McArdle Works over the country. I understand he's only to be nominal manager and is really to "learn the business" under old Mr. Hiram Huston, the McArdles' trusted "local representative." The youthful Dauphin is given command of an army—but under the advice of old generals strictly! However, you can guess what a spasm is happening here, with seventy million dollars (or is it seven hundred million?) walking around under one hat. I feel sorry for the poor agitated girls and their poor agitating mothers. The rich marry the rich; *we* sha'n't get him!"

She looked up thoughtfully at the mirror, frowned in sharp disapproval—not of the mirror—and continued: "It's really disgusting, the manœuvring to be the first to meet and annex him. Eleanor Gray and her mother are accused of having gone to New

York to try to be on the same train with him! Yesterday there was a rumour that he had arrived at the Jefferson Road Inn, which is to be his temporary quarters, and the story went all round that Harriet Joyce thought she recognized him there at tea and actually fainted away in order to make him notice her. My dear, I *believe* it! Really, you simply couldn't imagine the things that are going on. As for me, it is the piteous truth that this stupendous advent fails to stir me. I wish it could! But no, upon my life, I haven't a flicker—not the faintest flicker of ordinary human curiosity to know even if he looks like his tiresome pictures. These curiosities, these stirrings are for the springtime of life, my dear, while I—as I told poor Henry last night—I am autumn!"

Thus wrote Lily that most April-like of all maidens and within the hour went forth, looking like the very spring itself, to meet an adventure comparable to adventures met only in the springtime of the world. The scene of this adventure should have been a wood near Camelot, or the Forest of Arden, and Lily a young huntress in a leathern kirtle and out with a gilded bow and painted arrows for hare or pheasant. Then, if one of her arrows had pierced the thicket and

also the King's Son on the other side of it, so that she
came and took him, all swounding, in her arms, the
same thing in all true essentials would have happened
that happened to her to-day. The surroundings
would have been more appropriate—especially for a
damsel with a dead heart—than the golf course of the
Blue Hills Country Club, but the hero and the
heroine and the wounding and the swounding would
have been identical.

In particular, there was little difference between
James Herbert McArdle and a king's son. From
the time of his birth, which was announced by
greater tongues than those of royal heralds, these
greater tongues being the principal newspapers
of the world, he was a public figure. At the age of
four his likeness and those of his favourite goat and
dog were made known to his fellow citizens up and
down the land by means of photographic repro-
ductions in magazines and in the Sunday prints.
Lest there be fear on the part of the public that
he might alter beyond recognition as he grew up,
these magazines and prints continued reassuringly
to present portraits of him, playing in the sea sand,
or seated upon the knee of his portentous grandfather, or—with tutor and attendants—upon the

platform of his father's private car, and later, when he reached a proper age, being instructed in the technique necessary for driving his earliest automobile.

His first evening after matriculating as a freshman at a university was spent in dining and conversing with the university's president.   When, as a sophomore, he was found equal to a position in "left field" on the varsity nine, and the nine went out of town to play, reporters interviewed him and neglected to mention the captain.   When he had graduated and his father and grandfather began to prepare him for the ponderous responsibilities that would some day rest upon his shoulders, there were spreading "feature articles" about him everywhere.   Wherever he went, important old men hurried beamingly to his side, eager to be seen conversing with him; magnificent old ladies went beyond all amiability in caressing him; many of his contemporaries were unable to veil their deference; and lovely girls looked plentifully toward him.   All his life he had been courted, attended, served, pointed out, focussed upon, stared at, and lime-lighted before the multitude.   No wonder the poor young man liked solitude better than anything else!

When he contrived to be alone he protracted the experience as far as he was able; and to-day, having escaped from a welcoming committee and the mayor of the suburb that was to be his home for a year, he drove alone to the country club, which had already elected him to membership. Here he was delighted to find that the late hour and nipping air had divested the links of every player, and, attended by a lingering caddy who was unaware of his client's identity, James Herbert set forth upon a round of the course with a leisureliness unmatched by the most elderly member of the club.

It was a leisureliness so extreme indeed that it annoyed a player who arrived in full equipment a quarter of an hour after young Mr. McArdle had made his first drive on that course. Her equipment was too complete to please her, as it happened, for he had taken the last caddy, which was another item in her list of indignations;—Lily had found time to acquire such a list since finishing her letter. Most of the items concerned that unfortunate Henry, mentioned as having been dismissed on the previous evening. Henry had called; had been turned away at the door with "Not at home"; and then, by an unworthy pretext—though his lamentable state of

mind might have offered some excuse—he had se-
cured her presence at the telephone, where merely
what he said to her was furniture enough for any
ordinary list of indignations. She decided to cool
her temper by a solitary but vigorous round of the
golf course.

Lily was one of those favoured creatures who have
a genius for this most inviting yet most baffling of all
the pastimes of mankind; and persistence had added
so much to her native gift that a long shelf at home
was needed to support the tournament prizes she had
won. Various "ladies' championships" were hers,
too; and she was known among all the country clubs
for miles around on account of a special talent,
well practised, for marvellous little precisions of
accuracy. Moreover, Lily was what players have
been heard to call "conscientious" about her game.
She wished ever to excel herself, to play excellently
even when she played alone, and she was never quite
at her best when she had no caddy; therefore she was
annoyed with the gentleman ahead of her on that
account, as well as because of his leisure.

If she could play "all the way round" with a fine
score before darkness stopped her, Lily felt that her
irritations within might be a little soothed; but she

found them, on the contrary, increasing. She might have passed the laggard player if she had chosen; but his figure bore an accurate resemblance to that of a gentleman named in her letter as Captain Williams. Lily had her own reasons for avoiding any conversation with Captain Williams, to whom she had been as enigmatic, six months earlier, as she had yesterday been to Henry. She was almost certain, in fact, that the languid golfer was Captain Williams, and so kept far behind him—a difficult matter for one who wished to play at all.

She talked broodingly to herself, addressing him. "Old *Thing!*" she called him between her teeth. "Slow Poke! Aren't you *ever* going to hit that ball! Oh, my heaven, what are you doing *now?* Writing your score or writing a book? Snail! Tortoise!" And as his procrastinations continued, she called him worse. "Mule!" she said, and corroborated herself vehemently. "Mule, mule, mule! You're a mule once, you're a mule twice, you're a mule a hundred and eighty-seven times over—and that's only *commencing* to tell you what you are!" For now, as she waited and waited, withholding her strokes intolerably as the late light waned and waned, she hated him with that great hatred most human beings feel for all things unconsciously and persistently in their way.

But in the deepening twilight haze she felt safe to approach him more closely, until finally she was less than an arrow's flight away. He was upon the last of the greens by this time, and she, unnoticed, stood waiting for him to leave it so that she might drive her ball upon it. But here he delayed interminably. He lay prone upon the ground to study a proper aim, though he studied it so long that his purpose might have been thought a siesta; and when he rose it was to examine the sod by inches. Finally, having completed all these preliminaries and benefited little by them in their consummation, he remained standing upon the green, preoccupied with his score card. "You go on!" Lily said, dangerously. "You aren't writing a dictionary. Go on!"

But he continued to stand, amending and editing his card as though eternity were at everyone's disposal. The long red ribbons in the western sky merged with the general fog colour of the dusk, and he was but a hazy figure when at last he moved. And as he turned his back and lifted a slow foot to leave the green, Lily, impatient beyond all discretion, cut the air with her heaviest implement.

"Mule!" she said, furiously, instead of "Fore!"

and put that fury into her swing. Nevertheless, the
ball sped true in direction, though in the thickened
air it sped invisibly and would far have overshot
the mark if nothing had stopped it. Straight to the
short dark hair on the back of the languid player's
head the little white ball flew with fiercest precision,
and being hard, and on its way to a place much
farther on, it straightway rendered him more languid
than ever. He dropped without a moan.

XXVII

MIRACULOUS ACCIDENT

O H, MURDER!" Lily gasped, not greatly
exaggerating when she used that word. She
stood gazing toward him miserably, waiting
for him to rise; and then, as the stricken player's
inertia remained complete, she ran forward, screaming
to the caddy, who was disappearing toward the clubhouse.

He came back, and together they turned the prone
figure over so that it lay upon its back, revealing
an interesting young face of a disquieting pallor.
"I guess you must of killed him *this* time," the caddy
said, unreasonably, and then seemed to wish to solace
the assassin, for he added: "He ain't a member
though."

Lily was already on the ground beside her victim,
rubbing his hands. "Run!" she cried. "Get a
doctor! Run!"

She failed to recognize the fallen player, and so did
the steward and three waiters from the clubhouse,
which was just then vacant of members. James

Herbert McArdle's features were not so well known as those of the President of the United States, nor, probably, as those of the more conspicuous actors in moving pictures;—nevertheless, his face was familiar to those who now sought to identify it; and as they worked to restore the expression of life to it they were aware of elusive clews.

The steward said he was sure he knew the gentleman, who must often have been about the club, though he couldn't quite place him. The waiters had the same impression and the same disability precisely, while the trembling Lily herself was troubled by stirrings of memory. Either she had once known her victim, she thought, or else he was like someone she knew; but a white face inanimate, upturned to the evening sky, is strange even to those who know it most intimately. The likeness remained evasive, and the prostrate young man both unconscious and unidentified.

Lily was relieved of her first horror;—at least he was not dead. On the other hand, certainly he was not well. And when she drove that ball she had hated him. Of course she had not intended this dolorous stroke, yet when she made it, had she really cared whether or not it laid him low? She had not—and now regret shook her. Perhaps she would have felt it less profoundly had the maddening player proved indeed to be Captain Williams; but with the lifeless head of this well-favoured and unoffending stranger upon her lap, her remorse was an anguish.

She would not leave him or cease to do what she could in every humble way. She chafed his hands and bathed his forehead;—she helped to carry him to the clubhouse; and, when the hospital ambulance came, she went in it to the hospital with him. She stood in the corridor outside the door of the room to which they carried him there, and waited while a surgeon examined him. Indeed, she waited, weeping.

She knew the surgeon, and when he came out of the room she rushed to him. "Doctor Waite, tell me! Don't spare me!"

"He's got a concussion. It's no joke, but anyhow it isn't a fracture. Funny about nobody knowing who he is;—I'm sure I've met him, or else he reminds me of somebody, I can't think who."

"Doctor, he isn't—he isn't going to——"

The surgeon looked upon her reassuringly. "No. We'll pull him through. You quit thinking about

him and go home and get your dinner and then go
to bed and go to sleep."

"I couldn't," Lily said, choking. "I couldn't
do any of those things."

He laughed sympathetically. "Then I guess I'll
have to call up your mother and tell her to come and
make you."

But when not only her mother but her father, too,
arrived in hurried response to the telephone, they
could not get the tearful Lily to leave the hospital;
and they remained with her, engaging in intermittent
argument, until midnight. At that time Doctor
Waite informed them that the unknown patient was
in a torpid but not critical condition; he had mumbled
a few words to the effect that he wanted to be let
alone.

"And as that's just what we're doing with him,"
the surgeon said to Lily rather sharply, "and as you
can't do any possible good to anybody in the world
by staying here, I suggest that you take his advice,
too, and obey your father and mother."

Not until then would the suffering girl allow them
to lead her away; but so far as sleep was concerned,
she might as well have stayed at the hospital. So
might her father and mother, almost; for she was at

their door in her nightdress three times—three separated times, the last being at four o'clock in the morning.   "Papa, do *you* think he'll die?"

Mrs. Dodge wearily conducted her to bed again; but Lily only wept upon her pillow, and in whispers begged it to forgive her for not calling "Fore." Sunrise found her dressed; and in the chilly November early morning she slipped out of the house, crossed the suburban park to the hospital, and immediately heard news indeed.   Doctor Waite was already there, and with him were three other surgeons and a physician, all of them important.   He came to speak to Lily.

"All this distinguishedness for your unknown patient," he said, with a gesture toward the group he had just left; and, as her expression began to be grievous, he added hastily, "He's perfectly all right. At least he's going to be.   The importance yonder is only because he turns out to be so unexpectedly important himself."

"You've found out who he is?"

"Some*what!*" he returned with humorous emphasis.   "We've managed to keep your name out of the papers—so far."

"What papers?"

"All of them. Take your choice," he said—and he offered her two; but one at a time was enough for Lily.

Headlines announced that a "Mysterious Accident" at the Blue Hills Country Club had "resulted in grave injury" to James Herbert McArdle. The illustrious youth had lain unconscious and unrecognized until a short time after midnight, the more sober text of the report informed her. Mr. H. H. Huston, the McArdle representative, had been alarmed by Mr. McArdle's disappearance and continued absence, subsequent to the reception of an address by the suburban welcoming committee, and in the course of an exhaustive search Mr. Huston had caused inquiries to be made at the Blue Hills Country Club. Here it was learned that an unknown gentleman had been struck in the head by a golf ball driven with such force as to cause a concussion of the brain. The club's employees had withheld the name of the person responsible for the injury; but a reporter had ascertained that it was a lady and that she had accompanied the wounded man— "wounded man" was the newspaper's phrase—in the ambulance, and had "insisted upon remaining at the hospital until a late hour." Mr. H. H. Huston

had reached the hospital not long after midnight;
Mr. McArdle had just become conscious and revealed
his identity to the nurse in charge.   Mr. Huston had
said to a reporter that Mr. McArdle "positively
declared himself ignorant of the name of the person
who had caused his injury."   Altogether, there was
"an air of mystery about the affair"; and Mr.
McArdle's condition was still grave, though the
surgeons said that he would "probably recover."

It is to Lily's credit that the strongest emotion
roused in her by this reading concerned these final
two words.   She repeated them pathetically to
Doctor Waite.   "'Probably recover'?   'Probably'?"

He laughed.   "Don't you know newspapers?
Didn't I tell you last night he'd be all right?   We
wired his family an hour ago that there was no reason
for any of them to come on.   All that surgical and
medical impressiveness over yonder only represents
old Hiram Huston's idea of the right thing to do
for a McArdle with a bump on his head.   The young
fellow may have to stay here quietly for a week or
ten days possibly; but by that time he ought to be
pretty nearly ready to stop a ball for you again."

"Don't joke about it," Lily said, huskily.   "When
can I see him?"

"Think you better?"

"Why not?"

"The newspapers called it a 'mystery,' you know," he explained. "They'll probably be inquisitive. They might get your name."

"What do I care?" she cried. "Do you think I'd let that stop me from asking him to forgive me?"

"So?" the doctor said, looking at her twinklingly. "So that's why you want to see him?"

She stared, not understanding his humorous allusion. "Why, what else could I do?"

"Nothing," he answered. "I was only thinking I'd heard that a good many young ladies were anxious to make his acquaintance. I imagine you'll be the first, my dear."

"Well, oughtn't I to be?" she demanded. "If you'd done as terrible a thing as that to anybody, wouldn't you think you were entitled to ask his pardon about as soon as he was able to listen?"

"Without doubt. In the meantime I think you'd better go home and to bed again."

She protested, but proved meeker under advice than she had the night before. She went home, though not directly, for she stopped half an hour at some greenhouses that were a mile out of her way.

She sent to Mr. James Herbert McArdle at the hospital a prodigious sheaf of flowers—enough to cripple her rather moderate monthly allowance from her father—and the following morning, since the allowance was already so far gone, she did the same thing. Having thus fallen into the habit, she was as lavish upon the third morning after the accident, so that at three o'clock of this same day, when Doctor Waite took her into his patient's room, he seemed to be conducting her into a conservatory.

Like fair Elaine, James Herbert McArdle in a silken gown lay white and motionless, embowered among blooms; but his eyes glimmered in surprised appreciation when they beheld his serious visitor. Gray was becoming to the fair and slim Lily— her clothes didn't depend upon her allowance—and she was never more charming than when she was serious.

"My goodness!" said the frank convalescent, with a feeble kind of forcefulness. "I didn't expect anybody like *you!* I was sure it would turn out to be some old hag."

Lily was a little given to the theatrical, though only when occasion warranted it, as this one did if any occasion could. She swept forward softly, her sensitive face all compassion and remorse. She knelt beside the iron bed.

"Some day you may forgive me," she said, tremulously, and her voice was always stirringly lovely when it trembled. "Some day you may be able even to forget what I've done to you—but I want you to be sure that I shall never forget it or forgive myself."

"Here!" he said. "There's nothing to that. They tell me you came in the ambulance with me and hung around and did all sorts of things. And look at all these greenhouses you must have bought out! A person's liable to get a clip on the head almost anywhere these days. Let's shake hands—but not forget it."

"You can't——"

"I haven't got anything to forgive you for, of course," he said. "You don't forgive accidents; you just forget 'em. What I mean is, I don't want to forget this one—now I've seen you, I don't."

"Well——" Lily said, vaguely. "But I'd like you just to *say* you forgive me. Won't you?"

"All right." He moved his hand toward her and she took it for a moment. "I forgive you—but I think you ought to do something for me."

"What?"

"How long did the doctor say you can stay here?"

"Five or ten minutes."

"Well, then, I think you ought to come back to-morrow when you can stay half an hour or an hour."

"I will," she said.

But he had not finished. "And the next day, too. Maybe they'd let you read to me, or something. And as long as I'm laid up here—it won't be long, at that—I think you ought to come every day and help me pass the time. I forgive you, but I think you do owe me that much. And as soon as they let me take a drive I think you ought to go along. How about it?"

"I will," Lily said. "I will, indeed. I'll do anything in the world you think might make up a little for the pain I've brought you. Nothing could make me happier."

"That's good news," the young man told her, thoughtfully. "A clip on the head isn't necessarily such a bad thing, after all."

More and more he seemed to incline to this opinion; —in fact, he went so far as to assure Doctor Waite, three days later, that he preferred the hospital to the apartment old Hiram Huston was preparing for him. "I think I'd like to sort of settle down to the life here," he said. "It's nice and private and suits me exactly."

"Yes," said the doctor, thoughtfully. "It's a pity you're too important to do what you want to." And lightly, as if to himself, he hummed a fragment of frivolous song:

> "I don't want to get well,
> I don't want to get well,
> I'm in love with a beautiful nurse!"

The young man heeded neither the humming nor the remark about his unfortunate importance. He frowned, looking anxiously at his watch on the table beside his couch. "I wonder what's keeping her," he said, peevishly. "She said she'd be here with a book to read to me. When anybody does to another person what she did to me, I think the least they can do is to be punctual, especially when they've promised they would."

She of whom he complained was not far away, however. At that moment she had just been greeted and detained by two girl friends of hers who encountered her in the park on her way to the hospital. Their manner did not please her.

"Lill-*lee!*" they shouted from the distance, at sight of her. They whistled shrilly, and, as she looked toward them, they waved their arms at her; then came running, visibly excited and audibly uproarious.

They seemed to be bursting with laughter; yet when they reached her, what they said was only, "Where you *going*, Lily?" And before she replied, they clutched each other, perishing of their mutual jocularity. From the first, Lily did not like their laughter;—it had not the sound of true mirth, but was the kind of mere vocal noise that hints of girlish malice.

She looked at them disapprovingly. "I'm going to the hospital," she said with some primness. "What's so funny?"

"What you going to *do* at the hospital, Lily?"

"Read to Mr. McArdle," she replied. "He's better and——"

But their immediate uproar cut her short. They clung together, shrieking. "That's not *your* fault, *is* it, Lily?" one of them became coherent enough to inquire, whereupon they both doubled themselves, rocked, gurgled, screamed, and clung again.

"What's not my fault?" she asked.

"That he's better!"

With that, they moved to be upon their way,

still uproarious, still clutching each other; and as they went they looked back to shout at her.

"He won't get better very fast, will he, Lily?" one of them thus called back to her, and, without pausing, replied to herself: "Not if you have *your* way!"

And the other: "Eleanor Gray and Harriet Joyce have nothing on *you*, have they, Lily?"

They disappeared round a curving path, leaning upon each other from exhaustion; and Lily stood looking after them frowningly. There had been little good-nature in their raillery, and also there were mysterious and vaguely unpleasant implications in it—particularly in the final jibe about Eleanor Gray and Harriet Joyce. Miss Gray was the girl accused by rumour of having sought to put herself upon James Herbert McArdle's train, and Miss Joyce was widely supposed to have fainted with the deliberate purpose of attracting his attention. The implication of the mirthful pair just encountered that Lily surpassed both Miss Gray and Miss Joyce was plain enough—as if going to a hospital to read to a patient were a mere manœuvre of the type to which the Gray and Joyce manœuvres belonged! And as if one wouldn't gladly give a little of one's time to a hospital patient who has become a patient through one's own fault!   But more than mere rallying upon the hospital readings seemed to have been implied; and as Lily thought the matter over, she felt that something of the teasing pair's meaning evaded her.

She had the same feeling after an interview the next day with one of her nearest and dearest girl friends, who came to see her at home.   "I don't want to be intrusive, dear," the caller informed her, with sympathetic but rather eager gravity.   "You know me too well to believe I'd ask such a thing out of pure curiosity; but I've simply *got* to know how poor Henry Burnett is taking it."

"Taking what, Emma?"

"Lily!   You know what I mean.   I mean all this about you and Mr. McArdle."

"'All this'?"   Lily repeated in a tone of cold inquiry.   "I don't see that such a simple matter needs quite that sort of definition.   Naturally, I'm doing what I can to help him through his convalescence.   Oughtn't I to?   But perhaps you don't know that I'm responsible for his *being* in the hospital, Emma."

"Oh, yes," Emma said, quietly, and she gave her

friend a queer look. "Yes, everybody knows that, Lily," she went on in a thoughtful voice. "Everybody! Yes, indeed!" She paused, then reverted to her former topic. "I just wondered how poor Henry Burnett is taking it all."

"I haven't any idea what you mean," Lily said, impatiently. "I fail to see that there's anything for him to 'take'; and if there were, it would certainly be no affair of his. I have no responsibilities to Mr. Burnett."

"But you did! Weren't you almost——"

"That may be," Lily interrupted. "But I don't see him any more."

"You broke with him, Lily?"

"I did not, because there was nothing absolutely announced and definite to break. I simply decided not to waste any more of his time and mine."

"Why?" Emma asked.

"Because I found that I had no feeling for him; none for him nor for anything else—no interest in him or in any other man alive."

"Oh, Lily!" Emma cried; and then she sat openmouthed and round-eyed, staring in perfect incredulity. "Oh, *Lily!*"

"What's the matter?"

Emma still stared; but finally, being a true friend, she half gasped, "Nothing!" as she rose to go.

She was still round of eye, though her mouth had become decorous for a street appearance, when she left the house a few moments later; and Lily was not much better pleased with her friend Emma than she had been with the two taunting girls in the park.

Nor were these three the sum of all who displeased her. She went to a "tea," and easily perceived that she became instantly the centre of all interest;— but she did not like the interest. Whispering and half-suppressed laughter buzzed about her; eyes were furtively upon her wherever she glanced; elderly women looked at her and talked behind their hands; and she was uncomfortably aware of a wondering derision focussing constantly upon her. She came away shivering, marvelling at the pettiness of human nature that could make such a disagreeable pother over a girl's doing her simple best to atone for a moment's carelessness with a golf club. Moreover, before she got out of the gate she found herself surrounded by a group of newcomers, girls of her own age, who repeated almost precisely the performance of the two in the park. "How long do you think you can keep his head from fitting together where you broke it, Lily?'' This was the last thing she heard from the group near the gate, except for a loud burst of unfriendly laughter. She began to be seriously indignant.

XXVIII

A PUBLIC MOCKERY

NOT much time was granted her indignation to cool;—it became outright fury not twenty-four hours later; and the occasion of this change for the worse was a spectacular little performance on the part of the gentleman for whom her emotions had forever ceased to stir—that unhappy Henry so recently dismissed. And since Henry's performance took place "in public," according to Lily's definition of its background, her fury was multiplied in intensity by a number corresponding to the number of witnesses present at the spectacle.

One of these was Mr. James Herbert McArdle, who was seated beside her at the time. She was accompanying him for a drive, as she had promised him; and his choice for the excursion had been an open red car, noticeable also in contour and dimensions. The top was folded back, so that Lily and her escort, both richly shrouded in furs, presented to the world a fast-flying sketch of affluent luxury. A fleeting glimpse of beauty might be caught there, too; for Lily's colour was high, and sunshine glinted in her hair; amber lights danced from it and blue sparklings from her eyes as she sped by.

At one point, however, the fast-flying sketch ceased to fly, and halted, affording spectators more leisure for observation; but this, as presently appeared, was just the wrong point for such a thing to happen. The red car, returning from the open country, passed into the suburban outskirts, and Mr. McArdle directed the chauffeur to turn into the country club driveway. "I've got a fancy to see where our friendship began," he said to Lily. "I noticed the last green was near the driveway. Let's go look at it."

She assented, and they drove to the spot that interested him; but they found it inhabited. A score or so of people were there, watching the conclusion of a match evidently of some special interest as an exhibition of proficiency. When the red car stopped, the last shot into the cup was in the final crisis of action, and a popular triumph was thereby attained, as the spectators made plain. They instantly raised a loud shout, acclaiming the successful player, cheering him and rushing forward to shake his hand; though he, himself, seemed far from elated.

On the contrary, there gleamed a bitter spark in his eye, and his appearance, though manly, was one of so dark a melancholy that he might have been thought an athletic and Americanized Hamlet. Not speaking, he waved the enthusiasts away, tossed his club to his caddy and turned to leave the green; but, as he did so, his glance fell upon the red car in the driveway near by. He halted, stock-still, while a thrilled murmur was heard rustling among the bystanders. Everybody stared at Lily, at her companion, and at the morbid winner of the golf match. There was a moment of potent silence.

Then the sombre player advanced a step toward Lily and, looking her full in the eye, took off his cap and swept the ground with it before her in mocking salutation—derisive humility before satirized greatness.

A startled but delighted "*Oh!*" came from among the people about the green. They began to buzz, and silvery giggles were heard.

Lily's eyes shot icy fire at the bowing harlequin. "Tell the driver to go *on*," she said to McArdle.

"Who was that fellow?" he asked her, as they

drove away. "I had a notion to get out and see if I couldn't make him bow even a little lower."

"No, no," she said, hastily. "You shouldn't have. You aren't well enough, and, besides, he's only a ruffian."

"But who is he?"

"I've just told you," she said, fiercely. "He's a ruffian. His name is Henry Burnett, if you want something to go with the definition of him I've just given you."

"But what did he do it for? What made him bow like that?"

"Because he *is* a ruffian!" Lily said. Her eyes were not less fiery than they had been, and neither were her checks. "I believe I never knew what it was to hate anybody before," she went on in a low voice. "When I've thought I hated people it must have been just dislike. I'm sure I've never known what it was to hate anybody as he's just made me hate him."

"But see here!" Young Mr. McArdle was disquieted. "What's it all about? Telling me he's a ruffian doesn't explain it. What made him do it?"

"This," Lily said between her teeth. "For a while I thought I cared a little about him—not much but some—enough to let him know I thought so. Well, I found I didn't."

"How'd you find it out?" he asked.

"I discovered that I was absolutely indifferent to him, and that nothing he could ever do would have the slightest power to make me feel anything whatever. I told him so in the gentlest way I could, and since then he's behaved like the brute that he is."

"But is it true?"

"Is what true?" she asked, sharply.

"I mean," he said, "is it true you're indifferent to him?"

"Good heavens!" she cried, with the utmost bitterness. "Don't you see that I hate him so that I'd like to wring his neck? I would!" she cried, fiercely. "I could almost *do* it, too, if I were alone with him for a few minutes!" And she held up to his view her slender white-gloved hands, with her fingers curved as for the fatal performance.

Mr. McArdle seemed to be relieved. "Well, I guess it's all right," he said. "That is, if you're sure you don't like him." Then as she turned angrily upon him, he added hurriedly, "And I see you don't. I'm sure you don't." He laughed with a slight hint of complacency not unnatural in an important and well-petted invalid. "I think you kind of owe it to me not to go around liking other men from now on. I mean—well, you know how I'm getting to feel about you, I guess."

Lily sat staring straight forward at the chauffeur's back, though that was not what she saw. What she saw was the tall young man of the tragic face, mocking her before delighted onlookers. "I know what I feel about *him!*" she said, too preoccupied with her fury to listen well to her companion.

"I'm glad you do," he said, earnestly. "I wouldn't like to feel you were thinking much about anybody but me. Of course I know you've been giving me a good deal of your time; but the fact is, I'll want you to give me even more of it, especially the next week or so—before my mother comes out to visit me. Will you?"

As she did not answer, but still gazed fiercely at the chauffeur's back, he repeated, "Will you?"

"I could!" she said; but this was evidently not a reply to his question, for she again held up her curved fingers to view. "I could, and I would! If I were left alone with him for five minutes I *know* I would!"

"Let's forget him just now," young Mr. McArdle suggested. "I was telling you about my mother's coming out here to visit me in a week or so. My family's really pretty terrible about keeping tabs on me, you know—I mean, for fear I'll get engaged to anybody except my second cousin Lulu. She's one of the female branch of the family, you know, that married into the banks, and of course they all feel it ought to be kept together, and Lulu would be a great advantage. But she's homely as sin, and, so far, they've had a pretty hard time persuading me. You understand, don't you?"

"What?" Lily asked, vaguely. Then she drew a deep breath, clenched her curved fingers tightly upon the fur rug and said virulently to herself: "I could do it and sing for joy that I *had* done it!" However, in the ears of her companion this was only an indistinct murmur.

"I mean I suppose you understand about the family and all that," he said. "My mother's bound to interfere, of course. If you and I expect to see much of each other after she comes, we'll have a fight on our hands, because, of course, the family won't stand for my getting too interested in anybody out here. Naturally, they don't expect me not to

have a good time; but you know what I mean;—
they wouldn't stand for my getting serious, I mean."

He was serious enough just then, however; that
was plain. His voice was almost quaveringly plaintive, in fact, as he leaned toward her. "Lily," he
said, "I expect my mother would like you all right
if you were my cousin Lulu, or somebody in Lulu's
position; but the way things are—well, of course
she isn't going to. She's going to make an awful
fuss if I try to go about with you at all. But I'm
willing to buck up to her and see if we can't pull
it off anyhow. Honestly, I am. How about it?"

"What?" she said, absently, still looking forward
and not at him. "What did you say?"

"My goodness!" he exclaimed, blankly. "I don't
believe you were even *listening!*"

"I'm afraid I wasn't."

At that, a natural resentment deepened the colour
in this important young man's cheeks. "Well,
I should think it might be considered worth your
while," he said. "I don't put too much on being
James Herbert McArdle, Third, I believe; but at
least I might claim it isn't a thing that happens
every day in the world, exactly—my asking a girl
to marry me, I mean."

She turned to him, frowning. "Was that what you were doing?"

"I was telling you I hoped to make a try for it," he explained a little querulously. "When my mother comes and hears about this she'll send for my father probably and there'll be a big fuss—more than you could have any idea of until you really hear it. But I never took to any girl as much as I've taken to you, never in my life." Here his querulousness gave way to another feeling and his voice softened. "I'm ready to buck up to the whole crew of 'em for your sake, Lily. What about it?"

She looked at him blankly. "I don't know," she said.

"What?" he cried. "Don't you understand? I'm asking you to *marry* me!"

"Yes," she said. "I hear you say it; but so far as I'm concerned you might almost as well be telling me it's a pleasant day! I'm not in the right state to think about it or even to understand it."

"Why not?"

"Because," she said, "I'm so angry I don't know what I'm doing."

"Look here——" he began; but said no more,

and, in spite of her preoccupation with her anger, she was able to perceive that he now had some of his own. She put her hand lightly upon his sleeve and, simultaneously, the car stopped at the hospital door.

"Forgive me," she said. "I'm afraid I'm terribly rude. But don't you know there are times when you get so furious you just *can't* think about anything else?"

"Can't you?" he returned, coldly, as the chauffeur helped him down from the car. "I'm afraid I doubt if you'd *ever* consider what I was saying as of enough importance to listen to."

"I'm so sorry," Lily said; and in spite of herself she said it absently; so that nothing could have been plainer than that her mind was not even upon this apology, but altogether upon the offence she had received from Mr. Henry Burnett.

A special attendant of the convalescent's came from within the building and offered his arm. Young Mr. McArdle took it and gave a final glance at the flushed cheeks and fiery eyes of the lady who had already twice smitten him and thus smote him again. Something hot in his upper chest seemed to rise against this provincial and suburban young woman who was too busy being furious with a local nonentity to know what she was doing indeed! The affronted young man's last word was to the chauffeur.

"When you have taken Miss Dodge home I sha'n't want you until day-after-to-morrow. I don't care to drive every day."

Lily was borne away murmuring, "I'm sorry," again, but what she thought was: "I could! I could wring Henry Burnett's neck and sing for joy!"

. . . When the long red car drew up before her father's house, there was another machine standing at the curb, a small black thing of the hardiest variety and odiously familiar to Lily. She jumped out, and, shaking with rage and her desire to express it, fairly ran up the brick walk to her front door.

But here a housemaid sought to detain her, whispering urgently: "Mr. Burnett's in the living-room, waiting. Your mother isn't home and I didn't know how to keep him out. If you don't want to see him you'd better go round to the——"

Lily interrupted her. "I *do* want to see him," she declared in a loud voice. "I want to see him *instantly!*" And she swept into the room to confront the mocker.

But mockery was no part of Mr. Henry Burnett's present mood—far from it. He had come to apologize, and apology was profoundly in his manner as he rose from the chair in which he had been most dejectedly sitting. Dark semicircles beneath his eyes were proof of inner sufferings; he was haggard with his trouble and more Hamlet-like than ever; but now he was a Hamlet truly humble.

"Lily," he said, huskily, "I'd sworn to myself I'd never make another attempt to see you as long as I lived, but after what I did awhile ago I had to. I *had* to explain it. It was in vile taste, and you can't think any worse of it than I do. But you came on me suddenly. I hadn't dreamed I'd see you; then all at once I looked up and there you were—and with the man you threw me over for! I just couldn't——"

"Henry Burnett," she said, and her hot little voice shook with the rage that vibrated in her whole body; —"you used to be a gentleman. Twice within less than an hour you've shown me you've forgotten what that word means."

"Twice, Lily?" he said, pathetically; "I admit the other time—out at the club—but how have I offended you besides that?"

"In your very apology," she told him scornfully.

"You've just had the petty insolence to stand there and say I threw you over for Mr. McArdle!"

"But you did," he said; and he seemed surprised that she should not admit it. "Why, it's—why, Lily, everybody knows that!"

"What? You dare to repeat it?"

He looked at her in the most reasonable astonishment, his eyes widening. "But, Lily, I'm not the only one. Everybody repeats it."

"Who does?"

"Everybody," he said. "You certainly couldn't expect a thing like this not to be talked about, with the whole place in the state of excitement it was about McArdle's coming here, let alone what's happened since. I had no idea you'd deny it to me now, though I supposed you might to other people, as a matter of form. Of course no one would believe it could be a coincidence."

She stepped closer to him dangerously. "No one would believe what could be a coincidence, Henry Burnett?"

"That you threw me over just by chance the very day before McArdle came to town and you took that shot at him."

"I did *what?*"

"Hit him in the head," Henry explained. "Your name didn't get in the papers; but you don't for a moment imagine that everybody in town doesn't understand, do you, Lily?"

She stamped her foot. "Understand what? What are you talking about? *What* does everybody understand?"

"Your plan," he said, simply. "You don't think you can lay out a man like that—a man that every other girl in the place is ready to fight you for—you don't think you can do it in such a way as to make you the *only* girl who has a *chance* to see him, and then spend all your time with him, and day after day send him so many bushels of flowers that the florist himself gasps over it—and read to him hour after hour, and drive *more* hours with him—you can't do all that and expect people not to *see* it, can you?"

Lily's high colour was vanishing, pallor taking its place. "You needn't believe I don't hate you because I stop telling you so for a moment," she said. "But there's a mystery somewhere, and I've got to get at it. What do you mean I mustn't expect people not to see?"

"Why, the truth about how he got hurt."

Lily stepped back from him. "Henry Burnett," she said, "Henry Burnett, do you dare——"

Henry interrupted her. He had come to apologize; but what he believed to be her hypocrisy was too much for him. "I don't see the use of your pretending," he said. "The whole population knows you did it on purpose."

"Did *what* on purpose?"

"Hit him in the head with your golf ball on purpose!"

Lily uttered a loud cry and clasped her hands to her breast. Aghast, she stared at him with incredulous great eyes; but even as she stared, her mind's eye renewed before itself some painful pictures that had mystified her——the spitefully uproarious girls in the park; her friend, Emma; the buzzing "tea"; the group at the gate as she came out;——and there were other puzzles that explained themselves in the dreadful light now shed upon them. Uttering further outcries, she sank into a chair.

"Slander!" she gasped. "Oh, a *horrible* slander!"

"What?" Henry cried again. "When everybody knows the things you can do with a golf ball if you care to? When that professional trick-player gave his exhibition here, knocking five balls into five hats in a row, and all that, how many of his shots didn't you duplicate after you'd practised them? And some of the girls talked to the caddy McArdle had with him when it happened, and the boy said he didn't think you were over forty yards away when you hit him. Lily, there isn't a soul that knows you who'll ever believe you didn't do exactly what you planned to do. I don't mean they think you could do it every time, or that they're all certain you aimed at his head; but they all believe you tried to hit him—and succeeded!"

"And *you* do?" she said. "*You* believe it?"

He laughed bitterly. "Lily, it's clear as daylight, and I knew it when I looked up and saw you with him to-day. I knew you'd won what you were after. It was in his face."

Lily gulped and smiled a wry smile. "I see," she said. "It all works out, and nobody'll ever believe I didn't plan it. Yes, I think he proposed to me on the way home this afternoon."

"Let me wish you happiness," Henry said, and seemed disposed to repeat his satiric bow, but thought better of it. "Is the engagement to be a long one?" he inquired, lightly, instead; and this seemed to be as effective as the bow, for Lily sprang up, as if she would strike him.

"I could murder you!" she cried. "And, oh, how I'd like to! I'm not *sure* Mr. McArdle proposed to me; I only *think* he did. I told him I couldn't listen because I was too angry."

"Too angry with whom?" Henry asked, frowning.

"With *you!*" Lily shouted fiercely.

At that, it was his turn to utter a loud cry. "Lily, is it true? Did you hate me so that you couldn't even listen to him? Is it true?"

"A thousand times true!" she said, and, in her helpless rage, began to weep. "But I hate you worse than that!"

"And you sent me away because I couldn't make you *feel* anything!" he cried. "Lily, when will you marry me?"

"Do you think I'd ever be engaged to you again," she sobbed, "when you believed I'd do a brutal thing like that on purpose?"

"Lily," he said again, "when will you marry me?"

"Never," she answered. "I'll never marry any-body." But even as she spoke, the fortunate young man's shoulder was becoming damper with her tears.

XXIX

MRS. CROMWELL'S OLDEST DAUGHTER

ALL of the players except three had returned to the clubhouse before the close of the fine April afternoon, and, after an interval in the locker rooms, had departed either in their cars or strolling away on foot, homeward bound to the pleasant groups of suburban houses east of the country club. Westward lay the links, between ploughed fields and groves of beech and ash and maple, a spacious park of rolling meadows with a far boundary of woodland, and, beyond that, nothing but a smoky sunset. All was quiet; there were no sounds from within the clubhouse, nor came any from the links; and although no kine wound slowly o'er the lea and no ploughman plodded his weary way, the impending twilight in such a peace might well have stirred a poetic observer to murmurous quotation from the Elegy. Nevertheless, in this sweet evening silence, emotion was present and not peaceful.

There was emotion far out upon the links, and there was more upon the western veranda of the club-house where two ladies sat, not speaking, but gazing intently toward where the dim and hazy great sun was immersing itself in the smoke of the horizon. These two emotional ladies were sisters; that was obvious, for they shared a type of young matronly fairness so decidedly that a photograph of one might have been mistaken, at first glance, for that of the other.

A student of families, observing them, would have guessed immediately that their mother was a fair woman, probably still comely with robust good health, and of no inconsiderable weight in body as well as in general prestige. The two daughters were large young women, but graceful still; not so large as they were going to be some day, nor less well-favoured than they had been in their slenderer girlhood. They were alike, also, in the affluence displayed by the sober modishness of what they wore; and other tokens of this affluence appeared upon the club driveway, where waited two shining, black, closed cars, each with a trim and speechless driver unenclosed. The sisters were again alike in the expectancy with which they gazed out upon the broad avenue of the golf links; but there was a difference in their expressions;—for the expectancy of the younger one was a frowning expectancy, an indignant expectancy, while the expectancy of the other, who was only a year or two the older, appeared to be a timid and apprehensive expectancy—an expectancy, in fact, of calamity.

This elder sister was the one who broke the long silence, though not by uttering words, the sound she produced being an exclamatory gasp and but faintly audible. It appeared to be comprehended as definite information, however, by the younger sister.

"Where, Mildred?" she asked. "I don't see them yet."

The other's apprehension was emphasized upon her troubled forehead, as she nodded in the direction of the far boundary of the links. There, upon the low crest of rising ground capped with the outermost green, appeared six tiny figures, dwindled by the distance and dimmed by the mist that rose into the failing light. For the sun was now so far below the dark horizon that the last ruddiness grew dingy in the sky.

"Yes," said the younger sister, and her angry frown deepened. "It's they."

"Oh, Anne!" the older murmured. "Oh, Anne!"

"Yes, I should say so!" this Anne returned, decisively. "I certainly intend to express myself to *my* husband, Mildred."

Mildred shook her head unhappily. "If I only could to mine! But that's just what I can't do."

"I don't know," the other said. "I think in your place I should; though it's true I can't imagine myself in your place, Mildred. My husband has his faults, and one of 'em's the way he's letting himself be used to-day, but I can't imagine his behaving as your husband is behaving. Not *that* way!"

She made an impatient gesture toward the west, where the six figures had left the green and were now moving toward the clubhouse, three of them playing deliberately as they came, with three smaller figures, the caddies, in advance. One of the players detached himself, keeping to the southern stretch of the fairway; while the two others, a man and a woman, kept to the northern, walking together, each halting close by when the other paused for a stroke.

"Can you make out which is which, Anne?" the older sister inquired in a voice of faint hope. "Isn't it John who's playing off there by himself, and Hobart she keeps so close to her?"

"Not very likely!" Anne returned with a short laugh. "She's using *my* husband as a chaperon strictly, and I must say he's behaving like a tactful one. It's your John she 'keeps so close to her'— as usual, Mildred!"

Mildred made merely a desolate sound, and then the sisters resumed the troubled silence that falls between people who have long since discussed to a conclusion every detail of an unhappy affair, and can only await its further development.

The three players came nearer slowly, growing dimmer in the evening haze as they grew larger; until at last it was difficult to see them at all. Other things were as dim as they, the player to the south found to his cost; and, finally deciding to lose no more balls that day, he crossed the fairway to his competitors.

"I'm through, John," he called, cheerfully. "It's no use in the world trying to play out these last two holes."

"I don't suppose it is," the other man assented. "Julietta rather wanted to, though." He turned to the tall girl beside him. "Hobart says——"

"I heard him!" she said, laughing a light laugh, a little taunting in its silveriness. "Hobart's a well-trained husband. You know what that is, don't you, John? A well-trained husband is one who doesn't dare to call his soul his own. Hobart's been worrying this last half hour about what Mrs. Simms will say to him for keeping her waiting."

"You're right about that, Julietta," Mr. Hobart Simms agreed. "My wife's a pretty amiable lady; but I've kept her waiting longer than I like to, and old John's done the same thing. So, as he's probably in the same apologetic state I'm in, and it's ridiculous to try to play these last two holes in the pitch dark anyhow, I suggest we——"

The girl interrupted him, though it was to his brother-in-law that she addressed herself. "*Are* you in the 'same apologetic state' that Hobart is, John?" she asked; and there was an undercurrent in her voice that seemed to ask more than appeared upon the surface. She seemed to challenge, in fact, and yet to plead. "Are you as afraid of Mrs. Tower as Hobart is of Mrs. Simms, John?"

Mr. Tower laughed placatively. "My dear Julietta! Of course if you'd like to play it out——"

"There!" Julietta said, gaily triumphant. "You see he wants to, himself. I believe you're the one man I know who isn't terrorized by a wife, John."

She stepped closer to him, speaking through the darkness in a warm, soft voice, almost a whisper. "But then you're a wonderful man, anyhow—the most wonderful I ever knew, John."

"Oh, no!" He laughed deprecatingly, and, pleased with her, yet embarrassed by his modesty, coughed lightly for a moment or two. "Of course I'm not; but I do value your thinking so, Julietta. I appreciate it very deeply indeed."

"Are you *sure* you do?" she said in a hurried whisper, so low that he could just hear it. Then she turned briskly toward his brother-in-law, who stood at a little distance, waiting their pleasure. "Run along, Hobart, and please tell Mrs. Tower I haven't kidnapped him;—he's staying to play it out with me of his own free will. And please pay all the caddies off and let them go. We don't need them, and they're dying to get home."

He was obedient, and from the clubhouse veranda, where lights now shone, it could be discerned that the party on the links had broken up. The caddies ran scurrying by, their shrill outcries disturbing the air about them, and, in their wake, the slight figure of Mr. Hobart Simms appeared within the radius of illumination from the building.

"They're coming," Anne Simms said to her sister. "Don't let them see anything."

Mr. Simms mounted the dozen steps that led up to the veranda. "Dear me, Anne!" he said. "I'm afraid you've been waiting quite a time. I can't tell you how sorry——"

But she cut his apology short. "Where's John?"

"Old John? Why, I gave up; but he's decided to play it out. Old John and I started pretty late anyhow, and we were playing around with Julietta Voss, as it happened——"

"Yes," his wife said, dryly, "'as it happens' rather often! Where are they?"

"Just out yonder."

"Where? *We* can't see anybody."

"Well, they're there anyhow," he returned. "They'll be along in a minute or two."

Mrs. Simms rose from her chair. "Suppose you go and bring them," she said.

But before he could make any response, her sister intervened. "No! Oh, *no!*" Mildred cried in a voice of distress, and, rising, too, she caught Anne's hand in hers. "Don't send him! It would look as if——" She stopped, perceptibly agitated.

The surprise of the gentleman present was genuine,

though not so acute as that of an inexperienced man who expects ladies never to show unreasonable and apparently causeless emotion. "Why, what's the matter?" he said. "It doesn't seem to me that just because two people happen to get interested in the game——"

"Never mind!" his wife said, sharply. "If you intend to take your clubs down to the locker room you'd better be doing it."

"Very well." He entered the clubhouse through a French window that opened upon the veranda, and his surprise was somewhat increased when his wife followed him.

"Wait," she said, as she closed the window behind her. "Hobart Simms, I never dreamed you'd allow yourself to be put in such a position."

"What?" he said. "What position am I in?"

"I didn't think you were this kind of man at all," his wife informed him with continued severity. "I always believed you were intelligent—even about women!"

"Oh, no," he protested. "Don't go so far as that, my dear!" He laughed as he spoke, but despite both his protest and his laughter, his looks deserved what Mrs. Simms declared to have been her previous opinion of him. Bodily, he was still a feather-weight, and of that miraculous slimness which appears inconsistent with the possession of the organs neces-sary to sustain life; but his glance was the eagle's.

"I did think so!" his wife exclaimed. "I used to think you were different, and that women couldn't fool you any more than men could."

"Anne, what woman has taken enough interest in me to fool me?"

"Nobody. She doesn't take any interest in you; she only uses you."

"Who is she?"

The lady gave utterance to an outcry of indignant amazement at the everlasting stupidity of a man beguiled by a woman; for, in spite of the ages during which men have been beguiled by women, the women who are not doing the beguiling never cease to marvel that it can be done. "You poor blind thing!" she cried. "Julietta Voss!"

At this he was merely amused. "You're not feeling well, Anne," he remarked. "What you say doesn't sound like you at your best. I never heard anything so——"

Mrs. Simms interrupted him. "Who paid her caddy?"

"I did. I paid both hers and old John's, but I don't think we need——"

"What made you keep so far away from them? What made you play down the south side of the course and leave them so far over on the north? Did she ask you to?"

"Good gracious!" he exclaimed. "It just happened! They were playing the same ball, against me. Naturally——"

"'Naturally,'" she said, taking up the word sharply, "it was like that all round the course, wasn't it?"

"What of it? I understood you to charge me with being fooled by poor little Julietta——"

"Stop calling her 'little'," Mrs. Simms commanded. "She's a foot taller than you are!"

"Well, then," he mildly remonstrated, "with all that advantage, what would she take the trouble to fool me for? If she wanted to make love to me she could do it openly, by force."

At this, his wife's face showed sheer despair of him. "I just said that she doesn't take the slightest interest in you—except as a foil! This is the third time."

"The third time what?"

"The third time you've been manœuvred into coming out here to play with them. Good heavens, don't you *see* it?"

"No," he returned, meekly. "Tell me in words of one syllable, Anne."

Mrs. Simms complied, and in her response there was that direct brevity not unusual with her sex in the climaxes of bitter moments. "She's trying to get my sister's husband away from her!"

The bewilderment of Mr. Simms was complete. "Old John?" he cried. "Old John *Tower?* Poor little Julietta Voss is trying to get old John away from Mildred? Of all the preposterous——" His laughter interrupted his enunciation. "Why, that's the most far-fetched fancy work I ever—— But of course you don't mean it seriously."

"I do."

"But it's nonsense! Julietta's always ready to come and be an outdoor comrade for anybody; but it's only because she's such a good fellow she doesn't stop to care whether she's with old married men like John and me, or with the boys of her own age that she'd naturally like to be with a great deal better of course."

"She's almost my own age; she's over thirty,"

the grim Mrs. Simms informed him. "The 'boys of her own age' are busy elsewhere."

"Well, she isn't that kind of a schemer, no matter what her age is, and if she were, why, the last person on earth she'd pick out would be steady old John Tower. He's absolutely devoted to Mildred, and everybody knows it. And, finally, if poor Julietta is trying to break up Mildred's hearth and home, what in the world are you so sharp with *me* about? If it's John, and not me that Julietta's after——"

"Didn't I tell you she uses you as a foil? Who could criticize her for running after another woman's husband when his own brother-in-law is always chaperoning them? She knows there's talk——"

"She does? Well, I don't. You say——"

"I certainly do. Of *course* there's talk. There has been for some time."

"Does Mildred share your idea?" he asked.

"She does—most unhappily!"

"Anne, do you mean to tell me that as sensible a woman as Mildred's always seemed could actually let herself get worried about——"

"Any wife would," Anne interrupted, severely. "Especially with a husband as odd as John Tower. So far as women are concerned he's nothing but a grown-up child! He believes everything they tell him, and Julietta knows it. It's because he *is* so perfectly simple and naïve and trustful—with women—that Mildred is wretched about him."

"What's she said to old John about it?"

"Nothing."

"Why not?"

"Because if she did," Mrs. Simms explained, "it might look as if she were jealous."

"Well, she is, isn't she?"

"Not at all. She's terribly hurt, and naturally she's angry and rather disgusted to think her husband would let such a person as Julietta Voss have so much effect upon him."

Hobart's intelligent forehead became lined with the effort to solve the puzzle before him. "You say she's terribly hurt and she's angry and she's disgusted because she thinks her husband is letting another woman carry on with him; but she's not jealous. How would you define jealousy, Anne?"

"As nothing that a girl like Julietta Voss could make a lady feel," Anne returned, with no little heat. "Mildred is a lady—and I'm going back to her. Be kind enough to hurry with your ablutions, if you intend any."

He went away meekly to obey, and when he returned to the veranda he still looked meek, though
there was in his glance a sly skepticism readily
visible to his wife. She was sitting by the veranda
railing with her sister, who was staring forth into the
darkness in a manner somewhat pathetic; but, as
her brother-in-law thought her imaginings absurd,
his sympathies were not greatly roused. "Hasn't
that old Don Giovanni of yours finished playing it
out yet, Mildred?" he inquired.

Both ladies looked round at him over their shoulders, Mildred piteously, but Anne sternly. "There's
one great trouble with an unflagging humour," Mrs.
Simms said. "It never flags."

"Dear me!" he exclaimed. "If Mildred thinks
poor old John and Julietta—— Mildred, you don't
for one minute honestly and truly——"

But Mildred made a gesture of agonized entreaty.
"Please! Please!" she said in a low voice. "They're
coming!"

A peal of light laughter was heard from the darkness, and the figures of the two delaying players
became visible within the outer reaches of the clubhouse lights. They were walking slowly, engaged in
obviously cheerful conversation, and from the shoul-

ders of the stalwart Tower were slung both bags
containing the implements used in the game they
had been playing. It was characteristic and like
old John's punctilious gallantry, his brother-in-law
thought, to have seized upon both those bags the
moment the caddies were dismissed. Miss Voss,
almost as tall as he, was more than equal to carrying
her own bag without effort.

She had the figure of a distance runner in train-
ing, lithe, hard, and active; and there was something
lively, yet hard, too, in her tanned long face, which
was a handsome face in spite of its length.   But her
eyes were what was most noticeable about her, for
they were beautiful. They were brilliantly dark,
and at times seemed to hold little dancing lights
within them, as if they gave glimpses of secret laughter.   All in all, she was a cheery companion for an
outdoor afternoon, but by no manner of means a
tricky witch, Mr. Hobart Simms decided, as he looked
down smilingly upon her and upon that odd man,
his brother-in-law and junior partner, old John
Tower.

"Old John," of an age not more than Hobart's,
was queer, Hobart thought; but his queerness did
not alter the simple steadiness of character that made

his intimates think and speak of him as "old John." Moreover, his oddity lay mainly in his literal, simple truthfulness under all conditions, in his belief that others were as truthful as himself, and in an indefatigable formal politeness of manner, sometimes a little stately, that was really the expression of a kind heart.

The two came gaily up the steps, still laughing at something said out of hearing from the veranda, and Julietta gave a final fillip to their joke by reeling against her companion as they reached the top step. She steadied herself by clutching his shoulder, and seemed almost to hang upon him, for a moment or two, while she chid him. "Don't make me laugh any more, or I'll give you up as a partner and absolutely not play with you again to-morrow!" Then she turned briskly to Mildred. "I hope you haven't been waiting long for your poor abducted husband, Mrs. Tower. I'm afraid he's the kind of man who never gives up anything he sets out to do, even when he has to finish it in the dark. I suppose that's why he's a great man."

"Do you think he's a great man, Julietta?" Hobart Simms inquired in a carefully naïve manner.

"Everyone knows he is," Julietta returned. "Of

course you're a great man, John, since Hobart asks me!"

"At least, it's most lovely of you to say you think so," Mr. Tower responded, bowing his dark head before her gratefully. "I'm only a feeble assistant to Hobart here, who really *is* a great man; but it's charming of you to say I'm one, too. Really it's most kind of you, Julietta." He turned to his wife. "My dear, I hope you haven't been waiting long, and I hope, if you have, you haven't minded."

"No, not at all," she murmured. "But can't we go now?"

"Just a moment. I must take these bags to the locker room and freshen up the least bit. Julietta, if you'll give me the key to your locker I'll have your bag put away for you."

But Julietta laughed ruefully and shook her head. "Just leave the bag here. It takes every penny of my poor little allowance to keep me a member of the club. They charge too much for lockers. I told you the other day I didn't have a locker."

The kindly John struck his hands together in a sharp sound; he was shocked by his forgetfulness. "Dear me! So you did! Of course, you must allow me to make up for my omission. I'd meant to attend to that yesterday. Of *course* you must have a locker. I'll see to it at once and bring you the key."

Julietta said promptly, "How lovely of you!" and he went toward the French windows; but a murmur from his wife stopped him.

"John, it's very late. Couldn't you postpone seeing about lockers and things like that, and let's be starting home?"

"In just a moment, my dear," he said in the kindest tone. "I'll just arrange about a locker for Julietta and leave our clubs. It won't take a moment."

"He's so thoughtful always," Julietta said, looking after him gratefully as he departed. "I think I never knew a man so careful about all the little things most men don't seem even to be conscious of."

"Thanks, Julietta," Mr. Simms said, cheerfully, and was immediately aware that his wife looked at him with some tensity. She had not spoken since the arrival of Julietta and her companion upon the veranda. "Thanks for the rest of us."

"Oh, you!" Julietta said; and the dancing lights in her extraordinary eyes sparkled as she turned to him. "You're a great man really, as dear old John just explained, and we all know what everybody says about you and Julius Cæsar—or is it Napoleon? You've scattered fortunes around among your friends taking them into your corporations, the way he scattered kingdoms around among his relatives. You're so great you don't have to bother being thoughtful about little things."

"Julietta," he responded, "you sound like a testimonial banquet. I hope you'll convince my wife, though."

"She'd be the last to need convincing," Julietta returned. "Wouldn't you, Mrs. Simms?"

"I might be," Anne replied, dryly. "Hobart, I think you'd better run and tell John he's keeping us all waiting."

But the absent gentleman returned before his brother-in-law, moving to obey, could go in search of him; and he came with a key in his hand. "There, Julietta, if you'll be so kind as to use this——"

"You dear man!" she cried, enthusiastically. "Now just for that I'm going to forgive you for making me laugh so hard, and we'll finish that game to-morrow, because Hobart didn't play it out with us to-day. Don't you think we could all three be here a *wee* bit earlier to-morrow—say by four o'clock?"

At this, Mildred Tower turned to her sister in an almost visible appeal for help; and Anne hurriedly endeavoured to respond with the succour besought. "So far as Mr. Simms is concerned——" she began; but Tower, unaware that she was speaking, had already accepted Julietta's invitation.

"Delightful," he said, bowing. "Julietta, that will be delightful. I shall be here by four o'clock promptly. Thank you for thinking of it."

"You'll be sure to come, too, Hobart?" Julietta asked.

Hobart's wife began again, and her tone was emphatic. "So far as Mr. Simms is concerned——" But again she was interrupted, this time by her husband.

"Why, yes, Julietta," he said, amiably, "I'd like very much to play it out. I'll be here at four."

For a moment or two there was a silence during which his consciousness that both his wife and his sister-in-law were looking at him became somewhat acute. Then, without even a murmur of leave-taking or any sound at all, Mildred Tower walked quickly to the steps, descended them, and went

toward the waiting cars. Her sister, after a final
look, which swept scorchingly over both gentlemen—
though but one of them, her husband, was aware of
its heat—turned sharply away and hurried after
her.

Only the best of women are capable of doing
things so embarrassing, thought the philosophical Mr.
Simms; and then realized that his brother-in-law
was not embarrassed at all.

"Wait a moment, my dear," Tower called placidly
after his wife. "Julietta has been kind enough to
say we could drop her at her house on our way.
She's going with us."

No response came from the hurrying Mrs. Tower.

"My dear!" her husband called. "Julietta is
going to permit us——" Then, as Mildred disappeared silently into the interior of her car, he remarked with unsullied confidence, "She doesn't
hear me."

Julietta laughed and put her hand upon his arm,
looking up at him. "Do you think she wants me?"

"My dear Julietta! Of course she does. Everybody wants you. Why shouldn't she?"

"Perhaps she thinks I live too far out of your way,
and she's in a hurry to eat her dinner," Julietta said,

wistfully. "It isn't everyone that's too generous to keep thinking of food when someone needs a little lift. It isn't everybody who remembers all the little thoughtful things as you do, John, you know."

"Nonsense!" he exclaimed. "Mildred will be only too delighted to have you, though I do appreciate your kind opinion of me." He looked down at her hand, which was still upon his coat sleeve, and, taking it in one of his, tucked it under his arm. "You're charming, Julietta," he said, beaming upon her. "Indeed you are! Perfectly charming! Shall we go down and get into the car?"

It was time for the third person present during this little interview to depart, that person decided. "*Hobart!*" his wife called from her car, and her voice was threateningly eloquent.

Hobart delayed no longer, though he was thinking with some concentration just then; and, bidding Miss Voss and his brother-in-law a quick good-night, he went by them and hurried toward the summoning voice.

Descending the steps arm-in-arm, and talking, old John and Julietta did not seem to hear the word of farewell;—Hobart was some distance away when the scrupulous Tower called after him: "Hobart, did

you say, 'Good-night'? I beg your pardon; I was
listening to Julietta. Good-night, Hobart. Good-
night, Anne." Then, as Hobart got into his own
car, he could hear his brother-in-law busily talking
beside the other. "And now, my dear Julietta, if
you'll be so kind as to step in and sit beside Mildred,
I believe you'll be quite comfortable. There's an
extra rug, Julietta, if you——"

But Mrs. Simms had already spoken to her chauffeur, and the engine was in motion. As they drove
away, she and her husband could still hear the
thoughtful old John addressing himself to the subject
of Julietta's comfort, and replying to her thanks.
"Not at all, my dear Julietta; it's the greatest im-
aginable pleasure. And if you'll be so kind as to
allow me to place this other rug over your knees,
Julietta——"

The Simms' car passed out of hearing, and within
the dark interior its owner continued to be thoughtful. He was still certain that Mildred indulged
herself in mere folly when she worried about steady,
simple old John. But he was not so sure of the art-
lessness of Julietta;—the final little interview upon
the veranda had somewhat shaken his convictions
in regard to Julietta.

"I suppose you're pleased with yourself," Mrs. Simms said, icily, after an extended silence.

"I couldn't decline," he returned, easily. "You didn't give me a chance to."

"Hobart, that's really too much! You stopped me—interrupted me when I was in the very act of declining for you."

"That was the reason," he explained. "I couldn't let you decline for me. It might have looked as though I let my wife do embarrassing things for me that I haven't backbone enough to do for myself."

"How diplomatic!" she said. "May I ask your *real* reason for accepting her invitation after what I'd just told you about her? Perhaps, though, it was merely to hurt Mildred and irritate me. In that case, you made a perfect success of what you intended."

"It wasn't precisely that," he laughed. "For one thing, if what you and Mildred believe has any foundation, why, old John certainly needs a chaperon; and, for another thing, I wanted the chance to see for myself if there is any reason to believe what you told me."

"Oh, *so?*" She uttered a little cry of triumph, and laughed in the tone of her outcry. "So you're not so sure as you were a little while ago, when you

implied that my mind was wandering! So you see
there *is* something in it?"

"Only this: I admit the possibility that Julietta
might want to have him attached to her as a sort of
providing friend, to do little useful things for her
and——"

"'Little useful things'?" his wife said, scornfully.
"Don't you understand what type she belongs to?
Only a few minutes ago you paid her caddy for her,
and John rented a locker for her. Last week he got
her a new set of golf clubs, Mildred told me. Julietta
complained of her old ones, and he sent away for
the most expensive clubs you can get in the country.
When she said you put your friends into fortunes,
she meant more than just to flatter you about the
fortune you've put John Tower into; she meant you
to begin to get the idea into your head that it would
be pleasant some day to put *her* into one—or her
worthless old father, perhaps!"

Then, as Hobart laughed loudly at an idea apparently so far-fetched, Anne defended it. "Oh, I
know it was only her impulse and not deliberate, just
a chance shot of hers; but she never misses a possibility, and that possibility was somewhere in the back
of her head. Of course, it isn't you, but John that

she's playing for.   She'd *rather* have played for you;
but she didn't see any chance, of course.   She discovered John's weakness and did see the chance
with him."

"What weakness, Anne?"

"Why, the poor old thing's childlike acceptance
of women at the face value they put upon themselves,
and his quaint belief that they say everything they
mean and mean everything they say—just as he
does himself.   Mildred's helpless because he's such
a helpless idealist; he tells her the only thing he
can't bear in a woman is when she's so small-minded
as to speak slightingly of any other woman!   All
Mildred can do is to suffer and not speak.   I never
saw anything so pitiful as what she did when you
hurt her feelings so terribly."

"When I did what?"

"When you insulted her awhile ago," Mrs. Simms
explained with calm frigidity.   "She knew I'd told
you what she was suffering;—I'd just told her I
had.   And then she had not only to listen to her
husband accepting that girl's overtures for another
long tête-à-tête with him to-morrow, but to hear you
promising to lend countenance to it by being used

again as you've already been used three times. It was the same as either telling Mildred that she's a fool, imagining the whole thing, or that you approve of Julietta's little plans and intend to lend your aid to further them. You might as well have slapped my sister in the face."

"Dear me!" he exclaimed. "Don't look at it that way! I didn't mean——"

"Didn't you?" Anne had no compunctions whatever in punishing him to the best of her ability. "You'd already mocked her for suffering what no woman in her position could *help* suffering. Then, in addition to what she was already trying to bear and not show, you gave her some *more* to bear—and she couldn't trust herself to speak; she could only run from you!"

This was indeed a new light upon what Hobart had been masculine enough to think a mere example of woman's rudeness to woman; and in that light the speechless flight of the unfortunate Mildred now bore the colour of true pathos. Moreover, following his awakened doubts of Julietta, his wife's view of his conduct began to be uncomfortably convincing. He feared that he was going to be remorseful.

"Of course you don't dream I'm not fond of Mildred," he said. "I've always been very——"

"You show it strangely," Anne interrupted. She spoke with no softening of her resentment, though what she felt for her sister brought to her eyes the tears she had been withholding, and he saw them as a street light flashed through the glass of the window beside her. "Mildred's the kind of woman people do hurt, I suppose. She's so gentle and harmless herself, it must be a temptation! She's always been so lovely to *you*, I suppose you couldn't resist it."

"Oh, look here!" he protested, and his fears were realized; he was already remorseful. "You know I wouldn't have hurt——"

"Then why did you?"

"Well, if I did," he said, desperately;—"and, confound it, I'm afraid maybe I did—I suppose it was because jealousy is the kind of suffering that onlookers always have the least sympathy with. I'll beg her pardon, and, if I caused her pain, I'll try to make it up to her."

"How can you do that?"

"I don't know," he said, regretfully. "I'll just have to try to find some way."

"That wouldn't be very easy," his wife said.

"Could you get her husband back for her, if this girl gets him away?"

"But that *is* nonsense," he protested. "Julietta Voss couldn't get that far with old John—not if she had all eternity to try in!"

This was the position he took, and he maintained it during the rest of their drive, and at intervals during the rather stately dinner for two people that was the evening custom of their big country house. After dinner, however, as he sat down to coffee with his wife in the library, he was forced to adopt another view. His sister-in-law came in suddenly and dramatically, the fur cloak she had thrown about her for a hasty drive falling to the floor as she entered the door.

Anne sprang up from her easy chair. "Mildred! What's happened?"

For Mildred's pallor, and her visible struggle for composure, as she stood with both hands upon the back of a chair to steady herself, left no doubt that she came because of some definite happening.

Hobart moved to withdraw. "I imagine you and Anne might like to have a talk together, Mildred. I'll just——"

"No," Mildred said in a strained and plaintive

voice, "I've come for help. You've both got to help me somehow, because I can't stand it. I really can't."

He was distressed for her. "Anything—anything in the world——"

"I *hope* you mean it," Mildred said, staring at him with wide and desperate eyes. "If any one can do anything to help me it's you, Hobart, because you've always been able to do everything you've ever wanted to do. Maybe you won't want to help me."

"What?" he cried. "My dear girl!"

"No," she said, pathetically;—"maybe you won't want to. After the way you treated me before them at the club, I shouldn't be sure you'd want to."

"My dear sister, don't think that," he begged. "I see I did hurt you, and I only ask a chance to make up to you for it. What can I do?"

"Nothing!" his wife said, taking the reply into her own mouth, as she put an arm about her sister and stood facing him scornfully. "Nothing that will make up to her for what you did. That's something you can never do, because even you can't recall and do again what has passed."

Troubled, admiring Anne for the proud anger of her attitude, and secretly pleased with her "even you," he gave her a queer look in which there was a gleam of doggedness.   "I'll try, at any rate," he said; and then, more casually, he addressed his sister-in-law: "You drove over alone, Mildred?"

"As soon as John left the house after dinner," she said.   "I kept up till he went, and then I found I couldn't bear it any longer—I had to ask for help. After he put her into the car with me at the club, he asked me why I was so quiet, and I said I had a bad headache;—it was true enough, too.   She said that was 'too bad' and immediately proposed that we should 'all three' drive into town after dinner to a cabaret vaudeville and dance and late supper!"

"She did?" Hobart asked.   "Not just after you'd told them your head ached?"

"Yes.   She said the way to cure a headache was to 'be gay and forget it.'"

"What did you tell her, Mildred?"

"I said I couldn't and that John couldn't go either, because he had to be in his office early to-morrow morning.   He said no; he didn't need more than three or four hours' sleep, and he would be only too glad to escort Julietta, since if I had a headache, I'd probably go to bed, and he'd have nothing to do.   At dinner I asked him please not to go; *please* to stay

with me, instead. He said in his kindest way that
he'd be glad to, any other night, but it was impossible
this evening since he'd 'promised Julietta,' and
couldn't possibly break a promise. So he went—
and I found I couldn't stay in the house and think
it over any longer. Hobart, you mustn't go out
there and help them pretend to play golf to-morrow."

"Very well," he said, gravely. "I'll do whatever
you wish. But isn't it just possible you'd rather
have me with them? If Julietta really is the de-
signing person you believe she is——"

"If!" Mildred cried with sudden loudness. "'If'
she is! You don't understand, Hobart. This is
what happened in the car just before we reached her
house to-night;—it happens all the time. She made
a gesture—she always talks with gestures—and her
hand smashed against the door-frame and broke
the crystal of her wrist-watch. She said she was
sure the works were broken, too. It was a plain gold
watch, old and not very valuable, but she made a
great lamentation over it. John took it from her,
put it in his pocket, and said that since it was broken
in our car it was our place to restore it; she should
have a new one as near like it as possible to-morrow;
—it would be the 'greatest privilege' to obtain it

for her! She *knew* that was just what he'd do, and she broke it on purpose, of course."

"Mildred, you really believe——"

She stopped him. "You don't understand. It goes on all the time. And if she does this much under my very eyes, what doesn't she get out of him when they're alone together?"

"There might be something reassuring in that," Hobart suggested. "If she spends her energies getting these trifles from him—because of course that's all they are to a man in old John's position—doesn't that look as if her designs might be limited to——"

"No, it does not," Mrs. Simms interrupted, promptly.

"But——"

"No," his wife repeated. "Don't you see that the very fact of her wanting the trifles would make her want something a great deal more important, and that's to be in a position where she wouldn't have to work for them?"

"Well, then," her husband returned;—"if she expects to reach that position by supplanting Mildred, she has a ridiculous ambition!"

"Is it?" Mildred asked, unhappily. "If John

were any other kind of man, it might be ridiculous."
Tears came into her eyes that had been dry until
now; but she struggled with herself and kept more
from coming. "Isn't it ironical?" she said. "The
very goodness of such a man as John, his simple
kindness, his idealizing—the very things I've cared
for most in him—that they should be his weakness
and just what leaves him open to the easy cajoling
of a crude trespasser like Julietta Voss! Don't
you understand, Hobart? I know you didn't understand this afternoon, but don't you now? You
thought I was jealous of him, I know. Perhaps I
am; perhaps I do want to keep him for myself;
but I'm his wife; why shouldn't I? And I know I'm
better for him than she'd be. Oh, don't you understand? I want to *protect* him!"

Hobart came to her and took her hand. "Mildred,
old John hasn't the remotest idea you're suffering
like this. You've got to tell him about it."

"But I *can't*," she cried. "I can't let him think
I'm just a jealous woman, and what else would he
think of me if I told him the truth about her? That's
why I don't want you to go out there with them
to-morrow, Hobart."

"Of course I won't, since you ask it," he said, mystified. "Yet I don't see——"

"You don't?" his wife asked, sharply; and, in obvious pity for a poor understanding, characteristically manlike, she explained what she had instantly divined—her unhappy sister's reason for coming to ask him to help her. "Julietta counts on your being with them as the answer to the talk about them. She intends to have a defence against the talk—an answer that will help to keep people on her side—and if you break your engagement without any explanation she'll wonder what it means, and if we haven't *asked* you to do it; and she'll get John to find out. He'll ask you why you didn't come. Then you can tell him you stayed away because you're troubled about what Mildred may think. It's all you need say, and he'll speak to Mildred about it. That will give her a *chance* to talk to him."

"Is it what you want, Mildred?" he asked.

"Yes," she said. "It's the only thing I can think of. It gives me a chance to talk to him, that's all. It may make him despise me, anyhow. I don't know what he'll say, but I've got to do it;—I can't go on any longer not saying *anything!* Perhaps"—

her breath caught in her throat, and for a moment she could not speak—"perhaps he'll ask me for a divorce. Well, if he does, I'll give it to him!"

"No, no!" her sister cried. "You said you wanted to protect him!"

"If he doesn't love me any more, I *couldn't*," Mildred sobbed, for her struggle to control herself was lost now, and her weeping became convulsive. "Don't you see I couldn't? You can't protect anybody that's tired of you. If he's tired of you, how can you protect him against someone he's in love with?"

"My dear sister!" Hobart begged her, deeply moved. "Don't think it. Old John isn't in love with Julietta Voss any more than I am!"

"How do I *know?*" she sobbed. "He *acts* as if he is. What other way is there to tell? How do I know?" And, clinging to his hand, she sank down into the chair beside which she had been standing. "Oh, Hobart, you must help me; you must try your best to help me!"

"Indeed I will," he promised, with all the earnestness that was in him. "I'll do anything in the world, Mildred—absolutely anything!"

He meant it indeed; but over the bowed form of

the unhappy lady who clung to his hand, entreating him, he looked into the denouncing and skeptical eyes of his wife.   She needed no words, nor anything except those implacable eyes of hers, to tell him that his own recent behaviour was in great part responsible for the misery before them, and that he lacked the power to make up to Mildred for what he had done.

He adored his wife, and he took that look of hers as a challenge.

XXX

HE WAS far from convinced, however, that Mildred's necessity was as tragic as she believed. If it was, he would prove to his wife that he was a man of more resources than she thought; but it still seemed to him that old John Tower could be in no danger from the simple wiles of Julietta. For Hobart had accepted the theory that Julietta was wily; he had finally gone that far unconditionally before the unhappy evening was over; and he even wondered why he had hitherto been so blind when he looked at Julietta. But as for steady old John Tower—"No," he said to himself, as he drove into the city the next morning. "Absolutely impossible!" Yet in this emphasis there was that faint shade of doubt so often present when people buttress their convictions with "absolutely"; so he decided to buttress himself further by means of a diplomatic experimental talk with old John.

Arrived in the heart of the city at the great building that was his own, with all its thirty stories obedient to his five feet three inches, a Giant Jinn enslaved by a little master enchanter, he went, not to his own offices, but to old John's. "I just dropped in for a morning cigar," he explained.

His brother-in-law received him heartily.

"My dear Hobart, this is indeed a pleasure. Will you smoke one of my cigars or one of your own? I'm afraid yours are much the better."

"No, they're not," Hobart laughed. "Mine are much the worse. Your taste is a lot better than mine about pretty nearly everything." As he spoke he took a long cigar from the box that Tower was offering him, and lighted it. "You have better taste in cigars, better taste in furniture——" Here he seated himself in one of the set of seventeenth-century English chairs that helped to make the room the pleasant place it was. "You even have better taste on the golf links," he concluded, chuckling as if reminiscently.

"How so? You play a better game. You don't allude to my apparel for it, I imagine."

"That, too," Hobart said. "But I was thinking of something else."

"Of what, my dear Hobart?"

Hobart laughed, gave him a look of friendly raillery, mixed with jocose admiration, and said: "Don't you think I'm a good deal of a dunderhead? On your word, don't you, old John?"

Old John, beaming genially and amused by his caller's question, but puzzled by it, laughed with him. "On my word then, no. I haven't the slightest conception of what you mean."

"Just think of it!" Hobart chuckled. "Here we go, afternoon after afternoon, you and I, out to the links; and every single time, when we get there, I go roving round the course virtually all by myself, while you put in the time with Julietta! You and she keep together and play the same ball—and what do I play? It seems to me I play the Lone Fisherman! Honestly, do you think it's fair?"

"Fair?" Old John had become grave, and the other was surprised and interested to observe that a tinge of red was slowly mounting in his cheeks. "Let me understand you, Hobart," he said. "You mean that I've been monopolizing Julietta?"

"Rather!" Hobart continued his rallying jocosity, though inwardly he was disturbed by the spreading of that tinge of red over his brother-in-law's face.

"Don't you think it's about time I had a share of feminine camaraderie in our outdoor sports?"

"You mean, Hobart, that this afternoon you'd prefer to play the same ball with Julietta and have me play against you?"

This was not the question Hobart had desired to evoke; and his jocosity departed from him suddenly. "Well——" he said. Then, as his shrewd eyes took note again of old John's rosy face and of his gravity— already troubled as by some forthcoming disappointment—the Napoleonic Hobart came to one of those swift and clear resolutions, the capacity for which had made possible his prodigious business career during what was still almost his youth. Old John was indeed in danger, although old John was "too innocent" to know it, himself. And in the very instant of this realization, Hobart decided that he had found the opportunity to take up his wife's challenge and atone in full for his fault to her sister.

"Why—why, yes," he said, slowly. "Don't you think it's about time? You wouldn't mind very much, would you?"

Old John's large and well-favoured face grew redder than ever, though otherwise it was expressive of the most naïvely plain regret. "Ah—I suppose it would be fair," he said. "Julietta *is* attractive, as you say. In fact, I believe she is the most attractive girl I have ever known. I value her friendship very highly, Hobart. I came into town to a cabaret with her last night, and neither of us knew anybody in the place. We danced together and had a little supper, and danced some more, and talked—altogether until about two o'clock, I think, Hobart. And in all that time I never had a dull moment—not one! She is a most attractive girl, as you say, and I believe there's perhaps some justice in your idea that you're entitled to more of her companionship than you've been enjoying—for this afternoon at least. Since you put it as you do, suppose we arrange, then, that you and she play the same ball this afternoon and I play against the two of you."

"I believe that would be fair," Hobart said, his eyes sidelong upon old John. "It's settled then." He rose to go.

"I suppose so." Tower's gravity increased; but he brightened at a thought that came to him as his departing caller reached the door. "I suppose, Hobart, to-morrow—to-morrow——"

"To-morrow what?" Hobart inquired, staring at him.

"Ah—to-morrow——" Old John hesitated, then finished hopefully: "We might return to our former arrangement?"

"To-morrow?   Oh, yes, certainly—to-morrow we'll return to our former arrangement," Hobart said; and as he passed through the anteroom beyond he murmured the word incredulously to himself, "'To-morrow.'" He laughed shortly, and in his imagination continued the dialogue with old John. "Day after to-morrow, too, I suppose? And the day after that? And the next, and the next? Why, yes! Why not?" Then he became serious. "You poor dear old thing, there's got not to *be* any 'to-morrow'!"

He took the affair into his own hands for complete settlement; and at noon he went to a jeweller's and bought the most expensive wrist-watch in the place —a trifling miracle of platinum intricately glittering with excellent white diamonds. He put the little packet in his coat pocket, and at about five o'clock that afternoon he showed it to Miss Julietta Voss.

Old John Tower, absent-minded and not playing well, had driven his ball into a thicket fifty yards away from where Hobart and Julietta had paused;—

he was in the underbrush, solemnly searching, with his caddy.

"Something for you," Hobart said, tossing the little packet up and down in his hand.

She looked surprised. "For me? From you?"

"Yes."

"What is it?"

"Oh, nothing to speak of," he replied, airily. "I just happened to hear you broke that gold wrist-watch you usually wear——"

"I did," she said. "But John found another for me to-day—a new one exactly like it." She displayed her left forearm for inspection. "Isn't it lovely of him always to be so dear about all the little thoughtful things?"

"I don't know," Hobart said; and he quoted an ancient bit of slang: "There might be others!"

She shook her head. "Not like him!"

"Are you sure, Julietta?" He gave her a quick and serious look that increased her surprise. "You might at least take a glance round you to see."

"What on earth are you talking about, Hobart Simms?"

At that he gave her another quick glance—a personal glance, as it might have been defined, since to Julietta it seemed to convey an unexpected feeling concerning herself and himself. Then he looked wistfully away, and when he spoke, a moment later, his voice had not the briskness customary in his speech;—it was, on the contrary, perceptibly unsteady. "Julietta, I've been—well, don't you suppose a man might some day get a little tired of being —I mean to say, here I am with you, day after day —yet really *not* with you. You're so busy noticing old John all the time, you never take time off to be a little friendly with anybody else."

She caught her breath, staring at him wonderingly. "But you—you never showed me you wanted me to," she said, slowly.

"Didn't I?" He turned to her, smiling, and as he spoke he removed the paper wrappings of the small packet. "Other people might want to do some of the 'little thoughtful things' too—if they ever got a chance."

He put into her hand the green velvet box that had been inside the wrapping, and she opened it curiously; —then suppressed an outcry.

"Good Heaven!" she gasped, and stared at him. "Of course you know I couldn't accept a thing like *this!*"

"Why not?   You would from John."

"But——"

"You're wearing the one he gave you."

"Yes, but *this*——"

"It's nothing," he said.   "Of course, if you don't like it——"

Sorrowfully he extended his hand to take back the little green velvet box from her; but she retained it and stood staring at him, amazed and also profoundly thoughtful.   Like Hobart, she was a person who could make quick decisions.

"I never dreamed of this," she said.   "I thought you only came along with us because you thought it was a good course and because John asked you."

"And he asked me because you made him," Hobart added.   "And the reason you did was because you wanted me for a chaperon."

She laughed excitedly.   "You don't seem contented with the rôle, I must say!"

"How could I?"

"I never dreamed!" she said, and she looked at the watch upon her wrist and at that in the green velvet box.   "Queer!" she laughed.   "Now I have two!"

"Would you mind wearing mine?" Hobart asked, and he laughed with her.

"But he'll see it!"

Hobart's laughter became gayer and louder. "What if he does?"

"Perhaps you're right," Julietta said, and as she took the magnificent tiny miracle from the box, there began to shine in her eyes an exultation that could be ruthless. "Perhaps I'd better wear yours and keep his in my pocket."

"Perhaps you'd better," he agreed, still laughing. "Don't let him see the joke's on him till we get back to the clubhouse, though. If he asks you about it, don't tell him till then;—I want to get away first."

"Yes," she assented, thoughtfully. "Perhaps that would be just as well."

XXXI

THE ANNIVERSARY DINNER

WHEN he got home from the country club, something less than an hour later, his wife told him coldly that he seemed to be in high spirits. "You appear to have the happy faculty of not being depressed by the troubles of people close to you," she added. "However, your gaiety may be useful this evening, at Mother's."

"At your mother's?" he inquired. "Are we going there?"

She looked at him sternly. "What have you been doing that makes you forget such a thing? It's Father's and Mother's thirty-eighth wedding anniversary."

"So it is!" he exclaimed. "I'd forgotten all about it."

"Obviously. You'd better hurry and dress, because the dinner's to be very early on account of the younger grandchildren;—I sent them half an hour ago." And, as he did not move, she added, "Please get ready right away."

He still hesitated, for in his absorption in his plan
to atone to his sister-in-law and take up Anne's
challenge he had forgotten more than the anniversary
dinner. He had forgotten to consider in what
terms he would eventually inform his wife of that
plan and what already appeared to be its successful
beginnings. The present seemed to be a wise time
to say something about it; but he found himself in a
difficulty. Face to face with his wife, especially
in her present state of mind, which was plainly still
critical of him, he was convinced that she would
prove unsympathetic. He decided to postpone all
explanations, at least until they were on their way
to his father-in-law's house.

But, alone in the car with her, when the postponed
moment seemed to have arrived, he found the difficulty no less discouraging. He made an effort,
however; but he put it off so long that when he made
it they were almost at their destination.

"Oh, about that interview I'm supposed to have
with old John, to-morrow morning——"

"Yes," she said. "When he asks you why you
didn't join him and Julietta at the club this afternoon, you'll not weaken, I trust."

"'Weaken'?"

"Oh, you'll protest *now* that you won't, I know," she said. "But men are sympathetic—with other men, especially in 'affairs'—and John's terribly sensitive. I shouldn't be surprised if you failed to carry it through. I shouldn't at all!"

"But—but of course I shall," Hobart said, before he knew what he was saying. It was not what he wished to say; but he found himself apparently without control of his own speech, for the moment; and he realized that it would now be more difficult than ever to make the needed explanation. He attempted it feebly, however. "That is to say——" he began. "I mean—ah—suppose such an interview shouldn't——"

The car stopped.

"We're here," Anne said. "I hope you'll be as thoughtful as you can of Mildred. And please don't be too cordial to John. Let him begin to feel what you think about him."

But Hobart's determination, as he followed his wife into his father-in-law's gaily illuminated house, was to be as cordial as possible to old John and to seek the first private opportunity to request him not to mention their game of the afternoon. Unfortunately, the anniversary dinner was already in jovial motion;—Anne and her husband were late; the adults of the party had yielded to the clamours of the children and had just gone out to the dining-room. Hobart found himself between Mildred and Cornelia, across the wide table from his brother-in-law.

Old John was silent, and his sensitive face wore such visible depression that presently his father-in law began to rally him upon it. "Good gracious, John, this is a party, not the bedside of a sick friend! Why don't you eat, or laugh, or anyhow say something? You and Mildred both seem to think it's a horrible thing to be present at a celebration of two people's having been happily married for thirty-eight years. Is that what makes you feel so miserable?"

"No, not at all," John replied, gloomily. "I wasn't thinking of that. My mind was on other matters." And, being the singular soul he was, and of such a guileless straightforwardness, he looked across the table at his brother-in-law. "I was thinking of our golf game," he said, to that gentleman's acute alarm. "I mean the one this afternoon, Hobart."

Hobart heard from the chair next upon his right the subdued and lamentable exclamation uttered by Mildred; but what fascinated his paling gaze was the expression of his wife, seated beside old John. She looked at her husband for a moment of great intensity;—then she turned to Tower.

"So?" she said, lightly. "Did Hobart play with you and Julietta again to-day?"

"He played with Julietta," old John explained, and in his noble simplicity he continued, to his brother-in-law's horror, "*I* didn't seem to be needed. I've been very fond of Julietta, very fond indeed of Julietta. She broke her watch in our car yesterday, and so I took her a new one this afternoon and gave it to her before we began to play. Hobart brought her one, too; and she took mine off and wore his. The one I brought her was an ordinary little gold one; but his was platinum and diamonds—it must have cost a remarkable sum. It was very generous and kind of Hobart, because Julietta isn't well off; but the way she took it made me feel peculiarly disappointed in her. She evidently considers only the relative financial value of gifts, and not the spirit. She was quite different in her manner toward me. I cannot say that I value her friendship as I did."

"You don't?" Anne said; and she laughed excitedly. "Don't you mean you've decided she values my husband's friendship more than you thought she did?"

The unhappy Hobart, upon whom the wrong he had done to Julietta thus already began to be avenged, made an effort to speak; but beneath the table he felt a warm hand upon his knee, pressing warningly. It was Mildred's.

"Wait!" she whispered, rapturously. "I understand. I'll help you to talk to her later. It will be terribly difficult, but I'll do what I can for you—you angel!"

THE END